Dethfest Confessions

The Devil's Playlist

Do You Want to Die at Dethfest?

The stories in this anthology can be enjoyed on their own, but they are tied to the interactive novel *Try Not to Die: At Dethfest*. I wanted to know more about the bands that played at this heavy metal festival turned tragedy and put out a call to indie authors around the world. The fifteen stories will give you a good feel for the event, but nothing compares to going to the festival and seeing how many times you will die.

Mark Tullius

Foreword

Dethfest. The day that ruined my life and devastated so many others. It was billed as the biggest metal event of the year but turned into the largest U.S. tragedy this century. And no one claims to know a thing about why it went so wrong.

Friends warned me to forget about it, to stop searching for the truth, and I tried, but I've already lost too much. Kyle went searching for answers, and the next thing you know, Tess discovers his body in a bullshit fake-suicide. Kyle absolutely hated guns and *never* would have taken his life.

Now, I'm not saying these stories are factual, and you're going to see spots where the stories differ from my testimony in *Try Not to Die: At Dethfest*. Please understand, not only was I tripping along with so many others, I might have taken some artistic license to make shit sound cooler in the book. Plus, there were places the editors forced me to change things up, make it more digestible, keep from making enemies.

Each of these fifteen stories in this *Devil's Playlist* was arranged by someone closely connected to each band, and they come from United States, Canada, Germany, United Kingdom, Australia, and Finland.

Some of the stories are dead ends where no one's accountable. And more than a few stories are extreme— meaning, please do not read if you are bothered by graphic depictions of sex and violence. I labeled the four stories that crossed the line.

Remember, this was a metal festival. There was sex, drugs, and oh so much violence. That's not why we went there, or how it was designed, but there's no question that's what we got.

I hope you get what you're looking for when reading these tales. I know I did.

Jerry Toleman

FLAMETHOWER
BLUTTRINKER
MARY JANE'S MOTHER
SEXXX
BONERIVET
KLAAZ
FLESHPEEL
VYKYNG
Bare Knuckle Bastards
DETHROS
II
I
III
OMNES MORIMUR
NECROTITIS
SYSTEMIC COLLAPSE
GOTHIKA
Red Jolly Roger
DETHFEST
2023
SPONSORED BY:
Epheelas

Table of Contents

B is for Brother 1

Phantasmagoria Ursus 18

Pigsty (Remastered) 42

THE GOTHIKA DETHFEST INCIDENT 57

Eat Me (Extreme Warning) 76

Walk the Plank 90

A Horrible Day to Have a Curse 99

Die Forever (Extreme Warning) 116

Reappraisal 132

Faceless 153

It Stared Back (Extreme Warning) 172

Fighting Fire With Fire 185

All Men Must Die 201

Memento Mori 221

Grind Finale 239

About the Authors (In Order of Appearance) ....

B is for Brother

by
Daemon Manx

Good…you're finally awake.

I thought I lost you for a second.

Chloroform can be so unpredictable, and some people have zero tolerance for the stuff. Also, my guys aren't exactly surgical when it comes to delicate matters like extraction.

I imagine you're still a little starstruck. I mean, one minute you're watching from the crowd, and the next, you're headed backstage. Dream come true, right? Meeting the blokes from your favorite band, Mary Jane's Mother, and shaking hands with your idol, Davin Lee. Not to toot my own horn, but I'm kind of a big deal, and it's not the sort of thing that happens every day.

I picked you, my friend…spotted you right away. And you've got something we did.

Do it!

Shhh…Easy…You're scared, I get it. But struggling won't do you any good. Those straps are over two inches thick. You'll be able to breathe just fine if you relax. It's only a ball gag. But I'm afraid talking is out of the question, and as far as screaming goes…Well, you'll find it quite impossible. Not that it would help if you could.

Look around for a moment. Do you feel that?

That's right. We're in a moving vehicle, traveling west on one of the nation's infinite lost highways, and you, my friend, just scored the VIP ticket of your life!

B is for Brother

Welcome to my own private little corner of the world—or the Lab, as I like to call it. She's a beauty, isn't she? A true work of engineering genius. Over twelve inches of soundproofing insulate the exterior walls, and the floor has been fitted with a series of drains to help expedite clean-up, as things tend to get a bit messy from time to time. The overhead spigots can deliver over two hundred PSIs of chlorinated scrubbing power, and the runoff is sent directly to a set of holding tanks located underneath the vehicle. All this is nestled secretly between the band's sound system and light show, atop eighteen wheels of traveling madness.

Settle down, James. You don't mind if I call you "James," do you? I'll explain everything. However, I don't think you're going to like what I have to say. But nonetheless, I'm going to talk, and you're going to listen, James. It's only polite, after all the trouble I've gone through to get you here.

Now, that's better. Like I said, I spotted you right away. Call it a sixth sense, but I've seen that look a thousand times. The way you watched my every move, focusing on my fingers as they danced across the neck. It's okay—it's called "hero worship," and it comes with the job. Nothing to be ashamed of. It doesn't take a brain surgeon. *Ha, ha, ha*! Now that's funny. Like I said, it doesn't take a brain surgeon to fit the pieces together. You were wearing a concert tee from our first tour, Skunk Mountain. Man, those were the days. There aren't a lot of those bad boys floating around anymore. The guitar pick necklace was another dead giveaway, not to mention the tattoo. Got to say, I'm honored, even if it doesn't look all that much like me. It was pretty damn obvious, dude, you're a Davin Lee fan. Admit it, mate. I'm your fuckin idol.

What are we waiting for!

I said, *shhh!*

No, not you. Look, just stay with me, James. This isn't the time to get agitated. I prefer not to put you under again, but if you continue to squirm, you'll leave me no choice. Hmm…now where was I? Ah, yes.

First, it's obvious you're a musician, a fan of the band. Anyone could see that. Further inspection would reveal you to be an axe man, one who has been seriously influenced by yours truly. Well, like I told you backstage—though I doubt if you remember—I'm honored. I love my fans, especially the fellow players. You might say, there's a special place in my heart for blokes like you. *Ha, ha, ha!* More like a special place in my head, if I'm being completely honest.

Have you ever considered what draws an individual to their instrument of choice? What makes drummers choose to take up the drums, bassists to play bass? And what is it that drives an axe man to pick up their first guitar? Well, I've thought a great deal about it, James. I believe it goes far deeper than simple desire. Any musician worth his salt will tell you, it's something inside us. *Heh, heh, heh!* Deep down within our souls.

The common man doesn't hear it—the call from within. But for guys like you and me, the shredders, the masters of our instruments…Well, I think that type of dedication to the craft, that attention to finesse, is a gift handed down genetically. It's in our DNA.

I think that can be said for axe masters, at least. Drummers I'm not so sure about. Any Neanderthal can bang on a hollow log and form a rudimentary beat. And don't get me started on bass players. There are only four strings, for fuck's sake! The most untalented guys I've ever met in the business have all been bass players with their fat, dick-beater fingers barely capable of mastering a simple pentatonic. No, James. Guys like us are a special breed. And it's not just about the speed. It's about knowledge and technique. It's about drive and devotion, James. Those attributes aren't gifted to just anyone; they're certainly not wasted on bass players or drummers. That blessing is specifically reserved for only the greats. Men like Mozart, Beethoven, Malmsteen, Satriani…Davin Lee. And maybe you as well, James.

I don't know how it was for you, but I was a natural. I could blast out cover tunes by the age of eleven and was ripping flames across the fretboard, shredding note for note of "Sweet Child of Mine," before I hit high school. And I owe it all to my brother, Davey. Like I said, it's in our DNA.

Exactly. Now get on with it!

Patience…Patience.

I see you're confused. The look on your face tells me you think you know a great deal about me. That Davin Lee, lead guitarist for Mary Jane's Mother, is an only child and never had a brother. Well, you're half right. I *am* an only child, but I did have a brother—for a little while, that is. A twin, in fact, and his name was Davey. At least, it would have been if he'd been born.

The doctors told my mum she was having twins, and she was elated. They had detected two heartbeats which appeared strong and healthy at the time. Mum ate right, took her vitamins, wasn't a smoker or a drinker, and the development of both fetuses appeared to be on track throughout much of the first trimester.

But something happened at the end of the fourth month.

Mum woke up one evening in the grips of the most severe contractions. She was rushed to the hospital but started to hemorrhage on the way. The doctors managed to stop the bleeding and stabilize her. Finally, the contractions subsided, but when it was all said and done, they were only able to detect one heartbeat. Davey was gone…nearly.

It's a condition called fetus-in-fetu, and it's extremely rare. Occurring in only one in every 500,000 births, or so I'm told. It's a form of parasitic twin syndrome, where one fetus absorbs the other. Usually, the underdeveloped twin is found partially formed in the abdominal cavity of the other. The healthy twin typically strangles the blood flow to their weaker sibling and consumes what remains of the tissue. Upon birth, there's usually very little left—a tangle of hair in the form of a cyst or a small mass of bone.

Only, that's not what happened with me and Davey. Our connection was a bit more cerebral.

You talk too much.

Please…this is important. Every time you interrupt me, I lose my train of thought.

Ah, yes. The doctors had no idea of any of this when I was born. They believed what remained of my brother had been discharged along with the placenta and my mum had given birth to a single healthy baby boy. That was, until I turned seven and the headaches started.

You can't imagine the pain. Unbearable, I tell you. Not like the typical headaches you get in the temples or the throbbing kind in the center of the forehead. These were even worse than those blinding migraines behind the eyes, the crippling ones that make you sick to your stomach. They started out simple enough, like an itch in the back of my neck. You know that area where the skull meets the spine? Yeah, that's called the brainstem. Well, that's where it started. Just an itch at first, but, man, did it get worse.

It felt like a knot, like a balled-up fist punching me in the back of the head, only from the inside out. And the sound…Christ…the sound. I could hear it eating away at me. You know the sound Styrofoam makes when it's wet and you rub your fingers against it? That's what it sounded like inside my head. Only loud, like it was being blasted through a Marshall stack. *Ha, ha. This one goes to eleven.* I love that movie, James!

Mum took me to the doc, who recommended I see a group of specialists. They ran a series of tests, CT scans and MRIs, and that's when they found him—Davey. Well, what was left of him. The parts I hadn't fully absorbed.

They hadn't considered it at first, but the MRI results were quite conclusive. The headaches I was experiencing were due to not only an enlarged cerebellum, nearly double the normal size, but a foreign object emmeshed in the tissue near the top of my brainstem. As far as the doctors could tell, it appeared to be a small organ, possibly an eyeball. Davey's eyeball. Due to the acute location of the foreign object, they ruled out surgery and prescribed a series of medications, which did wonders to alleviate most of the pain...

Most.

The abnormal size of my cerebellum was a mystery they were unable to explain; however, the answer to that puzzle quickly revealed itself.

I stopped taking the pills when I turned nine—hated feeling sluggish and out of sorts, always tired and gloomy. I'd hide them under my tongue when mum gave them to me, then spit them out when she wasn't looking. I figured if the headaches came back, I would start taking them again; it was a risk I was willing to take. Well, they didn't come back, and I started to feel like my old self...better, in fact. I had more energy and a newfound clarity of thought. However, there was one side effect—that's when Davey started talking to me.

Tada!

You're thinking I'm mad. I assure you I'm not. Well...no more than I deserve to be.

It was nothing short of a miracle. Once Davey revealed himself, I was overcome with a wash of awareness, and everything began to make perfect sense. I had always felt different than the other children, like I had been chosen for a greater purpose—selected, if you will. And Davey's presence confirmed that.

At first, our discussions were brief, nothing more than a few words exchanged in our own secret brotherly language. But in the weeks and months to come, our conversations grew more in depth, and Davey's instructions became clear. You could say I was thinking with twice the clarity. That's just one of the benefits of being born with a double-sized cerebellum.

You do know what the cerebellum is responsible for, don't you, James? Well, you should. I'm going to go out on a limb and say you have an above average portion of brain as well. Certainly nothing compared to what I've been blessed with. But you wouldn't be able to play lead if you weren't gifted with a little somethin' something. I'm sure of it…I can smell it.

We can smell it. Do it. Do it now!

Now, Davey, it would be impolite to rush our guest.

You know, James. The word cerebellum itself means "little brain." Isn't that ironic? Considering the fact my *little* brain is indeed quite large.

Funny.

Yes. Well, the cerebellum has a great deal of responsibility. For starters, it's the part of the brain in charge of virtually all physical movement. Balance, posture, speech, not to mention coordination and muscle movements. Then there's the processing of emotions. It's where the pleasure and fear response are triggered. But my favorite function of the cerebellum is its attention to precision and motor functions…like learning how to play guitar.

B is for Brother

It was Davey who suggested we pick up the instrument in the first place. With so much pent-up energy and undirected focus, he knew we'd have to find something to occupy our attention. Honestly, some of the thoughts he was having…There was no way we could act on any of them—not successfully, at least. Davey has always possessed quite the eclectic appetite and can be rather disagreeable when he doesn't get what he wants.

Anyhow, I convinced mum into picking up a used acoustic, and that helped quench the cravings. For a spell. Like I said, I was a natural. Operating with the motor skills of two, it was a breeze. The scales made perfect sense; it was as if I could see them laid out before me on the fretboard. The patterns and licks came easily. My fingers grew stronger with each practice, and my speed and accuracy increased by the day. I was able to pick up songs I had only just heard and perform them note for note, never taking a lesson, and I surpassed other musicians twice my age. Playing kept my hands busy and even seemed to satisfy Davey's constant thirst for something new and exciting.

Tell him…Tell him already so we can do this!

I'm getting to that, dear brother.

You see, James. Davey was prone to making suggestions I simply wasn't comfortable with. While the guitar satisfied my own darker urges, it was only a temporary fix for him. We talked of his desires at great length. I expressed my concerns and listened to his as well. But it all came down to nourishment, something I had never considered. Davey's entire existence was localized within our shared cerebellum. The increased activity we now exerted due to our love for the instrument had begun to take its toll on my twin brother.

It requires an awful lot of energy to master the axe. I'm sure you know. It's draining of a very specific type of fuel, and that fuel must be replenished, by any means possible.

Any means, James.

The human brain is comprised of a sixty percent fat content, with salt, carbohydrates, water, and protein making up the other forty percent. If you've never tried it, let me tell you, it's delicious…and the nutritional value is unparalleled. Also, it's exactly what my famished brother required. There was no way we could continue to expend energy without replacing it. However, we both knew we couldn't execute his wishes without the proper skillsets…or the means of disposal.

Settle down, James. Settle down. It doesn't matter how hard you struggle; this is going to happen whether you want it to or not. Now, show a little respect and allow me to finish, or I will simply put you back under and rip the meat from your unconscious body.

Oh, come on. Crying won't change anything. Show a little dignity, mate.

It's music to our ears, brother.

You could say, Davey and I came to an agreement. I promised I would provide him with the nourishment he required if he provided us with a little something in return. You've heard of musicians selling their souls to the Devil in exchange for fame and fortune. Davey and I had a similar arrangement. We were still quite young at the time, and it wasn't very likely a teenage boy could successfully get away with murder. It wouldn't help for either of us to spend our lives behind bars. As promised, Davey delivered.

The speed and precision of my playing grew tenfold, and as I neared my eighteenth birthday, I was asked to join a band called Mud Bottom. I'm sure you've heard the story. The rest of the members were all older dand had been together for some time. They mostly played pubs and had set me up with a fake ID, which seemed to satisfy the bar owners. We were drawing decent crowds, and although the face on the license didn't even resemble me, most were inclined to overlook it. Afterall, the bar was making money, we were making money, and everyone was happy. Everyone except for Davey, who was eager for me to fulfill my half of the bargain.

Then it happened…

We had just finished playing our last set to a standing-room-only packed house, and who approaches me after the show? Bentley Dickers from Peace Frog Entertainment. He shook my hand, slipped me his business card so the other guys in the band wouldn't see, then leaned in and whispered, "Call me if you want to be a star, kid."

And the rest, as they say, James, is history. I called Mr. Dickers the following day. A week later, he set me up with an audition. The band was called Mary Jane's Mother, and they had recently lost their lead guitar player. It was no easy gig, Mr. Dickers told me. They called it stoner rock, but that tag doesn't truly do the genre justice. The position they were looking to fill was a demanding one, and they needed someone with knowledge of varying jazz scales and alternate time signatures. Someone comfortable playing freestyle, without limitations like set song structure or chord progression pattern. I could tell they doubted I was the guy for the job.

Well, we sure showed them.

They laid into the opening changes of "Chronic Silence"—you know it from the *Skunk Mountain* album. I listened for a few bars, allowing the groove and the mode to settle in, letting Davey resonate in the funk. Then we started playing. I made that Stratocaster cry like it was my bitch, and before I was halfway through the first solo, I had the job.

Brother…I'm starving!

We opened for Flamethrower that year, and *Skunk Mountain* sold over two million copies. Some might call it an overnight success story, but Davey and I knew that wasn't the case. For my dear brother, it had been an eternity—all those years pouring his very lifeforce into the art, sacrificing his health so we could reach the stars.

And it had finally happened.

Finally.

And now, it was my turn to deliver.

Until that point, I hadn't exactly understood my brother's needs and was a bit concerned about his appetite. After all, his hunger was my own, and whatever he digested had to be consumed by me first. But that wasn't what had stopped me from executing his wishes sooner. I wasn't squeamish about the idea of eating brains, just worried about getting caught. Our only chance of getting away with such an act—killing another human being and extracting the gray matter from their skull—would require not only a small entourage of trusted accomplices, but a great deal of cash and resources. Both of which I now possessed.

You mean our *appetite, dear brother.*

Ah, yes. I did say I hadn't understood my brother's appetite until that point. But something changed during the first few shows of the *Skunk Mountain* tour. Of course, it can be difficult to distinguish his thoughts from my own, his desire from mine. It's a symbiotic relationship, parasitic twin syndrome. And with a shared organ so predominant, the waters began to run a bit muddy. Naturally, there was a little bleed-through.

Naturally.

Suddenly, I understood his hunger, felt his craving as my own, and sought to satisfy that ravenous desire with a fever. The years of expended energy had drained us both, and the euphoric sensation of playing to thousands in sold-out arenas was the catalyst igniting the engine.

The first time was messy. Although I was eager, I was ill prepared for the undertaking. We had yet to perfect our method of extraction. Call it a learning curve. His name was Eddie, a young man about your age. Davey spotted him in the front row at one of the shows, like he did with you. Eddie was an axe man as well. It takes one to know one, and he didn't think twice when my guys offered him a backstage pass for after the show. Hell, everyone wants to meet a rock star.

We didn't use chloroform back then—something a bit more primitive laced in the water. But effective just the same. I have three men under my employment whom I trust implicitly. They've worked for me for years and handle all my extractions. But you already know that, James. Yes, you do.

Yes.

I'd bought a rather large piece of secluded property. My men delivered Eddie to the residence I had built specifically for the procedure, then left me to my business. We had strapped Eddie's body to a table, nothing like the dentist's chair you're tethered to. No, it was a stainless steel surgeon's table, and that was a mistake.

I got to tell you, I was scared shitless. Not as much as Eddie was, but scared nonetheless. There's just so much to consider when it comes to decapitation. It's not like they teach you this stuff in school. Honestly, there's an art to this sort of thing, and I had no idea what I was doing. Should I use a blade, a hand tool, a power saw? Sure, Davey was there for guidance and moral support, but he had never performed the act before, and it's not like he had hands of his own. All the heavy lifting was on my shoulders.

Being a novice in the game, I opted for a Makita Sawzall with a ten-inch reciprocating wood blade.

What a mess.

Yes, brother. What a mess indeed.

I stood behind the lad with my saw at the ready, and he freaked! Eddie started thrashing and bucking against his restraints. I thought he might break free. The closer I came with the blade, the worse he reacted. He bit down so hard on his gag, his teeth snapped off at the gumline. Then he lifted his head several inches off the table and threw it back hard enough to knock himself unconscious. It was a blessing, really, and probably the only reason I was able to go through with the procedure.

Once Eddie was out, I pressed my finger to the trigger once again, causing the saw to roar to life. I lowered the thrusting blade to within millimeters of the young man's throat and pushed downward.

Oh, yes!

It cut into the soft meat just below Eddie's Adam's apple easily enough. But then the saw jumped as it ripped open the trachea and hit his carotid artery. Turns out, wood blades aren't that efficient when it comes to cutting into flesh after all.

In a heartbeat, the blood was everywhere. It jetted out of the boy's neck like a pulsing fountain, covering the saw, the table, and me as well. My stomach jumped into my throat. The gore painted every surface, and I remember feeling like I was about to pass out. Still, I couldn't for the life of me take my finger off the trigger. Not even when the blade snagged on Eddie's flesh.

It was awful, the way his head thrashed in time with the thrust of the blade. The serrated teeth pulled his skin inside the housing of the mechanism, till it finally overheated and stopped working entirely.

I stood over the body, cannons thundering inside my head. The hilt of the saw, buried halfway through Eddie's neck, was now impossible to remove. I tugged and pulled without success. Thick coppery fluid covered me from head to foot. It tasted metallic, almost electric. Like the way fingers taste after they've changed guitar strings.

Brotherrrrr…I'm starving.

I started to panic, had no idea how to finish the job or if I even could. That's when Davey spoke up. He assured me everything would be fine if I did exactly what he said. And what a brilliant idea he had.

Brilliant.

Have you ever heard of the Gigli saw, James? No? Cat got your tongue? *Ha, ha*! It's the type of corded saw doctors used to perform amputations back in the day. They're usually made of stainless steel and consist of several individual wires braided together, fastened to either wooden or metal handles at the ends.

Well, I didn't have one lying around, but you know what I did have? That's right…A damn drawer full of used guitar strings. Davey showed me how to braid them together, which was easy to do. I gripped the ends using a pair of leather gloves and went to work on old Eddie. Wow…wouldn't ya know.

How about that?

Who would have thought how efficient a used set of Ernie Balls could be at slicing into flesh? I had the Sawzall free in no time and lobbed off Eddie's noggin like the head of a dandelion.

Then came the job of extracting the gray matter, which wasn't as difficult as one might think. Sure, the skull is thick and harder than a coconut, but we already had access to the part we were after. The cerebellum is located just above the brainstem, and if you remove the remaining tissue around the spine—or what's left of it—you can snap that sucker off using very little effort.

Pop!

It's downhill from there. All you have to do is scoop out the good stuff. I like to use a twelve-inch cocktail spoon. The added length offers enough leverage to really dig into the meat.

We've all seen the movie, but trust me on this one, James. Brains are best eaten raw. You don't want to braise them or serve them with fava beans and a nice Chianti. No, no, no, that's a sure-fire way to spoil the meal.

Davey prefers his served slightly above room temperature, fresh out of the container, long before the body has time to chill. Although I had my doubts, it's really quite delicious.

Mmmm.

I'm not sure how Davey knew precisely what we needed to sustain our gift, the exact nutrients required to replenish our depleted cerebellum. He's always been so insightful. Playing guitar at such a heightened intensity is exhausting. Arena and outdoor events take an even greater toll on us. Add in a heavy dose of carnage and chaos, like the shit that went down at Dethfest, and our need to feed becomes taxed to its very limit.

You should be glad you missed most of it, James. Things got crazy before we split. Cannibalism…Arson…There was even a damn bear. Yeah, you should probably thank me. No?

I didn't think you would, but you *are* going to give me something very few have had the honor of. You, James, are going to provide us with sustenance.

And that brings me to this little beauty right here. This is my Gigli saw, and she is something special.

Special.

The coil is made of four braided B strings. I know…How cool is that? You're wondering why I chose the B string? Well, for a few reasons. First, I found the E to be a bit too flimsy. Couldn't get the job done. And the lower strings, the G, D, A, and low E…Well, they wouldn't braid properly, and besides, the letter B holds a special meaning to Davey and me. Afterall, B is for *beautiful*, B is for *beheading*, B is for *brains*, and finally, B is for *brother*.

Now, brother.

Yes, now, brother.

Try to hold still, James. This will all be over soon. You're going to feel a little pressure.

Easy.

Easy, stop squirming. That's it. I'm afraid this is going to hurt, James.

Quite a bit.

Yes, quite a bit, James.

Now you're playing my song, brotherrrr!

A Confession about Confessions

As a long-time musician, I jumped at the chance to write this story for *Dethfest Confessions.* I wasn't sure what I would write at the time but knew I had to not only do justice to the horror genre, but pay tribute to the Gods of Metal as well. To be honest, I'm a bass player, not a shredder, and certainly not one with any exceptional skill when it comes to thumping out a few clumsy tunes.

I do, however, hold high regard for those who spend years mastering their instruments, coming to know them in the most intimate ways. And my story needed to touch on that symbiotic relationship in more ways than one. Having spent much of my youth playing in bands, surrounded by other musicians—eating, drinking, and breathing that lifestyle—I felt I could at least do justice to the music side of the story.

Then came the horror side of it. I had an idea for the direction I wanted to lean and toyed around with a few possible scenarios. This story needed to create tension. I wanted it to be disturbing, and the reveal had to be undeniably brutal. I don't know about you, but nothing scares me more than the idea of being rendered immobile while a madman hovers over me, talking to himself…maybe to someone else…as he prepares to do unthinkable, ghastly things.

But Davin isn't your average madman. In fact, it's questionable to say whether he is at all. Everyone is the hero of their own story. Who are we to judge what another must do to survive? I'm sure there's more than a few hungry souls out there like Davin Lee.

Now, that's a nasty thought…don't you think?

Anyway, I hope you enjoyed "B Is for Brother," and I hope you consider reading more of my work in the future. Until we speak again, keep your friends close and your brothers even closer.

Daemon Manx
2023

Phantasmagoria Ursus
by
Steve Stred

"Chugga, chugga, chugga. You hear those fucking hacks?" Baleen shouted.

"Hey now," Talon, Klaaz's vocalist, said, leaning against one of the amps backstage. "Fleshpeel done well for themselves."

The rest of the group known as Klaaz broke into laughter, Baleen grinning wider than the rest. They'd toured often with the Fleshpeel crew and were stoked they were both on the Dethfest bill. The band always tried to keep loose backstage, but this was their moment to crush the masses and take another step toward owning the crown, being the biggest metal band in the world.

It'd been a longer journey than they'd expected. Some setbacks early on, especially when Razor, their lead guitarist, decided they should have a live bear come on stage with them.

"Like a fucking mascot! The coolest fucking mascot ever!" he'd proclaimed, leaving the rest of the group to wonder what he'd been smoking.

Turned out, he was right.

Their "manager" found a dude who could get a bear cub, and they acquired the little fella through less-than-ideal means. The first time the bear was let loose in their rehearsal space, he'd climbed onto the drums and tapped a tom a few times, which led them to christen him Lars.

"Just like Lars Ulrich, the fucker didn't use any double bass!" Talon had said, and the group laughed until tears came.

The crowds fucking loved it, and whenever Lars let out a roar from on stage, the women would show their tits, and the men banged their heads even harder. If you asked Talon, they were living the dream. Most of the clubs were cool with it. Some refused, others weren't told prior to Lars being brought out, but all in all, he was an expected part of Klaaz's live show.

And getting a prime slot on Stage 1 at Dethfest was another feather in their cap.

Baleen, their bass player, went through some more warmup scales while his wife, Dee, worked on applying his stage makeup. Talon always loved watching her work. To think she somehow transformed the six-foot-four, three-hundred-pound man—who in real life had the lame moniker of "Karl McNeil"—into a semi-ferocious-looking whale was always impressive.

"Baaaaaaaaaaaleeeeeennnnn," Talon screamed, punctuated with a guttural yell at the end, making even Dee smile.

She patted and penciled Baleen's makeup on, knowing by the time the first chorus of their opening song hit, Karl would be sweating so much it wouldn't matter. It'd just be goopy slop pouring down his chin.

Razor ripped through his scales soon joined by Rabid, their second guitarist and his younger brother. Talon howled, watching Rabid doing his fucking damnedest to keep up to Razor.

"Aye, Rabid? Didn't you fill in with Misery Index for an eastern U.S. tour? What's with this shit? Show him what you're made of." Mongrel, their drummer, pulled out his kit and started to rattle off a rhythm, forcing Razor and Rabid to fall into a guitar battle out of sheer peer pressure.

The band—and Dee—were all watching and heckling the brothers, not noticing Asshat wandering over. Asshat was their tour manager, bear wrangler, and main roadie. They'd not yet grown to the level of having a travelling crew, but Asshat could get fans to volunteer and even some of the other bands' crew to pitch in. He had a way with people. Plus, he could always score drugs and shared them with whomever gave a helping hand. For many, that was incentive enough.

While the guitar battle raged on, Asshat handed Talon and Baleen two bottles of water, keeping one for himself. Dee, seeing the drink, motioned for it, which Asshat grudgingly handed to her.

"You got a problem?" she asked, seeing him noticeably huff.

"Nah, Dee. Just that was the last fucking bottle at catering."

"So? Go grab some from the crowd. They're handing bottles out like they're condoms."

"Sure thing, boss lady," he said, jogging away before her foot connected with his ass.

Fuck, she's hot, he thought, turning and smirking at her. *Can't believe Baleen's luck.*

Asshat knew the reason chicks sucked him off behind the tour bus was in hopes of getting on it, but he had his rules. No strangers on the bus. He didn't want the boys accused of anything. Not worth taking any chances. And if they smacked him when he told them they couldn't get on the bus? No biggie. He'd just been blown. Asshat had gotten his, and that's what mattered.

He pushed past a guitar player from one of the other bands and continued down the short steps, bringing him beside the stage. To his left was the cage where their big brown bear was currently snoozing and snoring away, having recently gorged itself on half a pig laced with a mild tranquilizer. The right led around to the front, where the photogs were and where any crowd surfers would be directed if they came over the security railing.

Asshat was in luck. Only a dozen feet away, in the crowd, stood one of those water guys handing out free bottles.

"Hey! Hey! Water-bottle guy!" he yelled, but the *vrrrrrmmmm* of the current band's bass drowned him out. "Hey! I need some water for Klaaz!"

A sea of heads swung in his direction when he said the band's name. A couple of kids recognized him, one guy trying—and failing—to get an "Asshat!" chant started.

"What'd you say, bro?"

Asshat looked toward the voice, finding a guy whose stature would give Baleen a run for his money. The guy had dreads down to his ass, a chin-only growth of hair that wanted to belong on Scott Ian's face, and eyes so diluted, Asshat didn't think the guy even knew where he was.

"I said, I need water for Klaaz! We ran out backstage!"

He swatted a few hands away, people pushing to take a selfie or attempting to swipe his "Crew/All Access Pass" from around his neck.

"Bro, I can get you the fucking water. How many you need? Ten? Twelve?"

"You think you can manage fifteen? We like to spray water over the bear before taking the stage. That way, he looks scary and shit." Asshat turned and smiled as a girl snapped a selfie. He paused and took another photo with a guy who looked like Kurt Cobain but smelled like Chris Barnes.

"Yeah, fuck, that's easy. Meet you here?"

Asshat looked around, finding Simon Worthington standing near the stairs to the backstage area.

"Simon," he yelled, then whistled.

The man turned and saw Asshat, then waved and walked toward him. Simon was one of the guys in charge of set-up and take-down for the bands, having cut his teeth working at Ozzfest back in the day.

"What's up, Andrew?"

Simon was also one of only two people in the entire heavy metal world who called him by his real name. The other was Bruce Dickinson, who refused to call anyone "Asshat."

"I need to get some water for Klaaz. This guy here is grabbing us some bottles. Can you get him back to the band once he gets here with the H20?"

"Is catering out?" Simon asked.

"No clue. We just don't have any backstage."

"Yeah, this'll be faster. Sure thing. I'll wait here."

So, it was settled. Asshat told the guy to grab the bottles and come back to Simon. Leaving them, he jogged back to where the band was still standing around. Though he was bummed he had missed the guitar battle, it was obvious Rabid had lost—he was currently changing a few broken strings on his guitar.

"Here, I gotcha." Asshat grabbed the guitar and went to work.

He gave no more thought to the guy getting water until the events played out forty-five minutes later.

*

Espen Rasmussen lived for order and control.

He was the unknown at big events like these. At least to the bands and to the fans who attended.

Espen was a sniper by trade, but since getting out of the military world, he had led a group of similarly minded folk who watched for threats or, as the briefing before the concert stated, "anything that could cause a casualty." What they didn't want— what *nobody* wanted—was a repeat of the events that happened on December 8, 2004. And while Espen had been a teenager then, he'd not been big into heavy metal, so he didn't know the history of the band. He'd heard of Pantera before, but not Damageplan.

That made no difference. His group was here to prevent any nutjobs from somehow getting on stage and making a name for themselves.

They also had a secondary objective, which had been practically yelled to them from the higher-ups on one of the last Zoom calls during a safety check briefing.

"And that *fucking* band Klaaz is bringing their *fucking* bear!" the man had screamed, face reddening. "If that brute gets loose, I want no issues. You fucking blast it before it can attack *anyone*! Got it?"

The call ended before Espen had a chance to reply.

He was intrigued. *A bear.* That was different. Iron Maiden had their big mascot, Eddie. Megadeth brought Vic Rattlehead out on stage. And Roger Waters was still flying a big pig above the concertgoers' heads. But a bear? *First time for everything,* Espen had thought, briefing his own guys.

On his watch, nothing was going to happen. He wouldn't let anyone storm the stage, and he sure as hell wasn't going to let a bruin make a snack out of any attendees.

*

"Andrew," Simon said, finding Asshat backstage. "This large, um…gentleman has those waters for you."

Asshat chuckled at how uncomfortable Simon was. He was a guy who liked to oversee, not mix and mingle, with the people who attended the shows. It was evident in his body language, standing beside the large guy who was struggling to keep the bottles from falling.

"Here, man, let me help you." Asshat quickly grabbed a bunch of the bottles before they fell.

"You can show him how to get back to the crowd." Simon offered a parting wave and hastily went back to where he normally stood.

"Thanks so much." Asshat extended his hand. "Sorry, what was your name?"

The man's hand snapped out and viciously shook Asshat's, threatening to tear his arm off.

"Name's Bryce, dude, but everyone calls me Bumps!"

"Nice! Great meeting you, Bryce." He caught a glimpse of Talon leaning against a stack of amps. "Hey, as a thanks, you wanna meet Talon? Take a picture with him? Not sure where the rest of the band's fucked off to."

"Fucking A! I'd love that," Bryce said, looking around rapidly.

"He's right over here." Asshat directed the behemoth toward the singer. Talon was always up for meeting fans, so he knew this wouldn't annoy him.

Asshat took a swig from a bottle of water, grabbed two more, and led Bryce over to the stack of amps. Talon was in the process of getting his stage attire on. His makeup was done, and he'd put on some of the animal furs he wore.

"You find some water?" Talon asked, not looking up.

"Yeah, here you go." Asshat handed him a bottle.

"Thanks for opening it for me," Talon said, which made Asshat pause.

He *hadn't* opened it.

Asshat glanced at Bryce, who had a shit-eating grin plastered on his face. He thought nothing of it, shrugging it off as a fan meeting the singer of a band.

"Hey, Talon, this is Bryce. He got us the bottles of water from out in the crowd."

"Well, fuck! Thanks, man! That's fucking great. You want a picture or something?" Talon stood, taking in how massive Bryce was.

"Photo'd be sweet!" Bryce handed his cellphone to Asshat and stepped beside Talon. He threw one thick arm around the vocalist, pulling him closer and raising his other hand high, horns in the air.

"Count of three, say 'Sharon's a cunt!' One…two…three!"

"*Sharon's a cunt*!" Talon and Bryce shouted together.

Asshat pressed the button on the screen a few times, knowing Bryce would appreciate catching the candid moments of them breaking into laughter.

"Really appreciate it," Talon said, shaking Bryce's hand again. "I gotta take a piss, but if I see the other guys, I'll send them over. Baleen was bitching about how hot he was getting, so I think they went to find a fan to stand in front of."

Bryce offered his fist, and Talon fist-bumped him back before scampering away into the underbelly of the stage.

"Hey, Asshat? If it's cool with you, instead of the other members…you think I could see the bear?"

"Sure. Just this once." Asshat knew it'd be easier and less time-consuming to show him the furry guy asleep in his cage than to track the band down. If he played his cards right, he might have time to find a hottie to suck his dick before the band went on. He looked at his watch. It was five minutes until they had to be on deck. Asshat nearly shit himself.

"*Fuck*. All right, times ticking. The bear is in the cage just around there," he said to Bryce, pointing. "Feel free to take a few pictures, but don't get too close. Then go see Simon again, and he'll let you watch from the side of the stage. I gotta get these misfits ready to go."

He left before Bryce knew what was happening and jogged off to find the band.

*

Bryce stood there, perplexed for a minute, before deciding this was his chance to meet Klaaz's bear so he better take it. He grabbed a few bottles of water, laughing to himself about what he'd done, and walked toward where Asshat had told him the bear was.

Sure enough, he rounded the corner and came face-to-face with a decent-sized cage. Inside, the massive bear was snoring away, its upper lips flopping around with each exhale.

"Holy fuck."

Bryce had never seen a bear in person before, let alone one this large. And this close.

"Hey, fella," he said, feeling foolish calling it Lars. He stepped to the side of the cage and set the water bottles down. Bryce wrapped his hands around two of the bars, wondering how he could touch the bear. It seemed to be pretty out of it, judging by how deep the snores were, and if the bear was anything like how his dad used to be, the louder the snores, the less likely it'd wake. It was how he used to snag cash, beer, and pot from his old man—wait until he was conked and then go on a scavenger hunt for goodies.

Bryce cursed his thick forearms, wiggling his fingers in an effort to touch the bear's fur. He'd somehow managed to get his arm in a decent amount, but when the bars pinched him hard halfway up his forearm, he realized he was fucked. Bryce tried to pull, twist, and jerk, but there was nothing happening. His arm was stuck. He couldn't even reach a water bottle. If he could, he might've been able to pour some water on his arm and make it slippery.

"Help! Fuck. Somebody *help*!" he hollered, pulling as hard as he could against the cage but only causing himself agonizing pain. The bars held his forearm firm, and his skin felt like it was being ripped off. No matter how loud he shouted, the band that was playing made sure no one heard.

A loud snort caught his attention.

Bryce slowly turned his head, dreading what he'd see. And what he found was what he was praying wouldn't be there.

The fucking bear was staring at him.

"*Help!*"

He screamed it as loudly as he could, but the bear, startled awake, roared, drowning out his pleas.

*

"Asshat, you put something in this water?" Talon asked, eyeballing the bottle after he took another drink.

"No, why?"

"Dude, my peripheral vision is getting fuzzy. Always happens when I take psychedelics. You positive?"

Asshat gulped. Deeply. *Fuck. Bryce.* That's why he was grinning like a maniac. That's why all the bottle cap seals had been broken. The giant fucker had spiked their water.

"You gonna be okay to go on stage?" Asshat asked, eyeballing his own water, not sure why he wasn't feeling anything. *Probably 'cause you dropped acid twice already today, numb nuts,* his brain answered.

"Ha! You think we're amateurs? Remember when we all did acid for, like, a week straight, up and down the East Coast, playing parking lot shows after each Hatebreed concert? I think a little fuzz will be just fine. Right, Rabid?"

The guitar player simply nodded. The grin he sported told Asshat he was feeling A-okay.

"You guys have three minutes until stage time. You ready?" Asshat asked.

Baleen pushed by him, patting him on the shoulder. He took a solid stance with his bass in front, legs wide, knees bent, and strummed the opening intro to Klaaz's biggest song, "Churn the Soil."

"Under an icy snowfall," Talon sang. "Under a clear, blue moon!"

Asshat's favorite tune. He gave Talon a high-five.

"You guys opening with that one?"

"Nah, we're gonna open with 'Mastodon.'"

"Whoa, whoa…wait." Asshat held his hands in front of him. "You ain't gonna go out there and say what you normally say, are you?"

"What's that?" Mongrel asked, appearing as though from thin air. "That they used to be a solid fucking heavy metal band and now they're progressive metal poseurs?"

The band broke into hysterical laughter, and Talon slapped Asshat's back in the process.

"Please don't," Asshat pleaded. "You guys have a legit shot here. You don't wanna piss the wrong people off."

"Whoa, look at Asshat growing some morals and some balls," Mongrel replied, getting another round of laughter from the group.

"I promise," Talon said. "We're gonna go straight into 'Mastodon,' followed by 'The Stranger,' 'WE WATCH,' 'Incarnate,' and close with 'Churn the Soil.'"

"Fucking great. That's awesome." Asshat felt a relief he hadn't expected.

"*Klaaz! One minute!*" a guy yelled. Fleshpeel's gear was hastily rolled past.

From nearby, they heard their bear roar, which pumped them all up, the band hooting and hollering and fist-bumping. Talon had his tongue out, wagging it obscenely, while Mongrel rapidly rotated his arms in circles, his face going deadly serious.

"Here we go, boys!" Talon yelled as their intro music kicked in.

Asshat went to get the bear, unaware of what had happened.

*

At first, Bryce didn't feel the bear chomp down on his forearm. He watched the teeth slice through his skin like a warm knife through butter. He watched the bear violently twist and jerk its head and neck, marveling at how smoothly it crunched through his radius and ulnar. The bottom section of his arm—including his hand—seemingly popped free of the rest of his body. Bryce even had a moment to blissfully appreciate the spurts of dark red blood pumping from the open wound, arching through the air, and splattering across the bear's eye and snout, even as the bear tore at the gristle that had previously been his arm.

Then.

Then the pain fucking hit, the shock set in, and Bryce slumped to the ground, hitting the water bottles below him. They easily fell between the bars of the cage, coming to a stop by the bear's huge paw. The lids rolled free and spilled each bottle's contents. The bear greedily lapped at the water.

Bryce, still cognizant enough to find it comical that this huge bruin was drinking spiked water, also knew he wasn't going

29

to live long enough to see the outcome. The bear, having slurped up all the spilled water, lumbered over to where Bryce lay on the outside of the cage and grabbed the stub of his destroyed arm, which remained partly in the cage. With no effort at all, the bear grabbed Bryce and pulled.

The bars initially worked as a block, preventing Bryce from being pulled inside, even as the pain became unimaginable. But that all went away with a sickening tear. The bear rocked backward. The rest of Bryce's arm had been torn from his body, the force enough to send the bear tumbling. Bryce screamed in agony and rolled away. With the pain and blood loss overtaking everything else, Bryce rolled further than he should've, going under the dark black curtains that had been placed around the bottom of the side stage to make sure people knew where to walk. He tried to yell for help as Klaaz's intro music began, but that was all he had. Bryce took his last breath under the stage just as Talon strode confidently into view and the crowd went nuts.

*

Asshat couldn't believe the mess he found when he got to the cage. They'd been assigned a bear "trainer" for the event, something to make sure the proper boxes were checked off when the insurance forms were filled out, but the guy was a Grade-A slacker, and seeing the state of Lars's area confirmed that.

"What the fuck, Lars? I thought you already finished the pig," he said, eyeballing the blood—oddly fresh—and the chunks of meat still stuck to its snout. "You ready to perform, big boy?"

Asshat kicked away a couple of empty bottles. The crowd had been throwing them everywhere all day, and he was getting really fucking annoyed by it at this point.

The bear cage sat atop a furniture dolly, a flat slab of wood with four wheels on it, which allowed it to be easily moved. As each wheel lock was popped free, Lars groaned and swayed, its eyes falling on Asshat. For a moment, Asshat thought the bear looked higher than it normally did, but knowing the amount of tranquilizer they had put in that pig, he wasn't worried.

He had started to push the cage to the side of the stage when the trainer appeared. *What was his name again? Fuck.* It didn't matter. It was showtime.

They pushed the cage over to where two of the Dethfest crew members would help position it on stage just as the first chorus of "Mastodon" would hit, the one that always made Asshat bang his head. "Fear the beeping, watch for those creeping, into the killing circle—*explode*!"

Even thinking about it made him nod his head.

"Here he is," he said to the two crew members once there. Asshat looked to see if Bryce was going to watch from the side of the stage, but when he didn't see him, he shrugged and started pushing.

Once the cage was in place, Talon jogged to his spot, and the trainer motioned for the door to be opened. As it swung, the bear lumbered out, roaring and racing toward Talon.

A thick metal collar was always around Lars's neck, with two chains attached to a reinforced clip on the stage floor. When the bear made it to the end of the chains, its momentum flung it off its feet, into the air, and it landed with a crash, just as Talon bellowed, "*Explode*!" again.

Asshat looked at the mass of fans, crowd surfers, headbangers, horn throwers—the typical metal show crowd— and grinned. This was different than usual. It was the sheer size of the crowd. Everyone was singing along, creating a moment he didn't think he'd ever forget. Asshat felt like he was going to hyperventilate, he was so nervous. He grabbed another bottle of water, ignoring that Bryce had probably spiked this one as well, and guzzled it in two gulps. Asshat wiped his face, a distinct fuzziness blooming behind his eyes, and smiled.

And then everything went off the rails.

*

Talon hated when the bear got ripped backward, knowing that collar around its neck hurt. What he didn't expect—this time, at least—was to see the bear get ripped backward and for it to be free.

That's when he saw Asshat stumbling toward the bear.

What the fuck?

*

Asshat could hear Lars, but he couldn't believe it. All around him was a spectacle of illustrated characters and musical notes dancing and jiving to the beat of his heart.

His heart.

It beat alongside Lars's, as though they were one and the same. *Lars needs to be free*, he told himself.

"Free me, Asshat," Lars said, before laughing and slapping his knee with a meaty paw.

He walked toward the bear, his mind struggling to understand why the two long snakes dangling from Lars's neck were biting the stage floor one minute and then flying free the next.

The bear roared and swatted at the air around it, at something no one could see. Even in Asshat's fuzzy state, mental dots connected.

So much blood. Empty water bottles. Bits of meat. No sign of Bryce.

The bear had fucking killed the dude. The bear had somehow gotten some of the spiked water.

Now, this bear, which had already been tranquilized, was tripping balls on whatever the fuck Bryce had laced the water with. And Asshat was tripping along with it.

A scream erupted. Asshat saw two things at the same time.

The first was the lazy, slacker trainer posturing at the bear, fists raised. Lars whirled toward him and swiped. The man stumbled backward, doubling over, blood pouring from his stomach. The second was the bear pivoting and looking Asshat directly in the eyes. He understood. This bear *remembered*. It remembered Asshat was the one who always gave it the drugged pigs. This bear held *him* responsible for being constantly doped.

This bear wanted to give Asshat a taste of his own medicine.

And there was nothing Asshat could do about it.

*

The rainbows and two-headed frogs mocking and floating in front of Lars were pissing it the fuck off. When Lars swatted a frog away, it felt heavier, thicker, as though a person had been hit, not a hopping piece of shit with a long tongue. Then, when Lars looked over, the bear saw that cocksucker who always gave him the pig. But this time, he seemed different. It was as though he was just a large slab of bloody meat with legs and arms.

And it looked delicious to the drugged brute.

*

The bear was on him in less than two seconds, and as its teeth cut through his skin and penetrated his skull, the last thing Asshat thought was how Lars really was some kind of monster.

*

"Code Bear!"

Espen had been scanning the crowd when Klaaz came onstage, but he'd set his binoculars down and turned away for a moment before all hell had broken loose.

When he'd whipped around, it was just in time to watch the bear charge and decapitate a man Epsen had met not that long ago. He went by the name Asshat, and he was supposed to be the guy in charge of the bear.

Well, that's not good.

"Move out. Safeties off," Espen commanded, pushing the other guys in his crew to go in front of him.

He lingered a moment, trying to see if he had a shot to take the bear down, but it roared, rolled over, and once back on its feet, stampeded through the side of the stage. It easily pulled itself over the tall, blue perimeter fencing.

"He's going to the woods!" Espen shouted into his mic. He hopped down the three short stairs from their lookout booth and ran toward where the bear had escaped.

*

When Asshat had his head ripped off, Talon stopped completely, staring at his friend's body while it twitched. Baleen positioned himself in front of Talon and took a step toward Lars, bass held high in case the bear turned on them. Mongrel, Rabid, and Razor continued playing as though nothing had happened, which made

Talon wonder how much more water they'd had to drink than he had.

They're high as kites, he thought, while they continued rumbling through their song.

The bear rolled off Asshat and immediately sprinted across the stage, leaving crew members to scramble out of the way. Talon had known bears were fast, but Lars surprised him with just how quickly he crossed the stage. Then the bear was over the fence and into the woods.

The crowd began to chant, "Klaaz! Klaaz! Klaaz!"

They immediately went into the next song as though Asshat wasn't currently being dragged off the stage, his crushed skull still leaking blood and brains trailing behind.

*

It struggled to understand what was happening.

All around the bear, giant, kaleidoscopic shapes swirled and dove, trying to grab it and steal it away into the vortex of long-armed trees overtaking the sky.

It pulled itself over the mound of dead animals, the blue bones from the fallen jabbing and stabbing, until it was on the other side, and it raced into the field of burning green eagle legs.

*

The security team followed the bear into the woods, even as the music resumed behind them. Espen had no care for whatever was going on at Dethfest. His task now was to track and kill. He needed to stop this bear from killing anyone else. Luckily, the location of the concert was rural, so he wasn't worried about any random hikers ending up on the wrong end of a pissed-off bear.

But he was worried the animal would pivot and return to the festival.

"You two," Espen said to Franky and Kyle, "flank the left. You two," he said to Johnny and Shane, "right. Flush it back around to me in the middle, and let's knock this guy down quick."

Espen pushed through the thick growth, and the other four darted in their directions.

*

"A fucking bear! I can't wait to tell the boys about this," Franky said to Kyle as they jogged into the trees to the left of Espen.

"You joking about this shit?" Kyle asked, not sure if Franky was being sarcastic or not.

"Yeah, a bear, bro! Like, what the fuck?"

"It killed two people." Kyle stopped to face him.

"Dude. It's a fucking bear. Did you expect it to do the Harlem Shake with them?"

"The what?"

"Fuck you young kids. You don't remember the Harlem Shake?" Franky asked.

Kyle looked at him for another second before shaking his head in frustration and turning to continue.

As he pivoted, a massive bear's paw swung through the air, the long, thick claws easily slicing through his face. His eyeballs popped on impact, his ear was ripped off, and before he died, he realized he was shitting his pants, just as Franky managed to get two shots off.

*

Espen heard two quick pops of gunfire—*crack, crack*—off to his left, followed by a deafening roar. He changed course, moving through the bush toward where Franky and Kyle had gone.

*

After killing Kyle with its paw, the bear had watched the two large bees fly at him and enter his upper left shoulder. Seeing the queen bee standing with the bee launcher, he roared in rage and lunged, grabbing the queen's left wing in his jaws and frantically shaking. The queen screamed, and while it screamed, it transformed into a long, thin stick bug, which the bear went about breaking and snapping in every possible place.

Once he'd rendered the bug into a pile of mulch, Lars turned and sprinted into the trees, his nose picking up the scent of the biggest honeycomb that had ever existed.

*

Espen came upon the remains of Kyle first, then Franky. Franky looked like he'd somehow tumbled into a meat grinder. His body had been crushed and turned to pulp. Espen stifled a gag. In doing so, he spied a splattering of blood leading off into the trees. The bear'd been shot, which would let him track it.

The bear went over the mountain, Espen sang inside his head, stalking off after the beast.

*

Crack, crack!
Aeeeewwhhhhhhhhhhhhhhhhh!

Johnny and Shane stopped when they heard the two shots followed by the agonizing scream.

"Hold formation," Shane said, a regimented asshole.

"Nah, man, we need to get over there. Espen said priority is to immobilize the threat. We can't do that from over here."

"Senior rank here. That's an order. You follow."

Johnny nodded, continuing in the direction they'd been walking.

From off to their left, they heard something barreling through the trees, something they knew could only be one thing.

"Hold position," Shane said, raising his firearm.

The trees shook as the thing got closer, and just as Johnny started to put some pressure on his trigger, a cow appeared, bringing a smile to both their faces.

"Fucking cow," Shane said. "Onward."

*

A cow raced by Espen, which would normally make him scratch his head, but in this case, he understood it meant he was close. He was still following the blood trail, making sure to keep his wits about him. Espen noticed something ahead, a brown *something* between two trees. Moving closer, he stood, firearm raised, when a deep chuffing sounded to his left, over his shoulder.

"Clever boy," he managed before the bear pounced, throwing him to the ground under its mass.

*

Johnny and Shane covered the terrain quickly and efficiently, always remaining within touching distance. When the trees ahead of them shook again, they both positioned, knowing the likelihood another cow would come through was low.

*

The honeycomb had mooed at Lars and then trotted away, enraging the bear. He'd followed it, stopping when he saw a strange-looking cob of corn standing in his way. Saliva dripped, and the smell of the corn overtook the smell of the mooing honeycomb. The bear leaped onto the cob. The butter flowing within never tasted so sweet.

*

Espen wasn't sure why, but the bear had slammed him to the ground and then continued to run.

Must be in pursuit of that cow, he thought, painfully getting to his feet and jogging after the bear.

*

The bear burst through the trees, the animal slamming directly into Johnny while Shane opened fire, hitting it at almost point-blank range over two dozen times. It still didn't stop the carnage.

The beast bit and slashed Johnny's limp body. He was rag-dolled around, the life having fled his mortal shell after the bear had ripped his jugular open on impact. Shane fired a dozen more shots before the bear roared and pivoted, swiping at Shane's legs and ripping both thighs open.

"*Fuck*!" he shouted, falling to the forest floor.

The bear was on him faster than a circle pit starting at a Lamb of God show, gnashing and slashing with a viciousness

Shane didn't think possible. He slipped into blackness even as the bear began to ingest the fingers from his left hand.

*

"Fuck!"

Espen heard the shout, knew it was Shane, and after having heard over three-dozen shots, knew somehow this crazy fucking bear was still alive.

The sound of meat being torn from the bone came first, then the distinctive noise of something being chewed.

Espen stepped into the small clearing, where the bear was feasting on Shane's dead body. Raising his firearm, he held his breath, sighted between the ears, and squeezed. The top of the bear's head exploded in a puff of red mist before the sound of the shot echoed around him and his ears hummed.

The bear flopped onto Shane's corpse.

Espen lowered his rifle and let out a loud, *"Woop!"*

He'd done it. He'd stopped the killing brute, and even though the four under his leadership had died, no other concertgoers had been injured, which was what mattered most to him and more so for the guy who'd hired them.

"Threat eliminated," he radioed to the festival crew. "GPS activated. We're going to need a cart and a few guys to clean this mess up."

"Roger that," a reply came.

He leaned his gun against a tree and sat at its base. Espen would wait here until the clean-up crew arrived. He looked at the bear, an unease growing. *In a horror movie, this is when someone dies*, he thought. *Their gun within reach, but they get cocky and slack.*

Espen stood, retrieved the firearm, and absently kicked at the bear's thick back paw. A nerve activated on contact, and the bear kicked back, the impact enough to cause Espen to stumble away. Windmilling his arms for balance, he tripped over Johnny's legs and fell.

The back of his head was easily pierced by the broken branch. The sharp chunk of wood popped through his left eyeball and sent the fluid-filled organ through the air.

Espen was dead long before the eye hit the ground.

*

With the closing strains of their last song, Klaaz gathered in a straight line at the edge of the stage, took each other's hands, and bowed, the crowd losing their minds over their legendary performance.

As they left the stage, each member jumped over where Asshat had died, a tribute they'd repeat on every stage they set foot on for the rest of their career.

Pigsty (Remastered)

by

Jay Bower

Cadaverous Blog Post Number…Who the fuck cares anymore?

The last post I made mentioned how my girlfriend, Lisa, and I were forced to go into hiding after the last Cadaverous concert. We were wanted by the authorities, and my work was not done yet. The desire to play music was so strong, I couldn't help myself from hiding within another band. Besides, it's what my demonic benefactor, Paimon, wanted.

An explanation is in order for what recently transpired at a music festival called Dethfest. I have no problem taking credit for things I've done, but what went down at Dethfest was not my fault, nor was it called for by Paimon.

It would be easy to pin the flaming massacre at Dethfest on me. I get it. Paimon has directed me to commit many terrible deeds. Though, to be honest, they're more acts of worship than anything else.

Even considering my demonic involvement, my current band is not who you might think it is.

Of all the bands at Dethfest, it makes sense to think Omnes Morimur is my band…but they are not. That would've been too easy. Since Dethfest went to hell because of those idiots, I can share who my band really was. We've since broken up and gone our separate ways.

My band was Systemic Collapse. Surprised? The most politically charged band on the planet was, in fact, the most bloodthirsty. Our political nature threw everyone off.

I met the rest of the guys through online forums. Hell, our drummer, Marcus, had been advertising on Craigslist that he was looking to play in a jazz band. Lisa informed me Paimon gave her guidance that he was the one, and I reached out to him. It didn't take much convincing to get Marcus to join.

Victor, our singer, came from the wedding circuit, where I met him at a friend's reception. His angst was real, though. He hated government, and when I presented the idea of the band, he jumped at it as a chance to give the establishment the biggest middle finger.

Our bassist, Lenny, was a different story. He was eager to start the band and had the metal pedigree to back it up, having played in countless cover bands and even roadied for Megadeth. The dude was anti everything: government, religion, drugs, alcohol…You name it, he hated it. He didn't give a damn about anything, as long as he was left alone and could play music.

They all knew me as Andrew VW, and I left it at that. None of them recognized that I was Gaige Penrod, and they certainly didn't realize my girlfriend, Monica Lewis, was Lisa Baker, though her alluring green eyes were a dead giveaway, had anyone been paying attention.

*

The day of Dethfest started like pretty much any other day for Systemic while we were on the road: wake up at noon, drink a bottle of vodka, down a handful of pills, eat shitty Mexican food, and prepare for the show. I don't drink or take any kind of drugs, but Marcus and Victor did. Lenny stayed in his room because…hate. He's the angriest person I've ever known.

An hour before we were to take the stage, Victor stumbled across the tour bus to where Lisa and I were seated at a table, discussing the merits of Red Jolly Roger, one of the other bands at the festival. I thought their pirate-themed act was cheesy, but Lisa found it enticing.

"You ready for the show?" Victor asked, sliding into the seat next to Lisa. He wrapped an arm around her, and she cringed. Victor always thought every woman was attracted to him, but Lisa had made it clear several times she was loyal to me and, even if she wasn't with me, Victor would never have a chance with her.

"Of course, I am. We're gonna blow their fucking eardrums," I said.

"That's my boy." Victor leaned closer to Lisa and kissed her cheek. "How about you, Monica? Think we're gonna tear it up?"

She tried to scoot away, but there was nowhere for her to go. "I know it. No one plays harder than Systemic Collapse."

"There ya go!" Victor pulled his arm from around Lisa, and I could see the relief in her eyes.

I'd hear about it later, that's for sure.

He leaned in closer, whispering, "I wanna play 'Pigsty.'"

"Fucking right, we are. This place is gonna go nuts when we do."

"I'm gonna make sure Lenny and Marcus know for sure that we are. Sometimes, Lenny…" He shook his head.

Victor didn't need to vocalize it. We all knew Lenny well enough to know he'd hate the idea but then hate that we didn't play it. He made no sense.

Victor patted Lisa's leg and left. She brushed off her pants as though acid were burning through the denim.

"He's gross," she said. "I'm going to enjoy gutting him if I'm ever called to it."

My eyes widened, and I leaned back in my chair, crossing my arms over my chest and admiring her.

"How crazy do you think it'll get? You guys haven't played 'Pigsty' in months. With as much security as the organizers have out here, it might turn ugly fast. I don't think they'll enjoy you guys screaming about how they're all pigs and deserve to die."

"Do you think Paimon is behind this decision?" I had not received a calling from him. The last sacrifice he'd demanded was two months ago.

She reached across the laminate table and grabbed my hands. Her green eyes softened, and a slight flush crossed her cheeks. "We're in this together. Our destinies are intertwined with his, and whatever he asks, we must fulfill."

*

Jose Mangin took the stage and introduced us. We stood just to the left, huddled together. I did a quick check with the rest of the band, glancing at each one in turn. Victor was amped like I'd never seen before. He bounced around on the balls of his feet, a massive grin crawling across his face.

"Damn, brothers, we're gonna rip this crowd! Are you ready?" He punched my arm playfully.

Lenny nodded. "I hate it, but fuck it, let's do it." His blank expression didn't give away if he was trying to joke or not.

My guess was he wasn't kidding.

"Let's crush it." Marcus held his drumsticks in his hand and raised them up like the Olympic torch. "On three," he said.

The rest of us grabbed hold of his hand, and he counted us down.

"One…two…three!"

We raced onstage, and Jose pumped his fist in the air, then slipped off to the side behind the speakers.

Victor took the mic and spewed out his hatred of the system, of government, of everything. It was like he was Lenny. I didn't really pay attention to the actual words—I knew him well enough. When I looked out at the sea of people, I searched for the only thing that mattered: Paimon.

Disappointment settled in when I realized he wasn't out there. I closed my eyes and concentrated on my thoughts, hoping to hear his voice command me to invoke.

We tore through two of our songs, building a massive wave of energy that felt dangerous.

When I glanced back out at the crowd, I was vaguely aware of Victor's words but caught enough to know when to start playing our song "Pigsty," the one we had been warned against playing.

I turned from the crowd and let my hair hang down over my face, obscuring it from view. As I deftly played "Pigsty," I began to wonder if Paimon would appear.

The crowd erupted into a mass of fists and feet. They'd been whipped into a frenzy by Victor's call and the band's furious music.

I snuck a peek through my hair, but still no Paimon. Since my first band, Cadaverous, ended, he didn't appear as often. But when he did, someone had to die.

The crowd grew more intense, feeding off Victor's raw energy and our brutal music. Victor continued to spew his hate, and commotion on both sides of the stage caught my attention. A burst of hope blossomed within me. Had my patron shown himself?

But then that hope was destroyed.

Police officers and security guards rushed the stage, determined to stop us.

I was yanked from where I stood. Victor was placed into handcuffs, and Marcus and Lenny were both shoved offstage. I had no idea at the time where they were taken. The crowd lost their minds, shouting and raising their fists high.

Lisa rushed to my side. "Andrew! Are you okay?"

One of the black-clad guards backhanded her and knocked her to the ground.

"Lisa!" I screamed, completely forgetting the well-crafted cover we'd been using for years.

A boot slammed into my stomach and winded me. A baton cracked against my back, and I crashed to my knees. An arm slipped around my neck and held me in a chokehold. I struggled to breathe. My eyes felt like they were going to bulge out of my skull.

Jose Mangin raced toward us. "Those stupid motherfuckers almost shut this party down! Get them the fuck out of here, with the others."

So much for being the metal ambassador, I thought.

I struggled against my captors, but they were too strong, and there were too many of them. One of them snapped the strap off my guitar. The crack of wood from the bolt being ripped out made me fight harder, though it was no use.

I prayed Paimon would rescue me and deliver me from these brainless thugs disguised as officers.

"You think it's fucking funny to kill a cop?" one of them snarled.

"We'll feed you all to the pigs, you piece of shit," another added.

A blindfold was wrenched over my head, plunging me into total darkness. I prayed harder for Paimon's interference, but he didn't stop the beating from the officer. Unseen fists connected with me, striking in random places, while I struggled to protect myself.

"Lisa!" I cried through the black fabric covering my face. "Lisa, where are you?"

She screamed, and I thrashed my legs, trying to push against my attackers.

A baton struck the back of my leg, and the sharp pain raced up the muscle, making it spasm. Then they lifted me off the ground.

"Hurry, before someone notices," one of them said.

I had no concept of up or down. Everything was shrouded in darkness. With the crowd still agitated and the other bands playing on Stages One and Two, I couldn't make out where Lisa was, and it sent my heart drumming against my ribs. Adrenaline coursed through me, leaving a tang on my tongue.

I couldn't breathe and feared they'd dunk my head underwater. It was an odd fear, but that's what I remember feeling at the time.

When I twisted, I was rewarded with a punch to the gut.

A vehicle door opened, and the next moment, I was tossed inside, landing awkwardly on what felt like a leg.

Lisa groaned, and the leg under me shifted.

"Lisa, is that you?"

"Gaige?" she replied in a weak voice.

It was so out of character for her, I was speechless for a moment.

"Where are we?" she asked.

With the black veil over my face, I had no idea.

An engine started, and a rumble vibrated my intestines.

"Is there anyone else here?" I asked, hoping that maybe one of my bandmates was there.

No one replied. I assumed we were alone and had to figure out a way to escape. Whatever these bastards intended on doing with us, it couldn't have been good.

We bounced around inside the vehicle as it sped away. I spoke to Paimon in my head, praying he would save us.

*

By the time the vehicle slowed, I had lost all track of time and all hope of leaving it alive. Paimon had neglected us, and I had no idea where the band was.

My thoughts lingered on Paimon. After all I'd done for him, I wondered if he sent these men to punish me. What could I have possibly done to deserve this?

"Lisa," I whispered, "are you okay?"

She shifted and groaned but finally answered. "I hurt everywhere. I don't wanna die."

Her weak voice triggered something in me, lifting the resignation clouding my decisions. There was no way Paimon was doing this. I refused to believe it. With all the blood I'd spilled for him, I found it hard to accept this was our fate. As dejected as I was when the vehicle stopped, I had.

"We're gonna get out of this." I didn't know how, but I'd be damned if I was gonna let anyone hurt Lisa more than they already had.

The men murmuring in the front of the vehicle spoke too low for me to make out what they were saying, other than a few snippets of words. After several turns and a few curse words, we skidded to a sudden stop. The vehicle shifted into reverse, and they cut the engine.

The doors opened, and immediately, a stench of shit wafted toward us. I gagged several times. The taste of it wouldn't leave my tongue. I breathed through my mouth, but it only made things worse. The black fabric was sucked into my mouth, making me feel as though I would suffocate. Lisa was doing the same, if the gagging sounds were any indication.

"Looks like these fucking cop killers are afraid of little piggies," one of the voices said.

"They better be. Ain't no one gonna find their carcasses out here. That'll teach those fucking woke-warriors to fuck with the police. Stupid pricks."

I was pulled out of the vehicle by my feet, and my head thumped against the bumper. Stars erupted in my head, then I fell to the wet ground.

"Come on, bring 'em over here."

Warm, wet mud and what I assumed was shit slipped up my shirt as I skidded across. Pigs squealed on either side of me, startled by our presence. I kept bumping into them, their strong legs kicking me.

The men hoisted me up and held me against something wooden. A pole or some kind of fence, I wasn't sure.

"Come on, piggies, let's eat," one of the voices said.

Without another word, something sharp slid across my throat. Lisa cried out. No doubt, they'd done something similar to her.

Hot, sticky blood gushed from my wound. It spurted with every beat of my heart. The pigs grew agitated, and the men who had taken us laughed.

"Look at that. The piggies like it!" one of them said.

I struggled to breathe, tried to twist out of the hold they had on me, but my strength faded fast. A pig at my foot sniffed and grunted, then bit my leg.

"Let me help ya, little piggy."

Another streak of white-hot pain seared across my leg as the man cut into my flesh. The pig grew excited and, enticed by the blood, started rooting around the wound, gobbling up the gore and biting at my broken flesh.

I tried to cry out for help, but my voice was gone. With my throat slit, I lacked the ability to vocalize my thoughts. Instead, I called out to Paimon in my head. I was his servant. He couldn't leave me to die when I was doing his bidding, could he? I had been chosen for a purpose. My service was not yet over. The end hadn't come; there was more to do.

Invoke with this. Blood and life, he said within my mind.

Hope!

He had heard me.

Focusing all my waning energy, I envisioned his sigil, flaming bright and dripping with blood, carved into the flesh of my unseen assailants. I didn't know exactly what they looked like, but I imagined two barrel-chested men dressed similar to what the officers had looked like before the hood was placed over my eyes. Their faces in my imagination were nothing more than blurred outlines.

Blood and life, I said silently.

I coughed up a mouthful of blood, and the pigs descended on me. Their noses fought against one another as they sought to taste my raw wound. I concentrated on Paimon's sigil, watching it play out in my head, burning into the chests of the black-clad men.

More, more! Paimon commanded.

I channeled all my energy, every ounce of my being, into those words which called my patron. Invoking his presence was the only way out of this. The lyrics to my song escaped my lips, and I ignored the pain speaking caused the gash on my throat. I cried out to Paimon.

"Invoke with this. Blood and life. Carve the image, spill the blood, call my name. My favor I will grant. My disciple you've become. Serve me and live. Fail me and suffer."

"What's he doing?" one of the officers asked.

My throat was in agony. It was like a thousand suns burned from the inside. I didn't think I could call out like that again. The invocation had to work. I had nothing left.

The men holding Lisa and me screamed.

"What the fuck?" one of them said.

A loud, meaty burst followed his question and then another scream. Something fell into the mud, the pigs wildly snorting and squealing. Then more screams.

"No, get them off me!" It was one of the officers.

The pigs had been whipped into a frenzy, much like the crowd we had played for hours earlier.

Another burst and another scream. It was the man holding onto me. He fell, but as he did, his hand raked against my blindfold, ripping it off my head. I blinked several times, trying to focus and get my bearings.

Blood ran down my chest. Using the blindfold, I wrapped it around my neck and hoped it was enough to stem the flow.

It was dark outside, but nearby floodlights offered plenty of light. We were at a farm with what had to be hundreds of pigs tromping in the mud and shit. Three metal barns to my left were surrounded by fencing that wrapped all around the yard.

Two officers thrashed on the ground, pigs surrounding them like vultures. One of the officers screamed as a fountain of blood burst into the air. A slight glow tinged his body, and I knew Paimon was there. Attracted by the scent of copper, the pigs turned violent, shoving and snapping at one another.

Lisa whimpered, and I spun on my heels. She was on her hands and knees, barely able to fend off two large black and white pigs nipping at her. I rushed to her side and kicked at the beasts, chasing them off. Dropping next to her, I yanked the blindfold off her head.

"Lisa! Are you okay?" I croaked with a barely audible voice.

I cradled her head. Bite marks oozed blood on her arms. Other pigs tried edging closer, but I chased them off with a swift kick. They started to back away and instead, attracted by the squirming and screaming men, moved closer to the officers.

Paimon stood amidst the carnage, devouring the men's hearts, one in each hand, while the pigs tore into the officers' bodies with wild abandon. A wicked grin crossed my face. The invocation had worked! Paimon had come for us after all and had found a sacrifice in the process.

Well done, I heard in my head. Paimon was staring directly at me.

I gave a slight nod, and he glowed brighter. Flames licked at his feet. Blood dripped from his teeth, and chunks of heart muscle dangled from his lips. He seemed to savor the gift. The pigs continued to shred the officers' bloody bodies, fighting for the scraps Paimon had left behind.

Well done, Paimon said once more. Then with the last bite of fresh heart, he vanished in a plume of smoke.

"Come on, we need to get out of here," I said to Lisa.

Each word spoken was like glass cutting against the inside of my throat. I helped her to her feet, but when she tried to take a step, she almost fell. Luckily, I caught her. That's when I noticed one of her legs bent at an odd angle.

"Is it broken?"

She looked up to me with tears running down her face and her lip quivering. "I...I think so."

I wasn't the strongest person, but she wasn't the heaviest. After scooping her up, I regained my balance. With the blood loss I had suffered, I was lightheaded but was able to carefully shuffle through the pigs, toward the black SUV just outside the pen.

I gently set her in the back. "Are you gonna be okay back here?" I moved the hair off her sweaty forehead.

"It hurts so bad."

"I know. I'll get you to the hospital." In truth, we both needed medical attention, but my focus was on Lisa.

She nodded and leaned against the side, her head tilting down and her fists in tight balls.

I had never expected either one of us to be in this kind of danger. We had the world at our feet because of our patron.

What happened at Dethfest was unexpected, but I was determined it wouldn't hold us back from continuing to serve Paimon. The deaths of the officers could've been avoided had they not been overzealous to protect their honor. Instead, they served a greater purpose, and for that, I was thankful.

I climbed into the driver's seat and was relieved to see the key fob sitting in the cup holder. When I pushed start, the engine roared to life. I looked back in the mirror at Lisa. Dethfest had almost lived up to its name for us, but I had someone far greater than death at my side.

I shifted into gear and drove away from the squealing pigs. Though I didn't know what the future held, I did know that with Paimon guiding me, my future was secure.

Jay Bower

Inspiration for the Story

Writing within someone else's universe is always challenging. Trying to strike the right balance of respecting the story "as-is" while adding your spin to it can be difficult. My hope is that my story "Pigsty (Remastered)" has done justice to *Try Not To Die: At Dethfest* from Mark Tullius and Glenn Hedden, honoring the spirit of the book and injecting my own flavor to the mix.

From the very beginning, I knew I wanted to tie it in to my novel Cadaverous, a Faustian tale infused with heavy metal, particularly that of the late 80s and early 90s. But how?

A major spoiler for those who have not read my novel: the main character, Gaige Penrod, survives the brutal ending, and the reader is left to wonder what the future holds for him and his girlfriend, Lisa. As I considered my story for this Dethfest collection, I kept coming back to Gaige.

I knew he'd need to hide from authorities after all the deaths his band, Cadaverous, was tied to. Escaping from the carnage, he'd want to continue to play music. After all, he did make a demonic deal for a wicked musical gift! So tying him to Systemic Collapse felt like the next logical step.

I didn't want to have Gaige join one of the occult-driven bands like Omnes Morimur. That would've been too obvious. With the political sensibilities of Rage Against the Machine, Systemic Collapse was the perfect ruse to continue Gaige's story.

Using that as my basis, I then went to work.

I used the name of the song "Pigsty" to inspire what I wanted to happen. I thought what fun it would be to have pigs involved in the madness. Let me be absolutely clear: I support those in law enforcement. I have many friends and family members who serve or have served within their communities. I do not use the term "pigs" to refer to law enforcement. It was part of the mythos of the political band Systemic Collapse which made them feel more alive and, in turn, inspired the horror of my story.

I hope you enjoyed your brief encounter with Gaige, Lisa, and his demonic benefactor, Paimon. If you want to really know their story, please check out my novel Cadaverous.

Thanks for reading!

THE GOTHIKA DETHFEST INCIDENT: AN INVESTIGATION

PROVIDED BY AGENT VIOLET MCMASTER

The following document exists as an aid to the ongoing investigation of the May 2023 Dethfest *performance of feminist experimental-hard-rock group Gothika, which ended in extreme violence. What you are about to read are entries retrieved from the online blog of Dani Kildare, the band's bassist at the time of the performance. These pieces detail the events allegedly leading to her untimely disappearance, as well as the murders of her bandmates following their appearance at the historic metal festival. Police officials are still unclear on the facts surrounding Kildare's disappearance and the disappearance of surviving transgender vocalist Dee Winters. Combined with further evidence found online, Kildare's writing paints a puzzling picture of an otherwise tragic event. We caution any who approach this investigation to do so with healthy skepticism, as these events are horrific and widely speculative.*

Entry #1: "DETHFEST, BABY!!!" from online blog, *Go Goth or Go Home*, 05/1/2023

Through the clouded view of the van's front window, the Dethfest stage resembled a dais.

Our dirtied white van came chugging over the hill toward the monumental stage, so imposing and far it still felt like it was miles off in the distance. I finally felt a smirk cracking along my lips following the 100 miles of frowns. *In a way*, the voice in my head mused, *the stage* is *a dais…to* Her, *from* them.

I snuck my head around to peer at my band members, all in a seemingly unguarded sense of anticipation. My eyes landed on Dee, whose head lay nestled in the headrest of the middle seat. I heard the faintest of snoring. It would have almost been adorable if she weren't trans and wasn't being led into darkness…

Now, listen. I'm no fuckin bigot, no matter what the internet tries to tell me. I'm mainly writing this post because the last few months have caused me to spiral and I need to get this shit out somewhere. No one will likely find or read this. I don't really care if it implicates me in any way.

While my sisters in the band are hardcore in their hatred for trans people, I could honestly care less what they do with their lives. As long as they keep their shit away from me and who I love, that's fine with me. Faux feminists of the internet would think this makes me as good as a bystander enabling fascists. Whatever. I say to the one or two of you—if even that—reading my blog: let me just play my fucking music in peace. That being said, I cannot juggle the guilt of their delusions anymore.

I should probably explain myself a little, lest I'm besieged by reactionary comments. I joined Gothika several months ago, looking for a band that wasn't swimming in testosterone and only performing what they thought of as "real metal." Translation? Music that's not FUCKING BORING. Metal these days sounds like the same derivative trash that's trying to be the next Slipknot, or Metallica, or Megadeth. It's simply shit.

The city I was living in at the time was like many: liberal enough to leave me the hell alone, while making the landscape not so blindingly white, but conservative enough so Social

Justice Warriors weren't screaming in your face every time you walked to the laundromat. One fine morning, I made my way down to the local café where I typically fire off frantic job applications and chug coffee like it's my last drink on Earth. They have these chimes hanging over the door that lilt a sweet song as you enter, and it warms my little black heart each time I go.

Upon this visit, my eyes caught a bright flyer pinned to the aging corkboard filled with ads– "CALCULUS TUTORING – DEMOCRATIC SOCIALISTS MEETING THIS THURSDAY – LEATHER DOM FOR HIRE – MISSING GERBIL" —they didn't judge. This flyer in particular was from a band called Gothika looking for a bass player to join their "fuck-you feminist ranks." What caught my attention was the bold print lining the bottom: "THIS BAND IS WOMEN ONLY. MEN CAN KINDLY FUCK OFF INTO THE SUN." I instantly ripped off a tab with their information and contacted the listed number. Two days later, I was jamming in a swanky warehouse with the four coolest chicks I've ever met in my life.

Sandra, Alex, Tiffy, and Jax—they look like the girl-rock band of your dreams. Svelte, with hair colors and styles ranging from sunflower blond, red like horror movie blood, neon biohazard-green shorn short to the head, and jet black, respectively. The number of buckles, leather, and hardware are enough to make the members of Kitty faint. Playing with them is like a magic spell that fills me with a welcoming warmth most millennials have been chasing since pre-9/11. For the first time in my life, I feel understood and welcome in a feminist space that isn't solely, *obsessively* focused on identity politics, pronouns, and pussy hats.

For about four months we would jam like this, following each other's natural instincts and cues, building upon riffs and time signatures that defied genre, playing in tunings that made the meninist gatekeepers at our shows scoff and boo. It was an adrenaline rush every time, and for a while, there didn't even seem to be the thought of a singer. We were a sought-after instrumental and experimental metal group. Everything we had to say we said through our music, like it should be.

But, like many good things, this would come to a crushing end because then I learned about The Ritual. There was this near-devilish gleam in their eyes when they finally told me about their extracurricular activities.

As I was saying earlier, the girls in Gothika are extremely hardcore. Their feminism should honestly be held as a benchmark; they are so devoted to the centering of all women everywhere.

"Dani, have you ever heard of the goddess Diana?" Alex drawled in her husky baritone, her hand trailing through the dark red of her hair, creating a flame hovering above her grin.

"You mean like Wonder Woman and stuff?"

"Oh, Dani, this is why we love you," came Sandra's voice so close to my ear I jumped. "Such a sharp sense of humor. No. We are talking about the ancient goddess of the earth and fertility."

"Oh, sure, yeah. Wasn't, like, that back during the ancient Greeks and shit?" I rubbed the back of my neck to rid it of the sudden goosebumps.

"Greek, Irish…Her influence spread far and wide in the earlier Pagan religions. Various civilizations would show her praise and give sacrifices to ensure the health of their crops and births in the villages." Alex continued to watch me.

I felt like I was in the direct eyeline of a hungry tiger.

"She sounds pretty fuckin' great. Way cooler than Jesus, am I right?" I'd never felt nervous around these ladies, so the creeping chill walking up my spine caused my hands to fidget in my lap.

"What we're trying to say is that we trust you and want to bring you even deeper into our fold," Tiffy joined in, a glint of something in her eyes that did not contrast to the sneer forming on her lips. "Me and the girls? We're disciples of Diana, and in the classic tradition, we pay sacrifice to receive her blessings."

"So, you give up eating for Lent or something? Go on hunger strikes, shit like that?"

Jax broke out in a grin that should have been too large for her mouth. "Not quite…How do you feel about transgenders, Dani?"

Gears ground against each other as I earnestly attempted to keep up with their words, heat intensifying at my neck. "Um…I mean, I don't really agree with it, but they leave me alone most of the time, so I don't care?" The final words squeaked out of me as a question.

"But, Dani, all these men are trying to masquerade in our shared pain, invading our spaces and co-opting *our* movement. God, you can't even call yourself a true feminist anymore without people bellyaching about 'inclusion'." Sandra scare quotes inclusion, pure venom practically dripping down her chin.

"I don't even feel safe using public restrooms anymore," Alex added passively, studying her nails as if bored by the conversation.

"They think they can attempt to wear us like a fucking costume, like some kind of serial killer!" Tiffy piped up.

"In other words"—Sandra raised her voice to cut off the others—"they are practically spitting in the face of all that Diana has given us over the centuries. They mock the power she has granted to our ancestors. While many may see it as a problem that could just go away if we ignore it, the girls and I know better. We must bring matters into our own hands."

I didn't move a fucking muscle because Sandra was watching me so intently, I assumed there were laser beam holes in my head. "S-so, what do you do?"

Sandra walked to me as slowly, deliberately, and dramatically as she possibly could, leaning in toward my face and practically whispering into my lips. The shiver returned.

"They, my dear Dani, *aid* us in our sacrifice to Diana…"

So, it goes like this: They put out flyers, much like the one they used to bring me in but instead asking for a vocalist.

"We're a kick-ass GRRL rock group looking for a vocalist that can add some grit to our already raging fire!! We are BIPOC, Trans, and Nonbinary friendly, with a strong message of feminism and intersectionality!!"

Reading it made me feel sort of uncomfortable. I'd seen signs like this before for groups who were looking to create inviting spaces, and while I'd witnessed varying degrees of success on that front, what the girls were offering had a rather…sinister air to it. Now being aware of their anti-trans stance, I couldn't understand the point in hiring a designated trans vocalist for a "sacrifice."

Supposedly it's something the girls have done for a few years. They hire a trans woman as their vocalist, usually when a big gig is coming up. It's all a part of this ritual, though they still seemed hesitant to tell me what it all involved. Smoke and mirrors, all in the name of this goddess Diana—or Danu, as I found out the Irish called her.

In this instance, we nabbed the gig at Dethfest. One of the biggest metal festivals on the global stage and the girls somehow managed to make enough noise the owners took notice and asked us to play. Now, according to the girls, came the tricky part.

We sat through quite a few tryouts until we found Dee, and there were some fantastic candidates, in my humble opinion. Only problem was, none of them were trans. I witnessed some terrifying sides of the girls as the months grew closer to our shipping out date. The growing levels of stress were leading to quite a few terse and hostile arguments, but then the unthinkable happened…

We heard from our guardian angel.

Dee came in on a chilly yet gorgeously sunny Saturday afternoon—all lanky, six-foot, punk rock of her. She sort of had a Joan Jett vibe, with the wardrobe of a feminine Joey Ramone. I honestly had no idea she was trans at first. She passed fairly well. Dee's also a *killer* singer, despite her more withdrawn introduction. She's the type of performer who truly comes out of her shell when the music queues. It's a power not many introverted performers wield. I know because I'm one of those performers who can't.

As I watched her wail into that microphone, a heavy and sticky dread dropped into my gut. Whatever it was the girls had planned, I knew it wasn't something this girl deserved, no matter what my feelings on trans people might be. Were they going to humiliate her? Hurt her? Like I said, I've got nothing against these people. I just don't entirely agree with it. That doesn't mean I think they should be used in some woo-woo activity to appease some ancient weirdo religion.

I never expected to feel this way, and even as this beat-to-hell rental van winds down toward this dais-esque stage, I'm not sure what to do with this growing anxiety.

Am I a bad person…?

Entry #2: "Dethfest, Day Uno," from online blog, *Go Goth or Go Home*, 05/02/2023

Well, a few of you were EXTREMELY vocal in the comments of my last post. Not sure I should be saying thanks to those who were excusing or even agreeing with my experiences. Some of you seemed a little *too* gung-ho about bad things befalling an innocent person, trans or not.

Look, I'm just trying to get through this weekend, and I'm hoping this whole ridiculous goddess-sacrifice shit is all just some elaborate prank for the girls to get their kicks. Even when I tried searching for anything involving the band doing weird shit before this, I couldn't find a thing. That being said, I'm not sure how much more I can take of the worried, far-off look in Dee's eyes. It's like telling Lenny to look at the flowers in *Of Mice and Men,* or that budding psycho of a girl on the one season of *The Walking Dead.* Are these still relevant references?

Regardless, it's not even my unease surrounding Dee's fate that's wigging me out, but even the way she's been acting ever since we got here. It's like the lights are on but nobody's home, yet in a more relaxed sort of way. Shortly after we unloaded, I found her in the field behind the stage, just kind of staring off into the distance and trees, hands in the front pockets of her hoodie, wind whipping her longer hair around in tangles. Her seeming so unbothered came as a stark contrast to the practically withdrawn girl I had met back home. I had to ask the rest of the girls if they dosed her with something, or some shit.

At dinner, Sandra and Alex were off talking to other bands, suddenly seeming super lax with their "fuck men" stance on most things. But hey, showbiz is showbiz, I guess. I decided to take this absence as an opportunity to interrogate Dee a little, as the girls previously discouraged any sort of fraternizing with "the offering." So fucking weird.

"Hey, Dee, how are you feeling?" I asked gently, saddling up beside her, but not too close.

"Oh, hi, Dani. I'm feeling all right. Just kind of taking everything in. How are you?"

God, she even sounded like a girl. And so damn sweet. Ugh.

"I'm fine, I'm fine. Just wanted to check on you. Big festival and everything. Is this your first performance, or whatever?"

"Oh, no, I've performed a bunch before this. I haven't really been able to appear this way in a while." Her shoulders were sort of tense, hands resting in her lap.

"You mean, like a girl?" *Fuck, I shouldn't have said that.*

She gave me a confused look, but not quite the one of anger or betrayal I would have expected. Still, there was something there I couldn't read. She looked down at her hands, and awkward silence fell between us again.

"Well, hey, I think you're going to do great. You've been killing it at practice."

I'm not entirely sure why I was trying to force some kind of rapport with a person I barely knew.

"I don't think the other girls like me," Dee said suddenly, just above a whisper.

A wave of nausea washed over me in an instant. The girls hadn't taught me what to do if "the offering" started asking questions.

"Wh-what do you mean?" I finally got out.

"They just don't seem to like me that much. I don't know. I've had a lot of interactions with cis women who aren't as accepting or progressive as they like to think." Dee pushed some of her hair behind her ear.

"Did they say something to you?"

"No, it's a general feeling. You can usually tell when people want nothing to do with you but still want the social capital of having a trans person in their band."

I expected anger in her voice, but she appeared to sink further into herself.

"I-I'm sorry, Dee…" I reached out for her shoulder, but before I could make contact, she suddenly straightened up, so I retracted my hand quickly. "Are you okay?"

"Yeah. Just exhausted. I'll be okay soon." She turned and smiled at me.

I honestly wish I had found comfort in the gesture, but instead, I felt that cold chill again.

"I'm gonna take a quick walk. See you in a bit?"

I nodded. Dee rose and made her way out of the eating area. I noticed her heading off toward the woods, but Jax had called my name, so I went to leave myself. When I looked back for Dee, she was gone.

Before we continue onward to Kildare's final entry, the investigative team provided the following social media post as supplemental material. This stands as one of the only pieces of evidence concerning Gothika's performance itself. While plenty of social media users continuously speculate over the strange events that occurred during said performance, the following user offers the most comprehensive description, as well as the clearest video, of the incident. Their name has been redacted from the report for anonymity and safety.

Entry #3: Posted on Instagram by @(REDACTED), 07/13/2023:

I've been wrestling with myself on whether to post this video or not…I know a lot of people will call bullshit, or say I doctored things, but with all the discussion about what happened at "Dethfest" during Gothika's performance, I want to share my experience and hopefully clear some air.

My partner and I were really excited for this performance. We'd both been Gothika fans for a decent amount of time, so it was a big deal for them to be appearing at this festival. We got VIP tickets and planned to camp out for the weekend—this was an anniversary celebration of sorts for us.

However, I would be remiss if I didn't talk a little about some of the weird stuff I noticed before the terrifying performance, and honestly, this is the first time I'm speaking about any of it.

Before the performance itself, my partner and I decided to check out some of the woods nearby, just to see the local trees, wildlife…that kinda stuff. We thought maybe there might be some cool trails for hiking. Anyway, at one point, we were observing some of the plant life when we heard someone behind us.

"They're beautiful, aren't they?"

I spun around to find freaking Dee Winters, the recently added lead singer of Gothika, standing a few feet away from us. Needless to say, my partner and I were fangirling hard. However, after only a few seconds, we could tell there was something…off about her. It was like she was there but also a million miles away. Even her smile was tight, not in an unfriendly way, but like when someone is deciding whether or not you're a threat, if that makes sense?

"Are you okay, Ms. Winters?"

Look, I didn't know what to call her, okay? What would you do if you came face-to-face with a musician you loved?? Regardless, her response was what weirded us out the most.

"All things will be okay soon, my child."

Um…what? I've seen interviews with her in the brief time leading up to Dethfest, and she was in no way as weird as she was acting in that moment. At this point, my partner and I were looking to get back to the festival, so we politely said our goodbyes. As we walked away, though, she said one more thing over her shoulder I'll likely never forget.

"We appreciate your praise, the trees."

I literally couldn't think of anything else to do. I just nodded, and we hurried away.

I tell this story because I think with a lot of the chatter that's been going on surrounding the disappearance of Dee Winters, and even Dani Kildare, I can't help but refer to this interaction. Maybe Dee snapped after years of putting up with cis people's bullshit and murdered her bandmates—I don't know. All I know is what I experienced, and I share this post and video to put my story in context. I'm turning off comments to respect me and my partner's privacy, as well as to ward off any inflammatory posting. Thank you so much for reading. <3

The user's attached video begins with much of the fanfare expected of a live performance: the crowd enthusiastically cheering for the band as the members show their admiration. Ms. Winters takes center stage, however, with a very reserved and solemn air. Even as the music begins, she remains inert. Once her vocal performance begins, the video takes a turn. Winters comes alive, sweeping her arms toward the crowd in grand, arching motions. The audience responds in kind, taking note of this further theatrical performance. The rest of the band seems somewhat confused by Winters's sudden energy but continue to play their instruments as normal. Following the end of this initial explosion of sound, the band plays a sort of interlude as their singer addresses the crowd directly. The audio quality is a little muddled, but you can hear Winters talking about worship, thanking the crowd for their "worship upon this Mayday," and so on. The earlier confusion evident in the other band members turns to concern and outright anger. Lead guitarist Sandra McCullin storms over and starts shouting over the music to Winters, who seems to outright ignore her and continue her address. Naturally, this enrages McCullin further, who yells even louder but abruptly stops. Her face goes slack before her head thrusts back, bright light shooting from her eyes and blood spilling freely from her mouth. It is quickly evident to the audience this is not merely a stage trick. The rest of the band completely lose their composure, screaming obscenities. McCullin's eyes appear to burn out of her head, the blood continuing to pour forth onto the stage. The user's phone becomes jostled around as the audience panics and runs from the field, ultimately cutting the video after several seconds and ending their coverage of the incident.

This final piece of evidence from Ms. Kildare's blog was uploaded following the attack onstage and, allegedly, leads up to her disappearance. Instead of a written post, this piece is an audio recording, likely directly addressed to her phone. Again, we warn any who engages with this report to proceed with caution, as the following recording is extremely disturbing.

Audio Entry: "Untitled," from the blog *Go Goth or Go Home*, 05/02/23

[The recording begins with some audio distortion, followed by the sounds of shuffling shoes, indicating running, and who we can ascertain is Ms. Kildare, sobbing.]

DANI: Fuck! Fuck, fuck, fuck…Oh my god…they're all fucking dead…Dee, what the fuck did you do…? She fucking killed all of them…*Fuck*!

[The shuffling shifts to the sound of shoes on grassland, the running slowing to somewhat of a stop, though Kildare's breathing still sounds panicked and labored. Far off sounds of screaming and panic can be heard in the background.]

DANI: What do I do…? Where can I go where she won't find me…? The woods? Fuck it, I'll entomb myself in a fucking tree until the police get here. Why not?

[Kildare picks up running again, grass shifting to the snapping of trees, crunching of leaves.]

DANI (in a lower register): I don't know if anyone will hear this. Fuck, I don't even know if this will actually record…Dee lost her fucking mind. (heavy breathing) I don't know how, but she fucking killed Sandra. She made her head fucking explode! She probably did the same to Jax. She immediately ran to take Dee down, but we were already getting the fuck out of there at that point…

[There's a pause as Kildare starts sobbing again.]

DANI: We tried to get to our phones so we could call the police…I don't even know how much of what I saw I can trust. Alex was right beside me, but she suddenly went fucking flying into a wall…God, her limbs…They started twisting everywhere…Her screams…We could still hear it, even as Tiffy and I were able to get back to the green room and our phones. We locked ourselves in, and Tiffy dialed for the police, figuring we'd probably be safe just holing up in the green room until help arrived. Or, I don't know, a fucking exorcist or something…Of course, the line was goddamn busy!

[A snap suddenly sounds nearby, causing Dani to freeze for a few heartbeats of silence. An owl hoots.]

DANI (quieter): Everything was okay until Tiffy started kind of resting her hands on the vanity, looking sick. Before I could say or do anything, her eyes burst into that fucking light…fire…whatever it was that happened to Sandra, with all the blood coming from her mouth…All that blood…I had no idea what to do, so I figured I'd just take my fucking chances and run for it. Thankfully, I didn't see Dee anywhere, waiting for me, so I just booked it as far as I could…And now here I am, a fucking sitting duck in the woods…

[Another snapping sound, seemingly closer than the last one but with a cleaner break, as if from a shoe. Dani starts crying again, though muffled, most likely from her hand over her mouth to stifle the sounds.]

DEE (softly, almost comfortingly): Dani? Are you out here?

[The sounds of Dee slowly walking through the undergrowth can be heard over Dani's panicked breathing.]

DEE: Dani…I was hoping we could talk. I know you're likely scared and confused, but I promise that your judgment is not as severe as the others.

DANI (just above a whisper): Judgment…?

DEE: I didn't see murder in your eyes, Dani. Despite your aligning with these girls, you don't seem as misguided and lost as they were. Though, Mason may not agree, may he?

DANI (voice shaking uncontrollably): What the fuck…?

DEE: Yes, Dani, I am aware of Mason. Just as I've been aware of the horrid acts your bandmates committed supposedly in my name. They were going to murder me tonight. They've murdered many before me in their supposed worship to Danu. They wanted to implicate *you* in this, Dani.

[Dani's breaths become even faster, whispering "what the fuck" over and over.]

DEE: Please. I want to speak with you. You showed me kindness where many have not. I'm not here to hurt you.

[Dani's whispers become intelligible but seem to be her weighing her options. A rustling sound can be heard as she tentatively inches away from the tree to face Dee. The woman can be heard sighing contentedly, supposing she has seen her bandmate.]

DEE: Ah, Dani…there you are, my daughter.

DANI: Daughter? What the fuck are you talking about, Dee? You killed our bandmates!

DEE: Killed? What makes my actions similar to the way those girls slaughtered hundreds of women in the name of religion?

DANI (softly sobbing): They said it was an offering to some fucking ancient deity…that trans women needed to be held accountable for invading women's spaces…

DEE: Are you trying to say the women they killed were not women? After all you've seen and experienced?

DANI: Stop…stop mentioning her…

DEE: Him, Dani. If you dare to speak of your friend, speak to his truth. Don't stoop to the level of those murderers.

DANI: *Shut up*! You could never understand…I loved him, and he abandoned me…They all did.

DEE: Had he abandoned you? Or did you instead abandon him in his time of immense vulnerability? Mason needed you. Humans focus so much on their own pain and fear, they completely ignore the needs of those around them.

DANI: I didn't do anything wrong…Everyone got wrapped up in this crazy queer-reactionary shit, and they abandoned me when I didn't just follow along.

DEE: Dani…I think we both know that's not true. Mason trusted you, and you turned your back on him, where others did what they could to protect him from a hateful world. You initially chose the path of the fearful and the violent, deciding to participate with those who refuse to acknowledge change, variance.

DANI (full on sobbing): Who even are you…? What are you talking about…?

DEE: Oh, Dani. I have been witness to thousands of years of humanity and worship. I have felt the entropy as your species asserted faith in their concepts of a sole god to construct their own structures of control and power. You've traded love and community for fear and subservience, allowing the weakest of will to form the ways in which you treat those who seek truth outside of these strictures. You've forgotten the love we once offered.

DANI (quietly through tears): Please…please…

DEE: Daughter, while swaths of the human species are averse to the chaos of their existence, I do not believe you are all past redemption. Despite the growth of destruction and imperialism, there are still many who find their way back to the forest, back to the gods who foster that larger community. I know you hold that desire within you. You are not the villain you feel you are, but you also cannot follow in the path of your hateful sisters. They willingly took the lives of innocents, as though their bigotry could win my favor.

DANI (weakly): D-Danu…?

DEE: Yes, my child. I am not a monstrous deity, but I will never excuse the spilling of innocent blood, regardless of identity. Humans are far too focused on binary distinctions to enforce their destructive power systems. Your bandmates harnessed these ideologies in an attempt to disguise violence as sacrifice. But there's no way they truly believed, being that they held the hubris that I would not find out or retaliate.

DANI (sobbing again): I'm sorry…I'm so, so sorry…

DEE (softly): I know, Dani. I know you are. I'm offering you a form of judgment that asks for your change. You need to want to change, to relinquish the hatred of your forebears. Relinquish your worship of gender, of the structures that have encouraged endless violence upon you and the ones you love.

[There is a moment of silence, with the wind marking the beats between Dani's answer.]

DANI: I do…I relinquish myself to you, Danu…

DEE: Excellent, my child. Open your eyes and look to me.

[The sound of Dani's quickening breathing escalates over the wind but is quickly overpowered as the wind whips to a high-pitched whistle, distorting the recording for moments. As soon as the sound ceases, there are only the continued whispers of the wind.]

This is where the audio recording ends, functioning as the last instance anyone would hear from Kildare or Winters following the legendary performance. Due to the fantastical nature of Winters's claims of being an ancient Celtic deity, the mystery surrounding her murder spree endures as a subject of debate to this day. The recent re-emergence of Pagan cultures has only exacerbated this, as alleged covens continue to learn about Danu, offering her various forms of praise. The deity has even become a form of queer and feminist hero or icon, acting as a "mother" to the larger queer and trans communities. While this investigation currently offers no answers, we remain optimistic the truth will eventually make itself known. Until then, worship shall continue.

Praise Danu.

Eat Me (Extreme Warning)

by

Caitlin Marceau

A Note from the Author

When Mark asked me to write a story for *Dethfest Confessions: The Devil's Playlist*, I eagerly accepted his invitation…and then I immediately panicked.

Truth be told, I'm not a fan of metal.

Don't get me wrong, I love Ghost, and I enjoy the odd Black Sabbath song, but when it comes to the music, metal has never been my thing.

But its *aesthetics*?

Not only is that a different story, but it's the point of inspiration for my addition to this anthology.

I love the showmanship that comes with metal. I love the costumes, the pyrotechnics, the gimmicks, the personas, the crowd work, and the full-on pageantry that accompanies some of these bands. And I couldn't help but wonder what would happen if the lead guitarist of a sex-heavy, glam metal band wanted to get *darker* with their music. What would that mean for their identity? What would that mean for their lyrics? What would that mean for their fans?

Most importantly, what would that mean for their band?

If you're looking for a story that's heavy on the music and light on the metal aesthetics…well, I'm sure there's another story like that in this book, but it certainly isn't this one. If, however, you want a wonderfully gory and f*cked-up take on devotion, consumption, and self, then I hope you'll enjoy this piece.

And if you don't, well, "Eat Me."

Eat Me (Extreme Warning)

I wave goodbye to the audience crowded around Stage 2 and dramatically blow kisses to them with both of my hands. I wink and smile at whoever catches my eye, making sure to play into my flirty persona before following my bandmates off stage.

"That was bullshit, and you fucking know it," I hiss under my breath once I'm sure the sound technicians have turned the microphones off and there's no risk of the crowd hearing me.

"It *was* bullshit, Shiloh. It's why we fucking cut you off," Salem whispers back at me, absentmindedly combing his beard down with his hand.

I shake my head and push past him, making my way to the metal stairs leading us away from the stage. We walk silently through the scorching sun and tall grass to where the band trailers are parked, waving to fans who manage to catch a glimpse of us from behind the barricades and privacy fences. My leather pants and skimpy lace corset feel uncomfortably tight in the summer heat, and even my normally comfortable Doc Martens are too warm for me to bear. Hair sticks to the back of my sweat-streaked neck, and I try not to think about how much my makeup has smudged down my face since starting our set.

I see our trailer in the distance—a banner with "SeXXX" written across it hangs off the side of the metal monstrosity in intentionally campy blood-red cursive and black detailing—and sigh with relief. I spot one of the Dethfest volunteers waiting outside of it with bottles of water glistening with condensation and nod my thanks as I grab two out of their hands and make my way into the cramped space.

I sit on the edge of my small cot and toss one of the bottles next to me on the thin mattress, cracking the other one open and chugging most of the water. I breathe deeply, gulping in air, before slamming the last of it back. Halfway through untying my boots, the rest of the band filters in.

"We need to talk about what happened," Moss, our drummer, says quietly. Despite her ferocious way around a drum set and the extraverted personality she puts on for our shows, the woman is generally soft-spoken and even a little timid. For as long as I've known her, she's avoided conflict like the plague, so for her to suggest we talk about the show means things are getting serious.

"Yeah, we do," I say, kicking my shoes off and standing up beside my bed. I pull the duffle bag out from underneath it and make my way to the bathroom in the back of the trailer. I slam the door closed behind me and begin to wash up, eager to get free of my restrictive costume and feel clean again.

"That was a real dick move of you to put us in that spot, Shiloh," Salem yells through the bathroom door. "We told you that we didn't want to play that song."

I zip the fly closed on my jean shorts, pull my baggy black T-shirt over my head, and open the bathroom door.

"Then it's a good thing you didn't have to! You didn't even let me get through the fucking chorus!" I spit.

Pushing past him, I throw my duffle back under my bed and sit on top of the small cot, pulling on fresh socks and slipping my feet into a pair of worn Converse.

"Because none of us were comfortable with it!" he shouts.

Moss and Piper, our bassist, sit together quietly on one of the long benches at the front by the door. Although they don't nod in agreement with Salem, they're not quick to speak out against him either, and he continues to yell at me.

"We've told you a thousand fucking times that we're not comfortable with the shit you've been writing! We don't play music about eating people and brutally torturing them! We play music about falling in love and getting railed!" He holds up his hands in frustration, chewing me out. "But you just *had* to perform that song anyway!"

"You guys try new fucking material all the goddamned time, but the second I do it, you—"

"When we try something new, generally, the rest of the band is in on it! Or we're just doing a quick riff during our introductions! We don't just start playing a random song in the middle of our set." Piper frowns, crossing her arms in front of her chest. "That song was gross, Shiloh."

"That song was *great*," I snap.

"It was freaking me out, and it was freaking the crowd out too," Moss says under her breath.

"Bullshit! They were into it, and you know it! You're such a liar, you little—"

"Stop arguing, Shiloh!" Salem's voice reverberates off the walls, reminding us all why he's the lead singer. "If we've told you once, we've told you a thousand times: we don't want to play whatever the fuck *that* was."

"You guys didn't even give it a chance."

"And we don't have to! We're SeXXX! We're all about flirting and fun and pop metal! We get people horny and give them a fun show! That's it! That's the schtick!"

"Maybe I want more than that!" I scream at them.

"Then maybe you need to find another band!" Salem shouts back at me.

I wait for Piper or Moss to speak up, to tell Salem he's out of line this time, but that moment never comes. Neither dares to meet my gaze, to look me in the eye, while I stare at them.

"Seriously?" I finally ask, voice barely above a whisper.

He sighs and leans against the wall of the trailer, running a hand through his sweaty hair. Salem finally shrugs and looks at me, silent, before eventually finding the words.

"If you can't get on board with our sound and what we want and if you keep pushing this heavier fucked-up shit on us, then yeah. You should find another band."

"And who the fuck is going to write most of your music for you? Who's going to put up with your shit, you talentless hacks?" I ask, failing to keep the fury out of my voice.

"Don't you fucking call us—"

"*We* aren't SeXXX. *I* am! This was *my* idea. These are *my* songs. This is *my* band. And if you don't like the direction *I'm* taking us in, then *you* can leave!"

"It *was* your band," Moss says quietly, "but it's bigger than just you now."

"*We're* bigger than you now," Piper adds, pursing her lips together and finally looking me in the eyes.

"If you want to find new musicians and call yourselves SeXXX, then go for it. We won't stop you. But if you think for even a second that using our name and writing the same mediocre shit that you've been writing for years makes *you* this band, then you're as dumb as the bimbo you play on stage." Salem crosses the trailer and looms over where I'm sitting. He looks down at me, his eyes as icy as his voice. "We've outgrown you, Shiloh. We've known this for a long time. We just were too kind to admit it. So, get your shit together, or get the fuck out."

I stand up, my body pressed against him, and hold his gaze. Even with him towering over me, I refuse to cower away from Salem or give an inch. I square my shoulders and stick my chest out, glaring up at him.

"Get out of my way," I say, seething with rage.

He opens his mouth, like he's going to argue about this too, but eventually, he closes his lips and stands aside. I push past him, making sure to slam my shoulder into his torso when I squeeze by, and make my way to the trailer door, throwing it open and storming out.

Snippets of a hushed conversation follow as the three of them discuss me.

"What crawled up…and died?" Piper asks.

"I…how she treated…us," Moss whispers to them.

"…just needs a good…'uck is all." Salem laughs.

I storm through the tall grass, passing rows of trailers, heading to the hidden festival entrance for the bands. One of the security guards spots me approaching the metal barricade and stands up a little straighter. He opens his mouth, and I shake my head at him, hoping to kill off any conversation before it can begin. As much as I normally try to make polite conversation with the people working at these events, I don't have the energy right now, and I want to avoid drawing unnecessary attention to myself.

Without my stage makeup and tight corset, it can be easy to pass by crowds of people without them immediately recognizing me. But if I'm spotted talking with security on this side of the restricted entrance, what little cover I have will be blown.

I keep my head down and pass by the guard, following the trail cut into the dirt and grass by what seems like a million festivalgoers. Another volunteer is passing out bottles of water to the crowd, and I grab another one, still thirsty despite slamming back two of them already. I twist the cap off and drink. Some of the cold water spills over my lips and down my neck, sending a shiver through me.

I walk past a few stalls selling merch, most from bands I know and some from bands I don't, and feel myself turning red when I spot the booth selling T-shirts and hoodies with "SeXXX" and our photo silkscreened across the front of them. At first, I think I'm blushing with embarrassment at seeing myself plastered across the stall, but I quickly realize that my hands are balled into fists and my jaw is clenched. I'm not red because I'm mortified; I'm red with fury at being betrayed by the band.

By being betrayed by *my* band.

"Over my dead body," I mumble.

Someone near the SeXXX booth looks my way. I wonder if I'm just being paranoid about them recognizing me, but when they jab their friend in the ribs with an elbow and nod their head in my direction, I know I've been made. Not wanting to get mobbed by a pack of fans, I turn on my heels and quickly put as much distance between myself and the booth as I can.

The hot summer air smells like smoke, sweat, and stale beer. As I walk around the grounds of the venue, weaving through the horde of festivalgoers, my stomach starts to growl, and I realize I haven't had anything to eat since early that morning. I debate going back to the trailer for free food, but knowing that that means having to face my bandmates, I resign myself to the painfully long wait in one of the food tent queues.

I get in line and cross my arms in front of my chest, trying to calm myself down from the rage I've been in since—

I stop and think about it.

I've been mad since my song was cut off during the concert, but I know that's not when this anger started. I want to convince myself that the feeling started a few months ago when they told me they were unhappy with the direction I was trying to take the band in, but that's a lie too. The truth is, I've been angry for a long time. This quiet rage has been building inside me for years—maybe since birth—but I've been so busy channelling it into my music that I never noticed how big it's gotten or how it threatens to devour me whole.

We've outgrown you, Shiloh.

I picture Salem's face and another wave of anger rolls through me. I breathe heavily, remembering the way his eyes twinkled with malice, the smug smile he tried to hide while threatening everything I worked for, and the way he stood over me, trying to make me feel small. The memory of him makes me seethe, and I wonder if he'd coerced, bullied, or manipulated Piper and Moss into seeing things his way.

God knows it wouldn't be the first time if he had.

My flushed skin feels too hot and too tight, and I pull at the neck of my T-shirt, fanning myself with the soft cotton in an attempt to find some relief as I wait for my turn at the food tent. The sun overhead is unforgiving, and it doesn't help to improve my bad mood. My stomach growls again, louder this time, and the smell of barbecued hotdogs and hamburgers has my mouth watering. Normally, I'm not a fan of the scent, but right now, I can't get enough of it.

The man in line ahead of me runs a hand through his thick black hair, the long waves tumbling down his back. They're gorgeous in the bright sun, and I'm tempted to reach out a hand and touch them. As if he hears me, he gathers his hair together at the nape of his neck, accidentally swatting me with it as he pulls it through the loop of his elastic, tying it up into a ponytail. He turns around and smiles at me, his honey-brown eyes pushing away the memory of Salem's cold blue ones.

"Sorry about that."

"No worries," I tell him, too busy admiring his full lips to remember that I should smile back.

He starts turning back but stops. His brows come together, and he studies my face. After a second, his eyes widen in recognition, and he smiles excitedly.

"No way! You're the guitarist for SeXXX! Shiloh, right?"

I open my mouth, ready to deny the claim. People within earshot begin to buzz with excitement while he continues talking.

"That song you were playing—the one during the intro thing you guys do—was fucking amazing! *So* hardcore. I loved it!"

I smile wide, my heart beating wildly and my skin getting even warmer with excitement. "You liked my song?"

The buzzing and whispering around me gets louder. A few of the people from the line leave their spots to crowd around me, each trying to get a view of my face to make sure I am who the man says I am.

"I fucking *loved* it!"

I take a step toward him, excited, my stomach growling loud and long when I catch a whiff of the man's sweat on his skin. It blends in with the smell of the meats wafting from the food vendors.

"Really?"

More people gather around us. Their bodies are warm, and between the heat radiating off of them and the sun, it's unbearable. I pull at my T-shirt again, suddenly hyper-aware of how the clothing rubs against my body and sticks to my sweat-dampened skin.

The man must feel similar. He wipes perspiration from his forehead with the back of his hand and pulls at the front of his shirt. I lick my lips and look at him, catching a glimpse of his stomach and hips when his T-shirt rides up a bit.

My stomach growls again.

"Fuck yes." His eyes are wide and unfocused as he looks at me. "It was unlike anything I've heard from you guys. I mean, not that I don't like your other stuff, but this…This was intense. Visceral."

I nod my head violently in agreement.

The people around us move closer. Their sweat, their breath, their skin, their blood—all of it mixes with the thick smoke from the grills inside the tent. I breathe deeply, enjoying the scent instead of being repulsed by it.

"That's what I wanted," I whisper excitedly, pulling hard at the collar of my T-shirt, the cotton ripping. "I wanted something raw and brutal."

"That line about peeling back flesh and devouring demons…" he trails off, standing even closer as his eyes take in my body. "It really made sense to me," he finally finishes.

Heat rolls off of his skin, and I feel dizzy, drinking in the smell of the man, placing a hand on my stomach that aches and groans with hunger, swallowing saliva as my mouth waters.

"I think that's because we're all hungry for something— acceptance, love, validation, whatever—and the only way for us to get it is if we're willing to consume the part of us—the demon—that's holding us back." I'm not entirely sure what I'm saying or that I believe any of the bullshit spilling from my lips. What I *am* certain of is the desperation growing inside me with each passing second.

"I wish you could have finished playing your song," the man says, his breath hot on my face.

"So do I."

My clothes feel so hot against my skin that for a second, I think they might be burning me. My stomach bellows, ravenous, and my body bristles with tension from both my earlier confrontation with Salem and the energy currently pulsing between myself and this stranger. My muscles are tense and feel like they're going to snap, like I've been coiled too tight.

The air is thick, and at first, I think it's so solid and heavy that it's pushing me around, making me rock on my feet. But when I look closer, I realize it's not the air moving me, but rather, it's the mass of bodies crowded around me, swaying and heaving together as one.

I stare at the man, his honey-brown eyes locking onto my own, and the movement of the crowd gets faster. It's hard to breathe, the air is like fire in my lungs, and soon, all of us are holding our breaths. The swaying gradually slows, and everyone comes to a stop, the world around us silent.

And then: chaos.

The crowd explodes into a frenzy.

They grab at each other, ripping their clothes off and fitting their bodies together however they can. All thoughts of modesty and decency are gone, erupting into a flurry of flesh and desire.

I throw myself at the man, clawing at his shirt. I tear it off of him and drop it in the dirt beside us before running my hands up his chest, my fingers tracing the firm muscles and soft curves of his body. He rips my shirt off too and unhooks my bra, kissing a trail from my mouth to my chest, his lips finding my nipples. I sigh, letting my head roll back on my shoulders, and let out a loud moan when his teeth pierce into me, biting off a small piece of my right breast.

It should hurt—on some level, I'm sure it does—but it sends a quiver of ecstasy through me. I grab a fistful of the man's hair, enjoying the way his smooth locks feel between my callused fingers, and guide his lips back up to mine. I kiss him deeply, delighting in the taste of myself on his lips, and I savour the way my warm blood runs down my chest, over my stomach, and drips onto my thighs.

He pulls his mouth away from mine and continues to chew the piece of my breast. I take one of his hands in my own and lead it to my mouth, kissing his palm. Slipping his index and middle finger past my lips, I suck on his skin before sinking my teeth into them. I chew carefully, not wanting to bite through the bone, and slowly strip his fingers of their meat.

The man moans and pulls me closer to him, grinding himself against me. He lowers his head and takes another bite, this time out of my shoulder. Someone presses themselves against me, and I shiver in delight as they roam my body, their sharp nails leaving deep cuts that bloom red in their wake.

Once I've cleaned the sinew from the man's two fingers, I guide his hand down, past the waistband of both my shorts and underwear, and between my legs. I pant softly, using him to rub myself, enjoying the sensation of the hard bones and hot blood against the softness of my body. Pressure begins to build and grow deep inside me, and my pulse thunders in my veins.

When I feel like I can't take anymore, I slip his skinned fingers inside myself and thrust against them. Soon, my eyes roll back in my head and my legs shake as more teeth pull at my skin. A wave of pleasure rushes through me, and I cry out in release, my mouth finding someone else's. We share a sloppy kiss, and they push the flesh they were chewing into my mouth with their tongue.

The man withdraws his hand and turns his attention to a woman next to him. She's covered in blood and is missing her nose, but nobody seems to care. They gyrate against each other, while another set of hands guides me deeper into the crowd.

As good as I feel, as right as I feel, there's still something missing. I'm still not whole.

I'm not *sated.*

I let myself get swept up in the fervour of the crowd, enjoying the way our bodies become one body. I see a pair of blue eyes watching me.

For a second, I think it's Salem, but when I blink, his face disappears just as quickly as I'd imagined it. Someone's hands dig inside me, working me open and pulling me apart. As I let myself quake with pleasure, I know what I have to do.

*

The air that's been hot on my skin all day finally feels cold, and I can't help but shiver as I approach the trailer. Although a light is on, nothing but silence emanates from inside the space. I slowly climb the small steps and grab the cold metal handle, pulling open the stiff door. Ambling inside, I look around, noticing both Piper and Moss aren't here.

Salem, on the other hand, sits on a nearby couch, lazily flipping through the pages of a book. After a minute of pretending not to notice my arrival, he finally looks up at me, and his bored expression turns to one of shock and confusion.

"Oh my God, Shiloh, what the fuck happened to you?" he shouts. He looks me up and down, his eyes finding all the places my skin should be but isn't. His gaze lingers on my naked breasts, and although he seems genuinely concerned for me, he can't help but stare between my legs at my exposed body.

"I want you inside of me."

"What?" he asks, practically choking out the words.

"I want you inside of me," I say again, crossing the space between us to straddle his lap.

"Shiloh, you're covered in blood and seriously injured. I think you're in shock. We need to get you to a hospit—"

I lean in and kiss him, grinding down on his lap, my lips pressing hard against his. At first, he keeps his mouth closed, resisting me. But soon, his hands are cupping the backs of my thighs, and his lips are pushing back against mine. I keep my eyes open as we kiss, savouring the look of confusion and arousal on his face. I smile to myself—knowing that I'll get what I want—and deepen the kiss, coaxing his lips open with my tongue.

Behind me, the door to the trailer opens, and Piper and Moss talk in panicked voices about the chaos outside. They mention something about the water, but I don't care.

I'm hungry, and only one thing will satiate me.

I continue to tease Salem and feel a rush of joy when he slips his tongue into my mouth.

Finally.

I bite down, moaning softly when my teeth crunch through his tongue. He starts to scream and tries to pull away, but that only helps me rip through his flesh and sever the tongue from his mouth. I don't bother chewing the tough muscle. Instead, I let the warm blood coat the back of my throat and swallow it whole.

Salem tries to push me off of him, his arms flailing wildly as he panics. His screams mix in with those of Moss and Piper.

I smile down at him.

"I've outgrown you, Salem," I whisper coldly and take another bite.

Walk the Plank

by

Robert Essig

I saw her backstage before the show, hovering over our singer, and I knew she was in trouble. Of course, I was right, but it had nothing to do with Jerry.

Tara was one of the contest winners who would be onstage while we played our popular song, "Walk the Plank," a fan favorite. I hope you don't think it was a radio hit or something. Ha! The Top 100 wouldn't *touch* Red Jolly Roger. In the echelon of heavy music, pirate metal is lower than Viking metal, if you can believe that. But despite being the redheaded stepchild of heavy music, we have quite a fan base. Turns out, people like songs about drinking rum and spilling blood.

Like I said, Tara was one of five winners of a social media contest for backstage passes and a chance to walk the plank that night—well, midday—at the show. I saw her and took an immediate liking to her, as did Jerry, clearly. He wanted to give her the old third peg leg, is what he wanted. I could tell. But she didn't seem to be buying whatever he was laying down.

A band like ours had a few groupies, but that was sort of a thing of the past. More a symptom of excessive times. We weren't that excessive, so we didn't exactly have women throwing themselves at us. Well, not the ones we'd actually be interested in.

Not like Tara.

Forgive me. I haven't introduced myself. I'm Don Thurston, better known as Donnie Massacre. I play bass.

The band wasn't my idea—the theme, that is. I wanted to play in a doomy-sounding metal band. Something groovy, like Corrosion of Conformity mixed with the Sabbathy tones of Sleep, maybe a little Gojira thrown in to spice things up. And we were kind of doing that until the other guys got this wise idea to play pirate metal. I was outnumbered. But our songs are pretty cool, so I can't complain too much. Not that anyone takes us seriously.

The winners of the contest were super fans, the types who come to the shows dressed in pirate garb, even talking like pirate caricatures. It's pathetic. The other guys eat it up.

Someone had brought this weird bottle out. It looked weathered, with that chalky sheen like it had been floating in the ocean for decades. Typical for our shows. Pier One Imports sells that kind of bottle for decoration. People buy them and fill 'em with rum, smuggle them into the venue and raise them high, especially when we play our song "Three Cheers for Blackbeard."

Two of our roadies were hitting the bottle pretty hard, considering free liquor to be a godsend when events like this only provided complimentary domestic beer. Those two had been with us for years. They had a club mindset, though, so a big festival such as Dethfest was mind-blowing for them. Maybe they were nervous. I don't know. Just tune the fucking guitars and make sure the sound levels are good. And they did that, but I'm telling you, there was something wrong with whatever they were drinking from that bottle. One of them went apeshit and found a saber, but he was apprehended before any real mayhem could happen.

That occurred about when we went on stage, but I'll get to that.

Those guys were trying to get Tara to drink from the bottle, and she wasn't having any of it. They were kind of obnoxious, so I butted in and told them to fuck off. It was a lighthearted term of endearment around the Red Jolly Roger crew. Nothing like telling someone to get fucked. Gets the message across quite nicely. You live with these guys day in and day out on the road, and you find out what gets on your nerves. And *their* nerves, for that matter.

I talked with Tara while sipping bourbon straight from the bottle. One of the bigger bands on the bill had a fucking rider a mile long calling for gallons of liquor, cases of wine, and a veritable sea of beer, despite the swill provided by the promoter. The craft table was an afterthought, but there was plenty to snack on. We'd known the band for years, having toured with them. They always demanded loads of alcohol so everyone could get good and loaded.

Tara told me she was in grad school. Not the type who typically favored our band. She was going to be a parapsychologist, so I made a bad joke about a periscope, and she fake-laughed. I'd had enough Jack in me to not really give a shit if I was stupid. Lemmy had said the chase was better than the catch. I'm not sure I agree, but the bass player has to work twice as hard as the singer, unless, of course, you were both the bass player *and* the singer, as in Lemmy's case.

She was into historical movies about Ireland and whatnot. I was only half listening. Sometimes it gets loud backstage, and snippets of conversation threatened to break my concentration. Her love for period-piece movies had developed into a love for pirates. Being that we try to have a pirate aesthetic to the music as well as the image, she was drawn to our band and had been a fan since our second album. Tara had come to the show alone since she didn't have a boyfriend and none of her college friends could be bothered to attend Dethfest, much less give a shit about a fucking pirate-themed metal band. We're the redheaded stepchild of metal, if I haven't mentioned that before.

I noticed she kept looking across the way. Backstage was an area covered with a tarpaulin roof to block the sun and plenty of misters to combat the heat. She was clearly distracted, which bothered me, but I also understood she was a fan and probably wanted to meet all of us.

"Are you going to be hanging out after the show?" I asked.

Some girls you just *knew* were hanging out backstage after. They wanted to fuck every guy in the band. That wasn't so apparent with ours, but I've definitely seen it with a few of the headliners. Tara didn't look like that kind of girl. She was just a super fan, and that's cool. Despite what people think about rock stars being cocks with legs, some of us are actually looking for a girl to have a real relationship with. There was something about Tara speaking to me on that level.

She nodded. "Yeah, I'll be hanging around for a bit."

Her gaze darted to someone behind me. Again. This time I turned and saw Jerry Holmes holding court with a group of adoring fans and hangers-on. Oh, in case that name doesn't ring a bell, Jerry is our singer, Captain Orlock.

I looked back at Tara. She was smitten, just like so many others who make their way backstage. Orlock wasn't so much a good-looking man, but played a part and played it well. He wore black makeup around his eyes at all times, which drove women crazy. And Orlock swaggered around like Jack Sparrow, which annoyed the hell out of me. It wasn't like he was piss drunk all the time. It was a fucking act, but fans loved it, and Orlock had no qualms about being the center of attention.

I said, "Captain Orlock likes to jerk off dogs just to see the red rocket," when a disturbance interrupted my bad attempt at a joke.

One of the guys who had won the Walk the Plank contest had smashed that ancient-looking bottle and held the mouth end in hand, shards pointing out like he was in a bar fight in some old movie. His teeth were gritted, eyes bloodshot and bulging.

"You fucking scallywags, back off! I'll cut every last one of you. I fucking swear it!"

The guy swung the ragged bottle in swift swipes like a dagger. People stood back. If I had something long enough, like maybe one of my basses, I would have swatted the damn bottle out of his hand and knocked the son of a bitch out.

One of our roadies who hadn't been consuming the unknown liquor stepped in while someone darted off in search of security. The crazed fan lunged at him and slashed his arm with the broken bottle. It looked painful. Little Guy—we called him that because he was huge and had a habit of calling everyone Big Guy—saw red after getting slashed. His face swelled, neck bulging with veins like thick cables. It was like the fucking Incredible Hulk or Andre the Giant. He swatted the broken bottle out of the fan's hand hard enough to break the guy's wrist and then wrapped his other hand around the fan's neck.

I'm sure Little Guy would have killed him had security not stepped in and broken things up. Our manager was going to have to call our lawyer. Again. It wasn't that we were some kind of badass rock band trashing hotel rooms like The Who or cutting it up like Pantera every night, but we had lawyers for this kind of thing. Depending on how much alcohol was in Little Guy's system, we might not see him until the next gig.

After the bad noise, I realized Tara wasn't standing near me anymore. She'd made her way over to Captain Orlock. Of course, she did. They always flocked to that asshole. Yeah, yeah, he's the singer, I get it, but the guy really *is* a prick. We were hardly riding any kind of fame, but whatever he could get out of it he took without abandon. He was the star of his own movie, and he let everyone know it.

Here I was, foolish enough to think I could find love on the road.

We all hung out, chatting and drinking and sweating. It was hot as a motherfucker. Did I mention that? By the time the winners of the Walk the Plank contest were huddled together and given instructions on what to do on stage when it was time, I'd had enough whiskey to talk to Tara again.

Some of you are probably wondering how it is I'm in a rock band, tour the world, and don't have the balls to talk to women. That's not entirely true, but drugs and alcohol certainly help.

She looked kind of down, and I figured I knew why.

"They say don't meet your heroes."

She shrugged. "What's that supposed to mean?"

"Orlock. He what you expected?"

Tara had these amazing hazel eyes, sad in that moment, and I felt I could have looked into them every night before hitting the stage. I could also see she wasn't the least bit interested in me.

"He was kind of an ass, but I guess that's how it is for the singer, right?" She feigned a smile.

I shrugged. "Doesn't have to be. Front Man Syndrome. Happens to the best of them. Even a dumb band of fucking pirates."

"I think you guys are badass. The pirate theme isn't dumb at all."

"We're not all like Orlock, you know."

"I mean, he wasn't *that* bad."

Walk the Plank

We were given a two-minute warning. Our warm-up music, "A Pirate's Life for Me," was playing. I grabbed my bass and then looked Tara in those beautiful eyes.

"Enjoy your time on stage." Then I leaned in and said softly, "Don't let the crowd open up on you."

I walked away.

The show went off without a hitch. There was some kind of scuffle way out behind the crowd involving security, but that was expected at a festival of this magnitude. Despite my disdain for Captain Orlock, he brought his A game. We opened with our latest single, "Blood and Rum." Orlock carried around a huge bottle with water turned red with food coloring, and he spit it on the crowd throughout the song.

At the end of our set, we went into "Walk the Plank." I wasn't sure at the time why only one of our roadies, assisted by roadies from one of the other bands, wheeled out the plank we set up center stage every night. Usually, our three roadies came out dressed like pirates, wheeled out the plank, and locked it in place.

Well, we'd lost Little Guy after the incident backstage, and as it turned out, our other roadie had brandished a fucking sword out in the audience while we were on stage. That was the incident I had seen demanding the attention of all those security guards.

One by one, the five…no, four contest winners—remember, one of them tried to kill us with a broken beer bottle—walked on stage when given their cue and approached the plank. They would step onto the wooden diving board for an epic crowd dive.

Tara was the last one. As she walked on stage, she looked at me with fear in her eyes. Maybe it was fear of being on stage. She'd seemed kind of shy. Or maybe fear the crowd would split apart when she jumped.

She approached the plank, stood at the edge, and gazed upon the crowd who'd gathered to hear a group of vagabonds play pirate metal. Tara looked down at the hands reaching up to grab at her feet, missing by mere inches.

We went through the chorus—what was *supposed* to be the final chorus when she was supposed to jump—but she seemed to be frozen in place. We played the chorus again.

Captain Orlock screamed, "Walk the plank, wench!"

But Tara stood in place, staring down at a boisterous crowd and causing us to play too long. Every minute counted at a festival, and this was our last song.

I continued to pound out the chorus on my bass, saddling up to the plank just as Orlock swaggered his way in that direction with his mic stand. He had this whole Aerosmith thing going, with shreds of bandanas and pieces of bone hanging from the stand.

We had the same idea. All Tara needed was a little push.

The mic stand and the headstock of my bass jutted out toward the poor girl, while she shivered in place like a cat stuck in a tree.

Up until now, I always told people it was Orlock's mic stand that nudged her first. But that's not true. It was the headstock of my bass guitar. Right in her ribs. It was a spontaneous decision driven by frustration. Just like so many others I met backstage, all she wanted was a piece of Captain Orlock. That shit had started to get to me. Nudging her into the pit was my way of sticking it to her.

What I didn't expect was not only her reaction, which was to flail her arms and legs as if she were *actually* walking a fucking plank over a tumultuous sea, but like something out of a rock 'n' roll bible, this sea of Red Jolly Roger fans split.

I fingered the final bass line, and we closed out the song, watching the flailing form of Tara nose-diving right into the compacted ground. From my vantage, it was hard to tell how hard she hit, but it didn't look right. Her body lay there in a contortion of arms and legs, her head cocked grotesquely.

I had to look away as the last notes of "Walk the Plank" rang out. Fans crowded around her, kneeling to assist, and that was it. Walking off stage, I was half ashamed by what I'd done and half pitying the poor woman who couldn't handle a simple stage dive and had turned it into a spectacle.

I didn't see Tara after the show, and by the time I thought about her again, I was liver-deep in whiskey and balls-deep in some leftover groupie. It was true, I'd been looking for a girl to settle down with, but that didn't mean I scoffed at a nice piece of ass when it came my way.

The following day, on our bus to the next gig, I was informed Tara had been taken to the hospital after our performance. She'd snapped her neck.

"Is she…?" I couldn't even say the last word, so I let it hang there.

"No. But she'll never walk again."

In my mind, the chorus of our song, a song we played every night at every show, rang over and over: *Walk the plank! Walk the plank!*

Some nights, when I'm having trouble sleeping, I think about Tara and remember the fear I put in her mind when I said, "Don't let the crowd open up on you."

Zachary Ashford

A Horrible Day to Have a Curse

by

Zachary Ashford

Even before I started, I knew the cops would soon be on my ass. You can't just load four dead musicians dressed as Vikings into the back of a stolen truck, hightail it to the harbor, throw the forementioned dead dudes into a random vessel, and send it, burning, onto the lake without attracting attention. That's just a fact. But, if you're asking me what I thought was going to happen when they arrived, the truth is simple. I thought I was going to fight them.

If you're asking whether that happened, and how the fuck we got to this point, you'll need to wait. My fallen brothers deserve to have the tale of their deaths shared far and wide. Those bastards at Dethfest wanted to put a lid on it, but my berserker rage will not allow this! The truth *must* be spread.

Let me give you some perspective…

I already had Anders in the boat and Gunnar in my arms when I heard the first siren. It wailed in the distance like the cry of a vulture. In normal circumstances, two months ago before we embarked on our tour of the world, culminating in an early slot at Dethfest, I would not have been in this situation. I loved the aesthetic, but I did not believe the Norse gods were real then. The things I've seen, though, well, they've made a true believer of me. A true believer in Old One Eye, the Allfather, Odin, the Ancient One.

You see, what I saw on the day of the Dethfest clusterfuck left me with no choice but to send my fellow bandmates off to

Valhalla in a true Viking funeral. They had died warriors' deaths, and they deserved to drink and fight in the halls of Valhalla!

But I was telling you about the sirens…

There I was, trying to throw Gunnar's fat ass into the boat when I heard the first siren. I thought they would be coming sooner than they did, but I have to tell you that first siren really put lead in my pencil. I hefted all six foot six of Gunnar onto the prow and dropped him over. By Odin's spear, I thought I was going to throw my back out, but thankfully, the power of strong ale, Jägermeister, and sheer determination meant I wasn't going to cry off from my task. I had promised him, in particular, and I would see that through.

As he crashed to the sole of the boat, the sirens faded into the distance, and I realized all was not yet lost. I could still get these warriors to Valhalla before the pigs came to test my mettle. Before I tell you that story, though, you must know how we ended up in this dire circumstance.

*

With our new album, *Blood Eagle,* recorded and the publicity machine well under way, we were set to film what would be our biggest and most expensive music video ever. We had seen the success Archspire had with crowdfunding, and we did the same for the "Plunder and Pillage" video. As a result, we were going big. *Real* big.

The video would feature the blót sacrifice of a horse, and although we knew it was a risk many might fail to appreciate the artistry in sacrificing a real horse for the video, we counted on it being a great way to get some free publicity. If we could get PETA and others complaining about us on social media, we could go viral in no time. Controversy sells records, and I still think that, in theory, the idea was sound.

In theory.

In practicality, it was very, very dumb. I don't know if you know this, but the average horse has fifty-four liters of blood in it and weighs nearly a ton. Killing one is not as easy as you'd think. Especially when you've got the fucking thing hanging upside-down from a tree.

Now, we didn't know exactly what the rules were for this kind of thing. At the end of the day, we were musicians playing roles in a band. We were not historians. As I said, we liked the aesthetic. It also helped that singing angry songs about shield walls, berserkers, and burning innocent women and children out of their churches so they can be raped and enslaved is pretty fucking metal. All of which is to say that our whole inspiration for the horse thing was a television show with the guy from that terrible *Warcraft* movie. We didn't know that if we got it wrong, we would anger Odin.

Now, we do.

So there we were, five drunk metal musicians in Viking costumes, standing around a live horse that had been tied up and suspended from a tree.

Now, I don't want to be patronizing, but horses are fucking huge and terrifying. So imagine what it's like when you've got this monstrously sized animal hanging there, thrashing and squealing, while a director with industrial lights and five heavily bearded morons act like they know how to sacrifice the poor thing.

Oskar, our vocalist, was the one who did the honors. He ran a blade across the beast's throat. Obviously, the horse bucked. It shrieked and spun like a tornado of hooves and buck teeth. It was total fucking chaos.

I backed off, disgusted, as the blood fountained. The bough of the tree supporting the horse creaked and cracked. I'm pretty sure I pissed myself a little, and I'm a little bit certain that Anders cried for his mum. Seconds later, the horse crashed to the ground, breaking its neck on impact. The blood kept gushing, leaking onto the dirt, where it ebbed away into the soil.

Initially, we thought nothing of it. It was only later, after we were done filming the video—sans blót sacrifice—when Gunnar said his aunt, the historian who started his love affair with the Edda, believed that if Odin knew of our mistake, he would be angered.

Well, after that, I began to think he was more than angered. I began to think he was *majorly* fucking pissed.

Things around the band were weird. For the *Blood Eagle* world tour, we were plagued by airport delays, lost equipment, and strange dreams. Everywhere we went, crows glared at us. Usually, they are noisy, but for us, they would only stare in silent judgement. This was as sure a sign as any that the Allfather was seeking recompense for the failed sacrifice.

In my dreams, I would see fire giants and Jotun trolls rampaging through the crowds at our gigs. I would see Fenrir and Jormungand every time I closed my eyes. Nevertheless, we plowed on.

The Dethfest gig was to be a major event for us in the United States. One in which we could show the world that our brand of Viking metal was up there with the best in the world.

And then the speaker fell.

*

So you see, I am certain our mistakes with the blót sacrifice are responsible for the horrors of Dethfest. Why else would such horrors befall this event? It wasn't like it was planned by the Astroworld publicists. This was a metal festival, and if there's one type of music that knows how to throw a festival, it's metal.

No, the only reason for the horror was the curse we earned at the hands of Old One Eye. I believe he and the treacherous Loki conspired to bring our world down around us and end our chances of conquering the sea of death metal fans who came to rock out to our brand of metal.

When that speaker fell, we were tearing shit up. Oskar was swinging his axe-shaped microphone stand like a berserker. Johan and Anders were hitting their harmonized solos, and Gunnar and I had locked into a powerful groove, capable of moving the swiftest longships across the great Atlantic.

I do not know which sprite possessed those who chose to climb the riggings and shake the speaker loose, but when it fell, so did the drapery by which the gods were hiding their intentions. An oppressive toxicity hung in the air. It crackled with an evil atmosphere, and infected all who were there.

Well…almost all.

We talked about this in our trailer after our set, and we decided to make sure we each had the bravery of ten men should we need to fight for our lives. I know that sounds extreme, but things were getting fucking hostile out there, and we really liked to drink. So drink we did. Like warriors who'd just raided Lindisfarne.

Eventually, several drinks deep, it was Johan who spoke of his nightmares. He too had dreamed of monsters and curses and fire. He too believed we had angered the gods.

"I thought I was the only who had been fearing this," I said.

An oppressive silence followed before the others admitted to the same concerns.

Eventually, Gunnar broke the awkward tension. "It was the ritual. I told you what my aunt told me, and I believe we have ignored the omens that have been all too obvious."

A pregnant hush settled on us then. Considering the thousands of metalheads spread out across the vast grounds and the decibels blasting out from the various stages, it was a moment of bizarre quiet.

"The world has been full of omens," Oskar said. "And we ignored them all."

"There is hope," Anders said. "Did you see the bolt of lightning that shot out from the speaker when it fell?"

"Those speakers are powered by electricity, Anders," Gunnar said. "You are drunk."

We were *all* drunk.

Anders finished his horn of Jaeger and wiped his chin. "Nevertheless, I believe that the bolt of electricity was a sign from Thor."

At this point, even I was prepared to admit Anders might have been *too* drunk. I finished my own horn so I could get on his level. I belched and told him to continue. The least we could do was listen to his ramblings.

"Put it this way," he said. "We don't know what is going to happen, but we know that *something* is going to happen. You can feel it. The air out there is alive with chaos and darkness. It raises the hackles on my neck, and I, for one, want to be ready for it."

Based on the fact I'd seen several fights break out in the crowd during our set, and those black Humvees were skirting around the perimeter of the festival, I figured he was right. I poured another drink and topped everyone else up. "So what do you suggest we do?"

*

In short, what Anders suggested was keeping our weapons by our sides and drinking some more. Now, if you didn't know much about us, you might be surprised to know that Oskar's mic stand doubled as a battle axe, and we all performed on stage with paraphernalia you'd expect to see at a Renaissance fair. Before you say anything, it's dumb, but it's also great fun. For every performance, we had a range of shields and bearded axes on-hand. Some bands play with fire; we played with replica weapons. It's a metal thing.

Throughout the day, more and more stories of violence, accidents, and gunshots, even of cannibalism, came back to us from other bands. We kept hearing shit was getting really fucking wild, but despite that, we kept drinking. It was a hot day, and we were thirsty, and our on-tour rule is simple: water is for pussies. It wasn't until we stumbled out of the trailer to go and watch Omnes Morimur perform that we realized how quickly things had escalated.

During their set, the fire giants arrived.

I know you will say there is no such thing as a fire giant, but fuck you. I saw them. The curse had become real, and Odin was playing his final cards. I cannot tell you if Surtr was there—I honestly don't think anyone would have made it out alive if he was—but while Omnes Morimur lost their fucking minds and fire raged, I saw shapes appearing in the inferno.

They were huge, monstrous, and as they ran through the crowd, burning fans alive and spreading their flames like contagion, we knew it was now or never. Drunk or not, we had to fight our way to freedom or die in breathless oblivion, taking as many with us as we could. This was all our fault, and if we hadn't tried to sacrifice a horse without doing the research, we would never have brought the conflagrations of Muspelheim to the festival.

Alcohol and adrenaline surged through my body. I drew my axe as Anders did the same. On either side of us, Gunnar and Johan pulled their weapons, and in front of us, Oskar raised his battle axe.

One of the fire giants came close. Beneath its flames, it possessed the body of a fat guy in a Cannibal Corpse shirt. The human screamed for help. Screamed for us to quench the flames. For the briefest moment, I wondered if some collective hysteria had inflicted us, if Loki was attempting to trick us into great evil, but it could not have been. We had a battle to fight, and silly questions would only slow us down.

The fire giant came closer, and Oskar swung his axe, driving it into the burning creature with as much force as he could muster. Spurting blood steamed as it splashed onto the blade, boiling under the intense heat. The rest of us fell on the giant, smashing and slashing until it was a charred and bloodied pulp.

Moments later, the fires were out of control, and the *rat-a-tat-tat* of gunfire rang out across the festival grounds. Behind us, near the trailers, several more fire giants were spreading their incendiary flames. Portable toilets melted, merch stands combusted, people burned alive.

We huddled, psyching each other up, and then we charged.

Oskar screamed, "Attacccckkkkk!" the same way he used to during the self-titled opener from our album, *Berserker Rage*, and we charged down the closest of the fire giants.

And that was when Johan met his end.

As he raised his axe, the giant blasted him with a ball of fire, engulfing him immediately. I couldn't help but watch as he collapsed, a charred ruin. I bellowed, and as the monster turned, Anders hurled his axe with precision I could not believe.

End over end, it rotated, seeming to travel faster with every loop, perhaps even guided by his precious Thor. It struck the fire giant between the eyes. The thing fell, smoldering, before it disappeared.

Oskar and Gunnar dragged Johan with them as they ran for a bay of trucks parked near the trailers. Our van was beyond them, right next to the VIP valet trailer. We had to make a break for it.

Gunnar, who could always hold his liquor better than the rest of us, pointed to a small group of fans hiding behind a merch stand. "Get them in the van. We'll have to get the fuck out of here."

I felt like Anders thought he should be driving, but it wasn't the time to argue. He let Gunnar heft Johan's corpse over his shoulder and joined the rest of us as we ran to help the survivors.

"Come! Run! Come with us!" I shouted.

Some began to head our way, but a commotion broke out amongst them. There was screaming and strange movement. I could see no flames amongst them, so I was unsure just what was happening, but as the majority of them ran for the trucks, I saw a small number of them had tackled others to the ground. They were ripping and tearing throats out with their teeth! The cannibal attack we heard about earlier must have spread!

We ran into the melee, striking with our axes and clearing the way for other survivors, but we were too late. The cannibals had already killed those they attacked.

I turned to Oskar. "What the fuck is going on?" I asked.

There was movement below him, and he screamed. One of the cannibals, obviously still alive, had latched onto his heel. She tore through it with her powerful teeth. Oskar fell, kicking out with his good foot. Anders struck the bitch in the face, caving her cheeks in, but Oskar was in a bad way. Ragged flesh wriggled in the wound. Blood sprayed. The psycho bitch had clearly severed arteries and veins. The blood pooled out beneath him. We helped him up and moved as fast as we could toward the van.

It wasn't fast enough.

A huge explosion sounded in the distance, and a black Humvee came sliding around the corner. Even as drunk as I was, I could tell it was heading straight for the gate, on a collision course with the civilians running in the direction of the van—and it had no intention of slowing down.

The Humvee skittled them like Finska pins and crashed through the gate, leaving our escape route open. Anders and I dragged Oskar to the van, knowing we had to get away if we hoped to see another sunrise. It wasn't until we reached it that we realized Oskar had bled out. I cursed Odin, knowing all of this was his revenge.

I still can't understand why no help came, why no one was able to call emergency services, or why the soldiers were there, but that fucking horse had been our undoing. What was supposed to be a blessing had been our death warrant.

We laid Oskar down, propping him against the tire, and I turned to Gunnar. "What the fuck do we do now?"

Gunnar was about to answer when sounds came from the back of the van.

"Anders," he said, "please tell me you locked the van when you put your ESP away earlier."

"Of course I did."

Which seemed like an odd claim to make because there was definitely someone in the back of the van. Gunnar wiped condensation from the glass and peered in through the back window.

"Then why are there two people fucking in there?"

I had to see. He was right. There were definitely two people fucking in there.

Gunnar pounded his fist on the glass. "Hey, you two, get the fuck out of there before you get jizz on my snare!" He ripped open the door, and the dude inside spun, seeing an angry Gunnar raging at him.

Mortified and instantly flaccid, he flopped out of the old grandma in the "Dethros" shirt and covered his failing johnson with his hands. Then his mouth dropped.

"What's your fucking problem?" Gunnar asked.

The dude wasn't looking at Gunnar. He was looking beyond him, to the biggest fire giant we'd seen yet. I swear on Thor's hammer, this thing was so big, I had to snatch the grandma's beer off her and take a swig to make sure I was actually seeing it.

A line of crows watched from the power lines as the giant approached.

Gunnar still hadn't noticed.

Anders tapped him on the shoulder. "Dude, forget the van. We've got to go. Now!"

I drew my axe. This thing and its mates had been responsible for Johan's death. Responsible, kinda, for Oskar's death.

"Fuck you!" I screamed, charging toward it. As soon as I got into throwing range, overcome with anger at everything that had happened, I hurled my axe, hoping for aim like Anders'.

I didn't get my wish.

The fire giant plucked the axe from the air and used it to slice through the power lines. The sparking wires trailed to earth, writhing like a kraken's tentacles. I grabbed Gunnar and dodged out of the way. Anders, the one who'd thought Thor was on his side, was not so lucky. One of the wires connected with him, frazzling him and blasting his body clear of the van.

The fire giant laughed and took another step toward us.

The couple in the van slammed the door shut and locked it.

"Truck! Now!" I screamed.

Gunnar didn't need to be told twice. He grabbed Oskar and tossed him into the tray of the nearest truck. "Get Anders!" he said. "I'll find the keys."

The monster took another step closer to us, enjoying the game far more than we were.

While Gunnar ran to the valet trailer, I dragged Anders' still-smoking body to the truck and lifted him into the tray. Gunnar came back as I took care of Johan. There were only two of us left. Our friends had died warriors' deaths, but we needed to live if we were to send them to Valhalla.

We hopped in the truck, and Gunnar keyed the ignition.

The fire giant gave chase.

*

Before I continue with how this clusterfuck ended and I was left to send my brothers to Valhalla alone, you have to know, once I had them all in the boat, I heard the sirens ringing the harbor on many occasions. There was no doubt in my mind the bastards were searching for me, but their inexorable coming could only speed my efforts.

Exhausted but resolute, I powered on, knowing their eternity would be worth my exertions. If the police *did* come, I would fight them to the death to ensure my brothers would drink with the gods and heroes of the distant past. So, once I had laid them all in the boat, I began to siphon fuel from nearby vessels and fill the tank with as much as I could.

And that's when the chopper arrived.

Those bastards with the black Humvees had tracked me. My experiences at Dethfest were to remain secret if they had their way.

The bastards...

*

And that brings me to our final escape through the festival fence.

I told you the black Humvee had screamed out of the festival, presumably to escape. If only that were true. Instead, the bastards were guarding the road out of town. I could only assume, with the perimeter breached time and time again by fleeing civilians, they decided to use their mercenaries to remove egress for any vehicles escaping.

We were just about to clear the fence. The fire giant pounded after us, flames trailing its wake. Gunnar smashed the pedal to the metal. We thundered out of there like Sleipnir, Odin's eight-legged steed, but the giant wouldn't relent. He stayed on our tail with the rapacious desire to end our lives.

Our failure to treat the blót sacrifice with the respect it deserved meant Loki's servants would only stop once we were all dead. The giant was a thing to behold, sprinting after us. I could barely turn my head from the rear window, but when a spotlight lit up the cab, I pivoted to see what the fuck was going on. Straight ahead of us, two blaring headlights flickered into life. A military vehicle was hurtling toward the truck.

Gunnar was blinded by the lights, but it didn't matter. Seconds later, gunfire raked our vehicle. This first sweeping attack failed to wound us, but the windscreen exploded into glass rubble, and Gunnar swerved. With the giant keeping pace behind us, he wasn't able to stop. All he could do was avoid a collision and hope the mercenary's terrible aim would spare us from death.

He completed half the job. With the giant closing the distance, Gunnar swerved the onrushing Humvee, but he could not avoid the second spray of bullets. This time, he took one of them through the chest.

The truck screamed past the black Humvee, and for a moment in time, the looks of abject terror on the mercenaries' faces were all I could take in. Seconds later, there was an explosion. They had crashed into the fire giant, and they all—the mercenaries and the giant—went up in a ball of flame.

Coughing, Gunnar, my friend, a true warrior, let the truck idle to a stop. He spluttered, and blood dribbled down his chin. "Tonight," he said weakly, "I will drink with Odin, the Allfather, who we have failed with our offering."

Knowing that only I could ensure the proper burial rites were observed, I took his hand in mine. "I promise this will happen, Gunnar. I will send you all to Valhalla on the smoke and flames of a funeral worthy of your tremendous courage and riffs."

He didn't respond. He was gone.

I dragged him out of the driver's seat and sat where he had breathed his last. With clear road ahead of me and the smoldering remains of our enemies behind us, I drove until I saw a sign for a recreational lake.

I'm not going to lie—Njǫrd would have been incredibly disappointed with this body of water. It was hardly the stuff seafaring adventures are made of, but it had boats, and I had the means to make fire. I have already told you my knowledge of Viking culture is rudimentary, but I had seen movies and knew a funeral worthy of the men from Vykyng required both.

*

So, now you know how I ended up here. How I made it out alive, at least as far as the harbor of De Soto Lake, so far from our homes in Gothenburg. It was a bloody and brutal day, and once I arrived, it took me many more hits from my drinking horn before I could bring myself to say my final goodbyes. Once I was good and drunk, I set to work, but you know everything now.

Everything, that is, apart from what happened once the black helicopter made its appearance.

Moments after its blades bit through the air, police sirens came howling into earshot. Blue and red lights soaked my surrounds.

The chopper hovered.

Not wanting to know what would happen if I didn't set the boat ablaze, I clambered into it and unhooked the mooring line. There was so much noise that I can barely tell you what exactly was said, but I can only imagine the shouting cop was telling me to freeze, to put my hands up, to remain silent.

Flashlights from the chopper danced across the ground, and if I squinted hard enough, I thought I could make out a sniper sitting in the open door.

I used one of the oars to push the boat out onto the marsh, pulled my lighter from my pocket, and raised my hands. The boat began to drift. The cops ran to the edge of the harbor, but the distance between us grew. A red dot crawled up my leg and settled on my heart.

Knowing it was a now or never moment, I flicked the lighter on.

The flame flickered in the breeze.

I raised my horns and leapt overboard, dropping the flaming lighter as I did.

When I stuck my head above water, the flaming boat was drifting into the middle of the lake. I was alone. The last Vykyng going solo.

The chopper was gone. The mercenaries onboard probably thought I was dead or that the cops would take care of the rest. Their blue and red lights flashed on the harbor, and their torch beams shone on the burning vessel.

I couldn't let them take me to rot in an American prison.

Full of piss and vinegar, knowing I had a tale to rival the bards who had inspired so many of our songs, I swam in the opposite direction. I knew not where I would come out of the water, but I knew my friends would see Valhalla's gates. I knew they would sup with the gods who had killed them, and I knew they would have eternity to drink and fight while they laughed about their final days in this realm.

As for me, I will continue to share my story, and I will continue to travel the world, performing songs about epic battles, Norse monsters, and terrible deeds.

While we will die, metal never will.

A Note from the Author

First of all, I want to say that I really hope you enjoyed "A Horrible Day to Have a Curse." When I was first asked to write about Vykyng, I was thrilled. I immediately jumped to the parallels between them and Amon Amarth. Secondly, after coming off the back of launching my debut novel, a very emotionally HEAVY horror novel about a death metal band, Polyphemus, I wanted to write something more fun, something in line with my earliest releases, the *Sole Survivor* books. Those are action stories with hordes of monsters, and I thought I could lean on that kind of vibe for this story, albeit one that doesn't dwell in the bleakness of Polyphemus. I also knew it needed to be a first-person story, which is something I don't usually write much. The end result was something I thought was a tonne of fun, while also bringing the metal with all the power chords and guttural vocals it could muster. As for the title, the more astute among you will be going, *but that's not an Amon Amarth reference...* You're right. It's not. It is a Black Dahlia Murder one, though, and those guys rule burrito supreme, and it just...*fit.* So, with that, horns up, you legends. Let's jump into the pit and have a blast!

Die Forever (Extreme Warning)

by

Simone Trojahn

Kuno Wolf, alias "der Wolf," does not feel well. The day has been fucked-up from the beginning. In order to get out of bed—which, for three weeks now, has been the cramped sleeping cabin of a tour bus hopelessly crammed with people and things—he had to throw back a Ritalin, which he washed down with a few sips from the bottle of vodka he took to bed last night after forcing a couple of sleeping pills through his dry throat.

He wasn't feeling very well six months ago, when he was persuaded by his manager to go on a six-week concert tour in the United States, and things haven't gotten any better since. The bus ride through America with his bandmates demands the pitiful remnants of his mental health, which was not too good from the outset. If Kuno is honest with himself, which nowadays only happens when he is sober—and he tries to avoid that at all costs—he must admit he has never really been well in the last two years since Anna broke up with him.

Of course, he also took refuge in his music, as befits a real artist. Unfortunately—and he didn't talk about it with his therapist, his manager, or even his bandmates; only Anna knew—Kuno doesn't feel the music, his lifeblood and greatest passion since his youth, as he used to. The gloomy self-written lyrics with which Bluttrinker inspires the masses come from Kuno's pen, but no longer from his heart.

And what would hurt an artist more than the agony of having lost access to his own soul?

Kuno can't explain how this could have happened. Also, he still plays his role so well, neither his bandmates nor the fans are suspicious. When he is on stage and half of his face portrays the wild, teeth-baring werewolf, "der Wolf," whose deep rumbling voice blows over the heads of the ecstatic sea of fans like a rough growl, inside he remains the lonely, pill-addicted Kuno who can't get over the separation from his soulmate.

Usually, he can ignore the pain in his throat, the sinking feeling in his stomach, and the constant trembling of his knees—at least, most of the time.

Today is different.

The Dethfest Festival marks the end of the Bluttrinker *Stirb ewig* Tour, but Kuno is so devastated now, not even the prospect of the flight back to Frankfurt, which is scheduled in a few days, reassures him. He would have loved to pack his things and flee immediately. Flee from the bus, from this festival, from this country, and from all the stages of the world. The only place he still wants to be—with the exception of a cold grave—is in Anna's arms.

But she will never again embrace him. He was stupid enough to betray her trust, just because his miserable bandmates told him it was good manners for a black metal band to bang a few awe-shrouded groupies after every gig. Kuno has never regretted anything more than those soulless backstage fucks with the nameless, black-painted sluts from the VIP lounge.

Anna could not, and did not, want to accept this any longer. She didn't care about fame. She didn't care about money. She didn't care about Kuno. Anna wrapped up his wonderful little boy and disappeared from his life forever. She doesn't even ask for maintenance—although Kuno could pay decently since the band's commercial breakthrough. After all, she has her pride and prefers to go to work herself.

The main thing is, Kuno has his sentence and is forced to live without three-year-old Linus from now on—the last remaining light of his pitch-black existence.

And what does the lead singer of a successful band do when he is depressed?

Naturally, he takes *more* drugs, drinks *more* alcohol, fucks *more* sluts, and roars his anger into the faces of his fans.

Just shit, if that doesn't make *anything* better.

Now he's on stage, wondering what he's doing here. While the guttural growl of the wolf comes out of his sore throat, he performs the latest Bluttrinker song and title of the U.S. tour, "Stirb ewig."

It sounds like Kuno wants to drive the lyrics into the brains of the masses with a hammer.

A few hours ago, during another band's performance, a large loudspeaker fell over and crushed a few people, but Kuno's hopes that the organizers would end the festival were quickly dashed. Even other incidents with several injured people, which were whispered about backstage, had not changed the progress of the event. Thus, despite all the irritating omens and vehement manifestations, Kuno could not avoid his performance, although he would have preferred to retire to the tour bus with a few downers and a bottle of booze.

Anyone who sees him jumping across the stage at this moment, with his hair twirling and his mouth wide open, would never have guessed what was going on in his head.

Suddenly, Kuno is hyper-aware of the warm air on his sweaty torso. His leather pants are so tight, they feel like a second skin. He takes a quick look at Karl, his guitarist.

"Der Henker" wears a black coat and hides his face behind a skull painting. He lives up to his nickname of "the executioner" and exudes a brutal dangerousness, tossing his bald skull back and forth with his tongue outstretched and his eyes wide open. A few meters behind him leans the hand-forged medieval axe, which der Henker swings menacingly above his head at the beginning of each performance before putting it down to start the show with a booming solo.

The Bluttrinker drummer, Otto—"der Mönch"—is quite at risk of heat stroke. At least no one can see he's sweating in his pig mask and monk's clothes, hammering his drums like a man possessed.

On the other hand, the attentive observer will recognize the perspiration on the neck and chest of bassist Bruno, who, like Kuno, is shirtless and wears red leather pants. How "der Doktor"—that's what Bruno calls himself on stage—endures under the ancient plague mask remains his secret. Kuno doesn't want to be in Otto's or Bruno's skin. He would probably have had to be removed from the stage long ago due to a claustrophobic seizure coupled with advanced dehydration.

Fortunately, thoughts are free, and Kuno's fans have no idea what a cowardly loser is hidden behind the masquerade of the dark wolf. Not even his band members know. Not that anyone is interested. As long as you play your role and deliver as expected, neither your person nor your actions will be questioned.

And yet…today, something is different.

The incident with the loudspeaker might have been an accident, but the mood in the crowd seems abnormal to Kuno. *Or is it me?* he asks himself nervously. What to do if he suffers a panic attack here and now in front of the assembled team? As the lead singer of a heavy metal band, his last hour would have struck. After all, people didn't come to watch the wolf transform into a shivering puppy.

Kuno's head sounds the alarm, and his throat becomes drier and drier…And what's going on in his guts? He doesn't have to go to the bathroom, does he? The rumbling in his stomach makes Kuno even more nervous. After all, he will be on stage for at least another twenty minutes…

With a rumbling voice, he sings, "Heute Nacht gehörst du mir…und du schreist wie ein Tier. Offenes Fleisch und rotes Blut—mein Messer raubt dir jeden Mut…Bleib ganz still und sterbe leise…Satan schickt dich auf die Reise…"

What's happening? A few people in the front row seem to have blood on their faces. Kuno looks into a sea of distorted grimaces, wondering whether the crowd is really going nuts or if his overloaded brain is playing tricks on him.

Seeking help, he looks around for his bandmates, but they are completely immersed in their world—one with their frightening costumes and noisy instruments. Slaves of the beat.

A woman in the front row holds something between her teeth that looks like a dripping piece of meat.

What is this? That can't be true!

Kuno averts his gaze from this madwoman. Who goes to a concert with raw meat in her luggage? He tries to concentrate on the essentials and, living up to his racing pulse, jumps across the stage as if out of his senses.

After that, he has to take a deep breath to continue singing. In doing so, he avoids any view of the audience. He has truly seen enough. With bared teeth, he squeezes out the lyrics of the next song. "Ich habe das Herz eines Drachen! Meine Zähne sind die schärfsten!"

Kuno closes his eyes and tries to let himself be carried away by the music, as he used to do. "Meine Seele ist verdorben, schwarz und tot. Dein Fleisch zerreißt, dein Blut so warm und rot."

He immerses himself in the song, feels the vibration of the bass in his body. For a moment, it's actually like it used to be.

Kuno is not a self-pitying shadow of himself, but "der Wolf!" His animalistic grin seems almost blissful. He finishes the song without opening his eyes.

While Karl, "der Henker," strikes up a fanatical guitar solo, Kuno begins to blink cautiously. He sees the stage, the lights, and his ecstatic band members in their gloomy robes.

Outside, the world consists of a billowing mass of indistinct blobs of color.

Suddenly, the edges of Kuno's field of vision darken. It's like someone is pulling a black curtain in front of his eyes. The feeling is accompanied by wild palpitations and a dull nausea. Kuno still tries to turn around to signal to his colleagues—or one of the security guards—but it's too late. The moment his extremities begin to tingle, Kuno's legs bend away from under him.

*

Kuno is lucky. His guitarist catches him before he falls, and his consciousness is only gone for a few seconds. A murmur creeps through the crowd. A security employee is immediately on the spot to lead Kuno to the backstage area.

The broad-shouldered giant directs Kuno to an armchair.

"Thanks, man. I'm okay," he gasps breathlessly.

"Here, take a sip." The security guard holds an open plastic bottle to Kuno's lips. It is one of the free water bottles they have been distributing to the festival guests all day long to avoid the heat damage from getting out of hand.

Kuno sips the bottle, realizing at the same moment that he is dying of thirst. His sips become greedier.

"You okay?" his broad-built counterpart wants to know.

Kuno nods hastily. "Yes, it's all right, man. Thanks again."

The security man nods, pats Kuno on the sweaty shoulder with his giant hand, and then disappears toward the stage, where Otto is yelling, "Fickt eure Mütter, ihr elenden Schweine! Wir sehen uns auf eurer Beerdigung wieder! Verdammtes Pack!"

A typical Bluttrinker's farewell.

Only, the shouts of the audience don't really fit in with a normal concert ending. Instead of asking for an encore, all they do is shout and shriek hysterically.

So be it.

Kuno doesn't have to deal with them anymore. And currently, he doesn't want to think about the headlines his involuntary departure from the stage will entail.

The rest of the festival and everything that happens afterward passes him by. In two days' time, he will turn his back not only on this wretched region, but on the entire continent and go back to where he feels at home, at least temporarily. Without Anna and Linus, it will never be the same again, but it will still be better than the homeless vagabond life he has led in recent weeks.

Relieved by the ebbing of his feelings of powerlessness and panic, Kuno swears, at this moment, not to be persuaded to go on a tour next time. Maybe he will even put an end to this madness completely and hang up the wolf's clothing once and for all.

*

A short time later, the appearance of his bandmates tears him out of his thoughts. The contented, sweaty faces seem strange to Kuno.

Pro forma, his condition is explored, but when it seems clear he is doing well, the conversations quickly drift in other directions.

Grinning, Bruno, "der Doktor," toasts him, while his plague mask lies next to him on the massive couch set dominating the backstage area.

Kuno reciprocates the gesture with his empty water bottle. Strangely enough, he feels tipsy.

Bruno was always the band member he could stand the least. Fifteen years ago, after performing with his former band in Denmark, the guy killed a fan who allegedly sexually harassed him. As a result, Bruno was convicted of manslaughter and spent seven years in a Danish prison. Kuno doesn't think Bruno was really harassed. Quite the opposite.

All those who know "der Doktor" also know that he screws everything with a heartbeat. If it were up to Kuno, the guy wouldn't be in the band at all, but in this matter, he was overruled by his colleagues when Bruno applied to them two years ago. In fact, the guy is a gifted bass player, and the rest shouldn't matter if you want to have a successful music career, but for Kuno, the whole thing felt wrong right from the start. After all, as a band, you feel like you're on top of each other twenty-four-seven, and he personally can imagine better things than spending his time with a murderer.

"I hope you're fit again, dude! The girls are already on their way!" Otto's voice reaches Kuno's ear. "Der Mönch" has taken off his cowl and pig mask and sits next to Bruno in boxer shorts. The lustful grin on his feisty face reminds Kuno of a real pig.

"What?" he asks, still hoping to have misheard.

"Have a drink! We're about to get fucked!" Otto laughs and throws a cold can of beer into Kuno's lap, so cold his heart stops beating.

"Come on, dude! It's time for you to relax!"

Kuno winces when, suddenly, two hands fall on his shoulders from behind. He puts his head back and looks into the skull of his guitarist Karl, "der Henker," savior of the evening.

"Thanks for jumping in so quickly, man," Kuno says.

"Of course!" Karl pushes Kuno's shoulders beyond the pain threshold. "And now, have a good time and drink a little color in your cheeks!"

Kuno joins in the general laughter and opens his beer. Although the brew here in the States cannot be compared with the culinary delights of the German art of brewing, the barley juice tastes surprisingly good to him. To the cheers and roars of his bandmates, he empties the can in one gulp and then grabs the next one. He's probably still dehydrated.

Finally, he can turn off his carousel of thoughts and relax a bit. In fact, it's been quite long since he last had such a casual time.

When the "girls" arrive a bit later, the party quickly approaches its climax.

The four girls are real fans and typical groupies. They reverently hang on the lips of their idols and admire their masks and equipment.

A tall, thin girl with a black pageboy hairstyle, who also comes from Germany, even grabs the executioner's medieval axe and pretends to want to cut off the heads of her friends with it, which causes wild laughter on both sides.

For a while, everyone sits together on the couch, running a joint around, drinking, talking, and laughing, until finally, a little blond in skull leggings and a fringed top takes the initiative and throws herself at Karl's neck.

"Der Henker," on the other hand, does not take long to ask and returns the groupie's kisses with wild fervor. Shortly after, much of his makeup can be found on her face, neck, and décolleté.

Half amused, half disgusted, Kuno turns away from this spectacle, only to be captured by the next one.

"Der Doktor," alias Bruno, the bass player, sits with his legs spread apart and looks with a lustful grin at a curvy redhead in ripped jeans, who kneels on the floor in front of him and fondles his crotch.

That was fast, Kuno thinks dully. At the same time, has to admit to himself he has lost all sense of time. So, what's fast?

There was enough time for the other blond to undress, except for fishnet stockings and high heels, and put on Otto's pig mask. The sight of her jumping around, her breasts bobbing, on the monk's exposed lap is more than grotesque. The whole thing has the character of a brutal accident—you don't want to look, but you can't help it.

Only when he feels a hand on his thigh does Kuno manage to tear himself away from the "piggy" spectacle.

The long, delicate fingers caressing his leather pants come from the black-haired German, whose name Kuno—like that of the others—has already forgotten. "Wir müssen nicht hier bleiben," she says, moving so close to him that Kuno can smell her perfume.

He certainly stinks of sweat—just like his un-showered bandmates—but neither the black-haired woman nor her friends seem to be bothered.

"I don't like to make out in front of others," she explains in a dark, smoky voice.

With her short hairstyle and tight black mini dress, she makes a dominant impression Kuno would like to exorcise from her. All of a sudden, he can't remember he was just the victim of a fainting attack. Now he feels like a hormone-charged bull who would like to fuck this little bitch's brains out.

Kuno hasn't been so strong and full of energy for a long time.

He grabs the groupie's hand and pulls her toward the bathroom. Where could you be more undisturbed?

Kuno takes one last look back. The happenings on the couch are in full swing.

Except for the little redhead, who has Bruno's cock in her mouth, all the girls are now naked.

"Komm mit!" Kuno urges the thin girl, who towers over him by half a head.

She giggles and follows him swiftly.

*

As soon as he closes the door behind him, the groupie starts undressing.

"What's your name again?" Kuno asks.

She stands in front of him as God created her—a skinny thing with small tits, certainly very flexible.

"I'm Mia," she says in a breathy tone. "And I love your voice." Then she gets down on her knees and looks up at him, wide-eyed. "Du großer böser Wolf."

Kuno can no longer hold on to himself. He bends down, grabs Mia's stiff nipples, and pulls her up by them.

The groupie moans lustfully. Kuno presses her against the wall, pushes her to the ground, and pulls her back up by the tits. He does this until she cries loudly and begs for mercy.

Suddenly, there's blood!

It sprinkles the white tiles and drips from his hands. Mia stands trembling in front of him. Blood runs down her pale body, and where there were just cute little tits, shreds of flesh now hang.

That's when Kuno notices the copper taste in his mouth and a dull pain in his jaw. The wolf has bitten.

That didn't really happen, did it?

He looks at the frightened Mia, whose flesh hangs between his teeth and under his long fingernails. She sobs and begs him not to hurt her anymore.

Unfortunately, he can't help it.

Kuno tries to think, but what's left of his brain is like a swirling fog.

With both hands, he embraces Mia's small face. Those eyes drive him crazy! He closes his own and slams Mia's head against the wall. First, she screams, then she can only whimper. And soon, she is silent.

Kuno continues anyway. Until there is no more resistance. He lets go of Mia, and her body slumps at his feet. The back of her head is just mud, some of the pink brain matter sticks to the wall, and there is more blood than Kuno has ever seen in his life.

Once they had a video shoot where they used a few liters of pig's blood; it smelled the same.

At that time, he had felt sick, but now, he feels nothing at all—not the slightest.

Kuno turns around and walks to one of the mirrors. He expects the sight of a desolate man and gets the bloodthirsty grimace of a werewolf.

With the realization that, from now on, he no longer has to feel or fear anything, a pleasant warmth flows through him, which not even the thoughts of his prodigal son can touch.

If Linus were here now, he would crack his little skull and drink his brain.

What the fuck are you thinking! What's happened to you! Kuno can't answer these questions. All he knows is, he feels great!

Without caring about the blood on his skin or even turning toward Mia's corpse, he leaves the bathroom and goes back to the lounge area, where it smells of men's sweat and sex.

Kuno wrinkles his nose and sniffs like an animal absorbing the weather.

Meanwhile, his bandmates are so busy with the surviving groupies, no one notices him. Kuno looks at the wild hustle and bustle on the couch without a hint of emotion.

Both the women and all the members of the band are buck naked. The blond with a ponytail sits astride Karl, "der Henker," whose skull makeup spreads over their bodies in the form of black streaks. She rides him with her head tilted to the side, the cock of Bruno, "der Doktor," who stands next to her, stuck in her mouth. Bruno's ass is being licked at the same time by the redhead crouching between his legs. And she, in turn, is being fucked by Otto, "der Mönch," who kneels behind her. And last but not least, there is the fist of the mounted guitarist, which is almost completely stuck in the pussy of the blond lounging next to him.

The grotesque scene is accompanied by loud moans and wild pleasures. Kuno, on the other hand, only wrestles a tired yawn from the sight. After a brief look, he walks past them, almost bored, and heads unerringly toward the executioner's axe leaning against the wall, for which dear Karl has paid a small fortune. There's nothing like a stylish appearance.

A few seconds later, in honor of "der Henker," Karl is also the first to feel the sharpened blade of his favorite accessory when the teeth-baring wolf, Kuno, splits his skull with it. Karl

Schulze, alias "der Henker," dies with his fist in one pussy and his cock in the other, killed by his own weapon.

It could probably have been worse.

Dead before he knows it, Karl's blood splashes on the two blonds he has just made happy. The one sitting on top of him can hardly spit out Bruno's cock fast enough. She turns around, eyes wide, and looks at her dead sex partner, his brain oozing out.

Kuno's next axe blow splits her body from her breasts to her belly button. She doesn't even get to scream before she slumps down on Karl's lifeless body, burying her protruding guts beneath her.

All the others scream. Bassist Bruno and drummer Otto push the redhead away and roar while Kuno hacks at the defenseless blond, who still has dead Karl's fist stuck in her.

Meanwhile, the redhead picks herself up, slips in a pool of blood, and lands on her buttocks. Kuno is on her before she gets back on her feet.

From outside, excited voices and cries for help reach Kuno's ear. Bruno and Otto have escaped him. Thus, it is only a matter of time before the cops will appear. Time that Kuno wants to use. Again, he sniffs the air like an animal, sucking the heavy copper aroma of blood into his lungs. In the tight leather pants, his erection is clearly visible.

Wide-legged, he builds up over the hysterically sobbing groupie, who raises her hands defensively.

Shrugging his shoulders, Kuno chops off her forearms. The buxom body of the redhead twitches spastically. She is covered in blood and roars like she's being roasted on a spit.

Kuno laughs happily and hacks at her knees. She is completely immobilized, and her limbs hang only by tendons and shreds of flesh.

And how she screams!

Kuno likes that. He throws his head back and growls. Finally, he has become what he was always meant to be.

Meanwhile, the buzz of voices outside the door is getting louder. He has to hurry.

Grinning, he leans over the mutilated woman's body, sniffs, licks, and bites heartily. The sweet taste of the tender meat puts him in a real frenzy. Finally, he lives up to his band name and becomes the incarnate image of his bloodthirsty lyrics.

True, this bitch will not take forever to die, but he is determined to make the process as long and painful as possible.

Kuno will start at the bottom and eat his way up at a leisurely pace.

And since the sheer madness at the Dethfest Festival has taken possession of not only Kuno, no one is coming to stop him.

The young woman falls silent as he sticks his head deep in her warm entrails, and she dies while he is enjoying her spleen.

Shortly thereafter, the wolf suddenly begins to feel like Kuno again. In an overwhelming bout of nausea, a disgusting mush of half-chewed tissue debris shoots out of him, and when Kuno realizes what his puke is made of, he can't stop.

Under painful contractions, his stomach carries up everything the wolf has just so greedily swallowed—a sea of flesh, blood, and vomit.

When the nausea subsides, he looks around and stares in horror at the four dead and the axe with which he had raged.

Kuno, who can think more clearly with every passing second, sinks to the ground, sobbing, and thinks about killing himself.

Unfortunately, he is no longer a wolf, but just a pathetic piece of man, weak, cowardly, and unworthy of his band's reputation.

Hours later, when the madness has fully cleared, he will be found like this—a frightened child babbling helplessly without sense or reason.

And that's exactly how he will end.

Reappraisal

by
P.W. Feutz

Zach W: Hey, Brian, sorry to bother you for the millionth time, but can you review the new reappraisal sent from Jimmy Miercoles for the band equipment he's been obsessing over? He's calling every day and still getting on my case about the PLI, even though I told him that's Annie's department. Apparently, the event organizer is pushing responsibility on the security company, who's pushing it on the bands. No surprise, fingers pointing everywhere. Anyway, Miercoles is trying to force this new paperwork on me, and I want to make sure we have all our ducks in a row when the investigation is over. Woo, death fest…

*

From "We Nearly Lost Who We Were: How Bone Rivet Stayed True to Theater Through Two Decades of Angst," by Wayne Mitchell, *Kerrang!*, no. 1524, 05 July 2014.

"We were a hard sell in America, for sure, and I don't want to alienate anyone, but it was tough to play for years to crowds who didn't speak our language, who didn't know who we were beneath the bones," Vinnie says. "Then back home, where I wanted to play more, we were always being compared to, y'know, GWAR, for instance, who we really respect and all, but it was always unfavorable. We just don't have their strain of mischievousness."

Dan chimes in to correct the bassist's choice of words. "*Transgressiveness*," he insists. "We didn't set out to rattle any cages. Our early songs are earnest as hell. Our entire output is. Looking back, you'd have thought we'd do fine in the '90s landscape, with the things we wrote, but the crowds couldn't get past the skeletons, which is why we nearly abandoned the concept. The hardest decision we made was to keep the suits for *Every Notch A Kill*, our first post-2000 album. We were already changing our sound, and we almost changed the costumes too. Because of all that apathy and ridicule as the scene transitioned from grunge to nu-metal and we fell farther behind, we nearly lost who we were."

The room grows somber, the band reflecting on the lead singer's words. It's easy to understand why. *Every Notch A Kill* was teased for months with album art featuring the quartet in unsuited silhouette, suggesting they'd show their true faces for the first time. When the release date arrived and the official album art revealed them painted in the nude as each of their respective, idiosyncratic, skeletal characters, the early internet pounced. "KISS banged The Misfits," wrote *Rolling Stone* in a side column review, barely passing commentary on the music itself, as if only to join the dogpile. The album tanked. The tour nearly bankrupted them.

Still, there's a reason we're talking about—and to—Bone Rivet today. True to form, they rebound from this dark passage with a bout of self-effacing levity. Drummer Randy Bottman, whose arms account for the bulk of his body mass, twiddles his fingers at Dan and lead guitarist, Eddie McCaa, the latter of whom flinches away.

"What would you string beans look like onstage without your gear anyway? Falling on your asses, not knowing how to move without the weight?"

"It's our way of being fair to the greats. Like we're driving from the women's tee so all the other guys don't look bad," says Dan, grinning.

Vinnie follows up. "That hardly matters. We're not suited up in the studio. What you hear on any record is the best we're ever gonna get, with or without that crap on."

While Dan, Vinnie, and Randy laugh, Eddie snorts, his gaze suggesting he's still reliving the band's 9/11-era nadir. There's palpable discomfort on the subject of their costumes' perceived limitations and, with it, a long-hinted-at internecine discord. Perhaps not everyone thinks the suits should've survived Y2K.

Asked what other long-standing issues the band has been able to weather over the years, Dan waves away the question. "We're just fucking around. We are the suits. The suits are Bone Rivet. End of story."

*

From direct examination of Daniel Whitney, State of Iowa v. Vincent Anthony Mazzarelli (S.D. Iowa) (2023).

WHITNEY: That puts us about ten to two. After the show, we went back to the lounge. It was broiling hot. We were drenched. The AC was heaven. Vinnie and I talked about the crowd's response, like normal, you know, the highs and lows. It was hard to get a good read that day because it was so miserable out.

So we went into the wings. Backstage was a hallway that ran the length of the stage behind the curtain, then a couple of hallways went straight back, with green rooms and restrooms lining each side. All made of partitions—pre-fab stuff. We were halfway down, facing the restroom. The green rooms themselves were split between a lounge up front and a dressing room in the back, separated by a door.

We didn't make it to the dressing room, just stripped in the lounge. Randy commandeered the couch, sweating like a beast. He was zoning out, scratching his temple with a drumstick. Eddie was upset with himself—got in an argument with Jimmy, but that's not unusual. I lost count of the notes he missed during his solos, but he can't help how much his fingers sweat, wristbands or not. It's not like anyone notices. He kills every time he's out there, but he's his own worst critic.

I remember a good twenty-plus minutes of relative silence before SeXXX came on. We had a meet-and-greet that evening at six, so the roadies packed up the technical gear and stage dressing and left our personal kits and instruments in the lounge.

At that point, we didn't know anything about what was going on around the festival. There'd been maybe one notable incident by then? Not even a blip on our radar.

*

From police interview of Vincent Mazzarelli by Detective Myron Olivet, Pottawatomie County Sheriff's Office, 25 August 2023.

VM: What? Oh. They came back. The—

DO: Who came back?

VM: The people. The…the VIPs. They had passes.

DO: Did you know what was happening outside when they came? Did they—

VM: No.

DO: Did they…Were they coming to you for safety or help?

VM: No.

DO: Were they coming to hurt you?

VM: No. It was planned. A planned visit. There were the two guys, uh—

DO: A few girls.

VM: Yeah, four girls, the two brothers, and the man with his son.

DO: The boy. Darren Vane. He was with Make-A-Wish or—

VM: No. He wasn't, uh, ill. He was disabled but not ill. And it was planned. They were expected, and they all had passes. There was no malfeasance when they arrived.

DO: They were expected.

VM: Yes. All of them. And Darren and his dad. The dad was a Darren too.

*

WHITNEY: We didn't experience anything unusual until the meet-and-greet. The first rumors trickled in around four or so, I guess, but it's such a heightened atmosphere. We didn't think anything of them. Look at Woodstock '99. That went on for three days. Cram all that chaos into three hours, multiply it by a thousand, and see if anyone takes you seriously.

So what did we do that afternoon? We were wiped out. We rested, ate, and most of all, hydrated. Our rider calls for sparkling water, Powerade, Gatorade, and because Randy was a complete weirdo, Orangina. We lose more water weight performing than a wrestler before a weigh-in, so we demand the stuff that makes us feel better afterward. I point that out because I want to be clear how regimented our process is, and to demonstrate that it strayed in no way from the norm at Dethfest. I get that Dethfest is notorious for the tons of crimes of passion that occurred, but those have, by and large, been attributed to one factor. So I reiterate, none of us touched that Epheasos crap, Vinnie included. I guarantee we were the most sober band of the bunch. We had absolutely nothing to do with the violence at Dethfest. The only reason we were anywhere near it was that it came with the guests. We were just doing our jobs. They brought it with them. Six o'clock, they brought it.

*

VM: The boy came in with water in his lap too. Went straight to the suits. Dad did the same, then the others. All staring at the suits. Eddie mumbled, saying, like, "we're over here," you know? But that's how it is.

DO: You let VIPs touch the suits?

VM: If they want, I guess. Yes.

DO: And the boy touched them?

VM: The dad brought the water.

DO: Uh huh. But the—

VM: They all had some. They must have. The girls, the guys.

DO: Okay, let's not focus on that right now. Let's—

VM: They started it.

*

Reappraisal

Brian C: Hey don't sweat the reappraisal. It's legit and aligns with the scheduled items attached to the instruments and equipment coverage. Only weirdness was the original appraiser (who *was* certified) is defunct and didn't close up shop tidily, so we had to make some calls and get Miercoles to have it reappraised. And in case Miercoles says otherwise, the reappraisal is for ALL the assets together, not each one individually. Lastly, no prob on the question. Keep asking when it comes to death fest. Lots of clients affected there.

Zach W: Yeah I know about the original reappraisal. I *made* those calls to verify and got an earful when Miercoles had to pay for the second appraiser. I'm talking about this NEW reappraisal he's sent in, plus a letter from his lawyer. Miercoles says to ignore the old one and, woof, talk about issues.

Brian C: Say wut? Forward it to me please.

*

From "Bone Rivet Plano 5/5/92 Review" by Tracy Reynolds, *Nihil-tastic Magazine Monthly*, no. 31, June 1992.

The Boners came out en masse Tuesday, May 5, in Plano for a dose of sap metal by those ultimate purveyors of medium-core marrow. Color me perplexed at the size of their fandom and where they come crawling out of. Do they Lazarus themselves out of the cemetery for these "One Night Only!" faux-exclusive shows, hork down the bile, and slither back to their grave holes, the most boring zombies of all time? I don't get it.

Eddie McCaa is the most exhilarating part of the show, only thing close to revelatory, if you count fighting your own costume as a revelation. He looks like he's at war with himself up there, and pathetically enough, his comically self-flagellatory gyrations are a better visual touch than the absurd number of sparklers and fire cannons they use to distract from the blandness of their music.

Highlights: McCaa on "Fractured" and Whitney warbling "Light My Fuse."

Lowlights: They remain a paean to mediocrity.

But really, Bone Rivet with or without the armor? The ultimate catch-22. Are they anything without it? On the other hand, what *could* they be without it?

*

WHITNEY: Yup, Flamethrower was on. Seven o'clock. That's when we really heard shit was going down. Meet-and-greet went long because of it. A security guy popped in, told us to sit tight. He barely seemed to know the details himself. There was some hollering and running outside, but that's a show for you. We didn't tell the VIPs. We were safe inside, didn't know what was happening outside. Just rumors about rumors. We didn't know the substance of them yet.

Then the dad, Darren Vane, got a nosebleed. A real gusher drizzling down his shirt. We got him a towel, and he sat on the couch, same spot Randy was sitting. I remember the sweat squelching out of the cushion under him. I remember feeling sorry for him…before what he did.

One of the girls was not okay with the blood. Two of her friends tried to calm her down, but she wasn't having it. She kept backing away from them 'til they practically had her cornered.

The fourth girl was upset too, chewing her nails. I guess, now, maybe she'd seen some shit, maybe started putting two and two together. It was a strange situation—us trying to play it cool and entertain the others. Some people can't stand the sight of blood, right? I thought that was it.

Randy tried to lighten the mood, went to Darren Vane and joked around, talked up how metal it was to bleed out backstage with us. The kid got worried and wheeled himself over. Ed, Vinnie, and I were talking to the two guys. They couldn't have cared less what was happening, but I was watching.

Vane was…sheesh. Rocket ship to space, man. He held out that bloody towel and stared at it, like a dipped photo in a dark room. And I didn't hear it—and Randy can't tell you—but I swear I read Vane's lips. He said, "Metal." Then he started feeling around his mouth.

*

VM: He pulled out his teeth.

DO: Who?

VM: Vane, senior, pulled out his own teeth. Snap, snap, snap. I followed the boy to him. He wrenched them out. Front teeth first. Randy laughed—like, in shock—then he grabbed Vane's arm when he went for another.

DO: Randy tried to stop him?

VM: Yes.

DO: Did he stop?

*

Brian C: Okay, this is a whopper. First reappraisal was basically a changing of hands from an out-of-business to a new appraiser, based on the original estimate from 15 years ago. He had to pay a fee, which oh well, but it's legit. This? This is tantamount to a second felony if it wasn't so ridiculous. First off, this appraiser is a total mystery to me, and absolutely no lawyer wrote that. So he's trying to inflate the equipment's worth based on its collectible value now that it's been destroyed? That's…not how insurance works. Like I said, stick to the book.

Zach W: That makes 2 possible counts of fraud if the police investigation doesn't go his way…And get a load of this…I have a feeling Miercoles saw the same thing: https://www.businessinsider.com/ebay-seller-in-hot-water-over-dethfest-bone-rivet-suit-auction-2023-8

*

WHITNEY: Vane went after Randy. Got his hands all up in his face, his fingers in his mouth, and pulled on his jaw. He knocked his own kid over. The girls lost it, started screaming. Ed and Vinnie and I, the three of us, jumped to Randy's defense. It took all of us to pull Vane off him. And it worked…for a minute.

Randy backed away and didn't lose his temper. I guess he was too stunned. He had a deep scratch across his nose and eye, and Vane nearly tore off his lower lip. So with Ed and Vinnie holding down Vane, I checked on Randy more closely. One of the girls helped too, and we saw how much damage Vane had done so quickly. There were deep scratches around Randy's neck, and Vane had bit him near his hairline, leaving a gnarly wound. The scalp was flapping. Blood was everywhere. It became…pandemonium.

The freaked-out girl ran for the door, but a security guard was right outside and pushed her back in because of, uh, whatever was going on out there. The two guy VIPs were worthless, which in hindsight is better than what they became.

When Ed saw how bad Randy was, he went off on Vane. Vinnie had to stop him, make him help the kid and get a medic. Ed, to his credit, listened. He got the kid up, helped Vinnie drag Vane into the dressing room, then barged past the security guard who'd stopped the girl from leaving.

At that point? It was every man for himself.

*

VM: I smelled smoke.

DO: What did you do then?

VM: The other guys became a problem.

DO: How so? What about Vane?

VM: The water.

DO: Please focus. What about Vane and—

VM: Vane was in the dressing room. Dan asked the two guys to help move Randy because I was holding the door shut. They…giggled. Then there were shots. In the hall.

DO: Was that the first you heard shots fired?

VM: Two of the girls bolted out the door. The other two were tending to Randy. Then Dan lost it on the guys. Screamed at them to help.

DO: And did they?

VM: One grabbed a barstool and swung it at the girls. The other, uh, charged and kicked Randy in the head.

*

WHITNEY: Screaming. Fighting. Blood and smoke. Um, it was that kick…It…That was…Randy's head hit the wall after he was kicked. That's the combination…That's the two things that caused the TBI that killed him. He was in my arms. I-I'm sorry, I'm…It's not easy to talk about. And because…Jesus Christ, it's that memory. He was in my arms and that happened, but it's so entwined with what I saw happening to the kid.

*

DO: Eddie wasn't there, right? It's just you and Dan on your feet.

VM: Right. Yes. Randy was down. I left the dressing room door. Dan and the girls couldn't take those guys. Too strong. I knocked down the one going after Dan. Got tangled up with him. That let Dan go after the guy attacking the girls.

DO: And Vane?

VM: Got out. I heard the door. Saw him go after his son.

DO: Go to help him?

VM: Hurt him. Knocked him down, started whaling on him. I got up, tackled the dad again.

DO: What about the other guys?

VM: Somehow, Dan and the girls subdued their guy. Other one was still moving. I had to drag Vane back into the dressing room. Kicked at him 'til I got a kidney.

DO: And the still-moving guy?

VM: He went after Dan. I almost helped but—

DO: But what?

VM: Darren was hurting himself.

DO: Darren? Junior? The kid?

VM: Yes.

DO: What'd you do then? Vince? What'd you do then?

VM: Got an idea.

*

From "Lipstick Chicks & Guitar Picks: The Completely Unauthorized, No-Holds-Barred Account of One Groupie's Crazy Odyssey Through The '80s Rock Scene" by Jeanie Lister, Sangreal Publishing (2003).

"That day came in 1987. We were at The Joe in Detroit, and I was racing down a concrete tunnel after Nikki.

"By that leg of the tour, roadies were popping uppers and snorting lines as regularly as you blinked or cleared your throat. It was like a caffeine addiction, a yuppie's wake-up fix. Nothing to do with partying. Having cut back myself, I felt like I'd never seen that kind of tolerance. Maybe I wasn't paying attention before. Maybe I had to be in the right frame of mind to notice. Iron Maiden in '87 certainly put me in it.

"Nikki was new to the game and wanted to be cool—do as the Romans do. Pills were left in plain sight, standard as a coffee station, piled in a bowl in the green room, like bleached Skittles. Earlier, lounging around as crew wandered in and munched them down with nothing but saliva, I watched her pop I don't know how many and wash them down with beer. Now here I was, flashing my VIP pass in people's faces for the first time in years, evading security, huffing and puffing as I tried to keep this raven-haired, pill-addled little sprite from slapping men's crotches and shouting out states like she was playing the license plate game. Maiden was in its encore, and I distinctly recall our chase soundtracked to the drum rolls from "Run to the Hills," that sliding scale on the skins that makes me think of a cartoon character's legs turning into spinning propellers as they bolt across an oil painting backdrop.

"Nikki was revved up. She'd just keep going until she was clotheslined by some three-hundred-pound gorilla security guard. I could see it already.

"I ran out of steam and watched her go, unwilling to play chaperone any longer, cringing in the face of her imminent capture, when something bright and shiny flew across her path from an open doorway, hit the opposite wall with an ear-shattering crack, and clattered to the floor. She skidded to a halt and stared down at the thing as it wobbled to a stop. I thought someone got into the hockey players' things. It looked like a shin pad.

"I was so caught up in her antics that I hadn't noticed the raging argument emanating from the doorway. It had reached that pitch of a fight where it's hard to parse the meaning amid the bullshit-this and fucking-that, like cutting meat from a fatty slab of bacon. But there was a lot of repetition.

"'I can't play like this. I'm not doing this anymore.'

"Out of the doorway came this lanky man with long brown hair. He was looking down and barreled right into Nikki. She sprawled to the floor on her back, her head bouncing off the concrete. The man was stunned and nearly lost his balance. I rushed to Nikki and got her on her knees. He offered a limp hand in aid, but I didn't accept, and he withdrew it. I recognized him then. He was the guitarist from the first opener. They'd jumped on the wagon when we hit Michigan and had just been booed mercilessly for their skeleton getups and mediocre power chords for the third show in a row. The crowd bobbed their heads ironically and threw beer onstage.

"Now I know it was Bone Rivet, and that they found their 'Boneheads' eventually. Just not in Detroit. Definitely not Detroit. I could've swore I heard him sniffle. When this mean-looking little man emerged from the room and asked what happened, the guitarist, Eddie McCaa himself, stormed down the hall.

"The other man crouched by Nikki and said her eyes were rolling around in her head. Then I noticed the wet heat on my chest. Blood. Tons of it. I got her to the ER, but I didn't stick around. I didn't want questions. Honestly, I knew what I looked like, and I was embarrassed. A few days later, I called the hospital pretending I was her sister, and they said she'd been released with a minor concussion. I never saw her again.

"I'm sure I saw plenty of bad things like that and had either been too high, wasted, or crazed to care. But that one hit me hard. Maybe all the bad things had finally added up, like a pile of dirty laundry I couldn't ignore. I'd been so far around the block that every shocking new sight, escapade, near miss, close shave, or bombshell I witnessed couldn't be swept under the rug like the ones I'd already seen. I was noticing real consequences for once.

"The '80s didn't end that night for me. It wasn't that dramatic. But it was the beginning of the end. I was getting old, and for once, I wondered if I'd make it all the way to 1990."

*

WHITNEY: This girl and I had our hands full. Randy and the other girl were out on the floor, but me and her were up and fighting. She was kicking at the first guy, keeping him back while I wrestled with the other one. Ed was gone. Vinnie was duking it out.

It's all a blur.

*

VM: It seems crazy. I was, uh, a hairsbreadth away from throwing out my back. It was twinging bad. I'm old, man. Man, I'm old. And the fighting…These guys and the fire. Guns going off. There was—

DO: It was chaotic, yeah?

VM: It was chaos. And the kid hurting himself on top of it? So I got my suit, starting taking it apart.

DO: Uh huh.

VM: And I started strapping the kid in.

*

WHITNEY: With me wrestling this guy and the girl wrestling hers, we rolled into each other's fight, and then it was like cats in a bag. Limbs everywhere. But it worked to our advantage. The guys got hung up on each other. The Epheasos crap started working in our favor, and they went for each other.

I scrambled up and saw Vane charge out of the dressing room and spear Vinnie into the suits. I was done at that point. I was utterly depleted.

But man alive, this girl, she had her head on straight. With the smoke and gunshots and all that, she noticed the dressing room was clear of danger. She rushed in and shouted back that we could break through the AC panel at the top of the wall. Without missing a beat, she picked up a guitar and smashed the unit until it fell outside.

*

VM: The kid helped put it on. Stopped hurting himself. He was talking. I got him all kitted up.

DO: What'd he say?

VM: He was, uh, chanting. "Me-tal. Me-tal."

DO: And then, uh—

VM: I got hit from behind. Went flying. That's when my back gave out.

DO: But you say he helped put it on? How much did he help?

VM: I…He really seemed to want to be in there.

*

Brian C: Hoo boy, that's evidence you're hawking there, krebmedallion74. I wonder how he got a piece of that thing anyway. Everything's in lockup. Gotta be a fake, like some melted PVC or something. I don't get what Miercoles thinks he's doing. In the first place, his claim can't process til the investigation's over. And second, he's gotta know he's never gonna see that junk again to sell anyway.

Zach W: I suspect the prospect of some hefty legal fees isn't helping.

Brian C: Then they shouldn't have handed us such an obvious case of fraud. Absolute chaos erupts at this festival, some bands' entire kits get destroyed, and bone rivet's the only one with an absolute cut-and-dry case of defrauding their insurer?

Zach W: Dude it's not just the fraud. It's pretty obvious they melted their costumes on purpose. But it's what they found inside one of them. How closely have you been following this case?

*

WHITNEY: I didn't see anything else between Vinnie and the kid. But I can tell you this. The suits never left the room. Not while we were there. And forensics shows the fire didn't reach our room, so what else can I say?

And that girl, she was a real hero. She got her friend on her feet and helped her out the opening. I grabbed Vinnie from the pile of armor and tried to make him help with Randy, but his back was fucked. Sorry. Busted. So the girl helped instead. All the while, these guys were fighting and slobbering all around us. We got Vinnie out the opening, went into the lounge again, dragged Randy to the dressing room. And miracle of miracles, the two of us lifted him through.

*

VM: I was already wracked with pain, then Dan tossed me six feet on the ground.

DO: So that was your last contact with the boy? In the lounge?

VM: Yes. I didn't move him or any of the suits out of there. So maybe it was Vane? One of the other guys?

DO: But why would Vane move all the suits down the hall? Vince?

*

WHITNEY: It would've made all the difference if Ed hadn't gone for help. Maybe he'd still be with us if he stayed. They found him just feet outside the room, bullet hole in his side, smoke filling his lungs. He probably got hit right when he ran out. I bet we'd have found him in time if we got a chance to search, but once we dropped Randy outside, Vane and those guys came after us. I got the girl out, followed her, and there was no going back in.

*

VM: It was the water.

DO: Please, Vince. Why would they move all the suits? Vince?

VM: I just wanted to keep the kid safe.

*

Brian C: Zach, just looked this up. This is officially escalated to Cindy. Just stick to the book. If Miercoles initiates contact, assure him all the pertinent information has been collected and you can't comment on the claim until the authorities have concluded their investigation. If he gets agitated, let me know. You're done with bone rivet for now.

Zach W: Woo death fest

*

From "Dame Hades Victorious in Battle of the Bands" by Joy Niedermayer, *Delaware County Daily Times*, 23 October 1982.

Drexel-Hill-based rock group Dame Hades emerged the grand jury prize winner of Friday night's Greater Philadelphia Battle of the Bands following a ground-shaking performance in a show featuring thirteen local groups. The band also won the Audience Choice Award following a rapturous five-minute standing ovation, forcing the emcee to cut short the segment and decree Dame Hades winner by default.

Dame Hades consists of Upper Darby High School students Winston Foley, Peter Kronenwehr, Edward McCaa, and Anthony Tommaseo. They rollicked through a four-song set consisting of three originals interrupted by a rumblingly anthemic, Led Zeppelin-worthy cover of ABBA's "Fernando," which earned the night's most raucous cheers.

According to lead singer Kronenwehr, Battle of the Bands was the group's first public performance, having only played private parties for friends prior to Friday.

Following the victory, lead guitarist McCaa, whose inexhaustible finger work drew audible gasps from the crowd, said, "We've never tested ourselves in front of a crowd like that.

You think you know when you're good enough, but there's no telling until you see a bunch of strangers react."

Asked what the future holds for the band, McCaa said, "We definitely want to keep playing. I just want to get better and better. I want to be the best in the world at what I do."

A Note from the Author

There's a rich history of epistolary storytelling in horror, or at least a number of high-profile works that employ the technique, like *Dracula* and *Frankenstein*, which may create the impression it's more widespread than it is. Stories assembled from several subjective sources can introduce mounds of raw emotion, mystery, and uneasiness, and there's a special thrill to piecing together those sources into a cohesive, horrific whole that's hopefully greater than the sum of its parts. That said, am I the most qualified to comment on the connection between epistolary writing and the horror genre? Probably not. But I'm a fan. And perhaps influenced by my recent enjoyment of Elizabeth Hand's pseudo-oral biographical *Wylding Hall* (which incidentally traces the tragic end of an English rock band) I wanted to try my, uh, hand at the technique. The magic stroke I needed was one little comment from Mark, a comment that hinted at a deeply held grudge, which kicked the plot into gear. With that serving as my inspiration, my collage of sources came together to suggest what really happened to Bone Rivet that fateful day.

P.W. Feutz

Faceless

by
Renee S. DeCamillis

The new-moon night hangs heavy and dark over the city. No stars twinkle in the cloud-choked sky. I hope the threat of rain makes me look less suspicious with my hood pulled over my head and all my hair tucked inside. Must mask my identity.

With a quickened trot and a small leap, I make it across the not-so-busy cobblestone street and up onto the brick sidewalk. I glance over my shoulder again before stepping into the recessed doorway.

Capone's, a hidden speakeasy. Not the trendy, eye-catching tourist trap like the many bars of the same name across the country. No. This place moves when too many people find out about its location. Perfect for my needs. I pull open the red, windowless steel door and enter the dimly lit stairwell leading down to the basement, hoping the journalist who asked to interview me is able to find this place, that he's not expecting— considering my band's fame—to meet me at a five-star lounge. More like a dive bar, which would normally make me feel right at home. But not tonight.

At the bottom of the stairs, I face the black metal door with the small, square, slide-open window. After I give the rhythmic three-knock code, the little window scrapes open.

A baritone voice croaks out through the opening, "ID." When I hold my license up to the window, he says, "Buddy, I need to see your face or *you* ain't getting' in."

Slowly, I glance over my shoulder to confirm the stairwell and entryway still remain empty before turning to the window and pulling my hood back a bit.

Though I can't see his face, I hear the smile in his voice when he says with a laugh, "Well, I wasn't expecting to see that pretty face under the hood."

The window slams shut, the knob turns, and the hinges of the thick door creak as it slowly eases open.

The shadowy velvet-and-mahogany-smothered lounge floods my sight, and the scent of cigars assaults my nostrils—no-smoking laws don't make it through the door of this private club. I step inside. The door slams shut behind me, and a strong sausage-fingered hand grips my shoulder.

"Hold up," thunders a gravelly voice.

I turn, look up. The guy stands about six three to my five three and at least twice as wide as kid-sized me. The bouncer, or "doorman," "doorkeeper." But to me, he's just Pasquale.

"Hey, Maya. It's been a while. Good to see you. I didn't recognize you under that huge hoodie."

With a finger to my pursed black lips, I wink, pull my hood forward.

"Yeah, let's keep my presence on the down-low, if ya dig."

He cocks his head and looks me in the eye, brow furrowed.

"I was never here." I nod, eyebrows raised, making sure my message comes across clearly.

Pasquale agrees. We fist bump.

"Oh, yes." He flashes me a crooked smile, clears his throat. "Hello and welcome to Capone's." Pasquale waves his arm toward the shimmering mahogany bar and steps aside for me to go get a drink. Reaching out behind him, he grabs his hat off the stool beside the door, then performs his signature move. He flips the hat end-over-end up his muscular arm and plops the pinstriped Fedora onto his slicked-back black hair, crooked—true Al Capone style.

"You're the best," I whisper before walking away.

Good thing it's a Monday. On my way to get that stiff drink I so desperately need, I see only two people, shrouded in cigar smoke and sitting at the bar. A couple nuzzled close together on the far end. Probably having an affair. None of my business.

After tipping back a shot of tequila, my peripheral vision catches sight of a man sitting alone in the back corner of the room, hand resting on a notepad and a cell phone stacked on the small round table in front of him. A pint glass of pale ale sits beside his notebook. His vest and bowtie shine like neon signs in this joint. No doubt the journalist.

Nice. He followed my request to sit in the darkest corner of the bar, away from the front door.

I order a margarita and head over to him.

The table is a two-top. I don't sit in the seat available.

"Do you mind?" I nod toward the empty chair, the one with its back to the door.

He smiles and stands. "Not at all." The reporter reaches out his hand. "Thank you for agreeing to meet with me, Maya. I'm Chase Levitt."

We shake.

From the small dispenser hanging from my over-the-shoulder satchel, I squirt hand sanitizer into my palm, cleanse my hands. I take no more chances, not since the Dethfest carnage.

Chase steps over and pulls the empty seat out in long-gone gentleman-style for me to sit down.

"No, I mean switch seats. I never sit with my back to the door."

His smile melts, replaced with a look of irritation or dread or who knows what, but I don't like it. One wrong word from him and I'm gone. And I'll leave him for Pasquale to take care of for me.

With a flatline smirk, he slides his notebook and cell to the other side of the table and sits in the seat I refuse. As soon as I set my drink down and my ass hits the red velvet cushion of the other chair, I reach out and snatch his cell phone.

"Whoa. What the hell?"

I stare him dead in the eyes, seeing my reflection in his thick, black-framed glasses. My eyes look like black holes ready to devour this star-chasing hipster. "No phones." I power it down and slide it into the back pocket of my jeans. "You can get it back from the doorman after I leave. Not a second before."

"Seriously?" The question squeaks out of his five-o-clock-shadow face.

My stare never wavers.

"Okay. Whatever you say." His soprano voice defies the Adam's apple bobbing in his long, skinny throat as he swallows his nerve. He really should start drinking that beer, or he may lose his eagerness to write this article once I start spilling the horrific details.

I plant my elbows on the table, lean toward him. "You need to understand the risk of this meeting. Some of the other bands have received death threats. Family members have gone missing. I'm interviewing bodyguards to hire. If you underestimate the dangers I face meeting with you, I walk, and you get no story. Got it?"

Obvious tension hikes his shoulders up as he takes in a deep breath and nods. He pulls a pen from the inside pocket of his paisley print vest, opens his notepad, and sits at the ready. "Okay. No BS. I'm ready. Tell me everything you know, everything you and your bandmates witnessed at the infamous Dethfest metal music festival."

*

"Chase, I'm just gonna cut right to the...uh...chase..." I wink, take a big gulp from my margarita. "You know, no bullshit, no fluff. I can assure you right from the get-go that what sent that festival over the edge into psycho-fest came right from that fucking bottled water. No doubt in my mind. I mean, come on. A fucking pharmaceutical company? At a metal festival? Really? Anyone with half a fucking brain should see the sketchiness of that *alone*. And you can go on and say all the '*Yeah buts*' you want, but there ain't no convincing me or my bandmates otherwise.

"But, yeah, yeah, I know how you journalists work. '*Give me the juice. Give me the attention-grabbing, gut-wrenching details.*' You want evidence. Testimonial. Eye-witness accounts. Well, I hope you don't have a queasy stomach. I gotta ask...Chase, do you like horror?"

I raise my glass for another gulp of inhibition-eraser and hold eye contact with the journalist, awaiting his answer.

"Not much of a horror fan, but I'm a huge metal fan. That's what piques my interest to report on this story. I'm on your side. I want to tell this story as *you* saw it, as *you* know it went down. Trust me, I..."

I pound the table with the side of my clenched fist. Waves ripple across his pale ale and dribble over the edge, pooling in a visible ring on the cocktail napkin under the glass.

"'*Trust me*'? Really? Well, you say you're a 'metal fan'..." Yes, I use air quotes around that term. Why? I think he's lying. I already smell the BS. "...But you're obviously no fan of my band, Fleshpeel. If you were, you'd already know—I trust no one. So, let me put it to you this way…"

"I'm so sorry. I mean no disrespect. I really am a fan of Flesh…"

"Damn. And *now* you're interrupting me? Chase, Chase, Chase…do you really want to hear my story, or do you want me to get up and walk out right now?"

Frozen mid-speech, mouth still open, he nods. Then he takes a wide-eyed swig of his beer, grabs his notepad and pen, and leans back.

"As I was saying, I'm only here to tell my side because the truth needs to get out. People need to know. Epheasos, that hypocritical pharmaceutical company, can't get away with this shit. They're trying to blame it on the music, on metal, on everything but…"

I stop and shake my head in disbelief as well as amusement. Chase has his hand raised, like a fucking school kid wanting to ask a question in class.

Okay. He has assigned us our roles.

"Yes, Chase. Would you like to ask a question?" I ask in my best faux teacher voice.

He clears his throat. "Yes. I have two main questions before you go into the details of what you witnessed. First…Did you or any other members of Fleshpeel get any violent or other unusual urges during the festival? Second…Did you or any of your bandmates ever drink the free bottled water Epheasos employees were allegedly passing out at the show?"

"'*Allegedly*'? Man, there's no fucking '*allegedly*' about any of this shit. Epheasos employees were everywhere at the festival, passing out free bottles of their water. They even had their employees cleaning up all the empties, and they repeatedly urged everyone through the loudspeakers to 'Rehydrate, Recycle, and

Rock'—brainwashing everyone into doing their fucking jobs for…Shit." Irritation practically sets my head on fire when I realize the implications of what I just said, so I sit back, take a haul off my margarita. I need to just get it out onto the information highway no matter how much it scares the fucking shit out of me to speak up.

After setting my drink back onto the table, I take a deep breath and just let the whole story spill.

"Okay, this shit is getting heavier the more I think about it. So, yeah, like I was saying, Epheasos employees cleaned up all the evidence, and whatever they put in the water not only drove thousands of metalheads to commit brutal acts of violence, but they also drove them to help clean up the evidence of foul play. That message that kept playing over the loudspeakers fucking *made* people help them clean up that evidence, *made* them feel like they were helping the environment by tossing all the empty water bottles into the *Epheasos* recycling buckets. And before the show ever ended, Epheasos hightailed it right out of there, leaving the authorities to deal with the carnage they fucking created. Man, I could spit fucking daggers just thinking about it.

"And no fucking way did anyone in Fleshpeel drink that laced water, not even our roadies. Evan, my band's lead guitarist, is adamant we only drink Liquid Death in public. Not only does it fit the band's image—another thing Evan is adamant about, upholding our image at all times in public—but the company also sponsors Fleshpeel. So we drink nothing *but* Liquid Death when we're on tour and whatnot. So, no, no tainted water for our band or our crew. It goes against our rules. But let me tell you, almost every person I saw draw blood or act violently had been drinking Big Pharm water. And what I witnessed…

"Wait. I need to back up. Me and Jerry, our bass player, go grab some grub a few sets before we go on since Jerry is so fucking obsessed with the Far-Out Falafels food truck, and we notice a bunch of black Hummers parked around the festival in inconspicuous places and a bunch of jacked military-looking dudes wearing all black with automatic rifles slung over their shoulders. We see one of the Hummers, manned by one of the men in black, out in the woods when we stop to eat and check out Mary Jane's Mother's set. There was some scientist-looking guy in a white lab coat too. True fucking story. This happened *long* before anyone drew blood, at least as far as I know.

"So, Chase, how does Epheasos expect people to believe that the National Guard didn't show up until *after* the chaos started when tons of people saw these military men and their giant…uh…Hummers long before the blood spilled and fires burned?"

I don't wait for Chase to answer my question before moving on. And honestly, he doesn't look like he dares speak right now: chin to chest, pen in his mouth, glancing up over his glasses toward me.

"Okay, so, I'm going to skip all the hearsay, all the crazy shit I heard from a bunch of the other bands and roadies and sound techs, and just tell you what I actually saw and heard myself.

"The first few songs of our set were fuckin' slammin', total face melters. The crowd went crazy—crazy *good*—singing and moshing and crowd-surfing. Typical metalhead shit, ya' know. Then we went into the fourth song, 'Take a Bite,' and by the time the solo came around, people started going fucking nutty.

"Evan kept checking out a couple of hot Goth chicks up front at the stage barricade right before our set got started, which is what keeps them in my radar during our set. By the time we hit the stage and our first song kicks in, the widening mosh pit spreading out behind the two hotties shoves 'em right up against the stage barricade in front of him. But they seem fine with it; they keep headbanging and screaming along with the lyrics. True Fleshpeel fans. Best shit ever! And Evan, he lights right up, like he just snorted some rails, looking right down into all that cleavage while he's shredding on his Schecter. His heaven.

"But then, 'Take a Bite' rips through everyone's eardrums, spirals their minds. The lovely Gothies keep right on headbanging and singin' along…

"Acid-sheet skin, I take you in
Tear off a chunk, clear out the junk
Spiral eyes swirl, take on the world
Embrace the night, it's time to
Take a Bite
Take a Bite
Take a Bite
Take a Bite

"…Until the solo kicks in. I go right over to Evan, you know, trading riffs with him. Then his solo grand finale takes off. That's when I see it go down. The taller Goth chick, with hair down to her ass, leans down and bites a chunk out of the shorter chick's shoulder. Bites it and fucking eats it! Blood running down her chin, dripping all over her cleavage.

"The short chick actually looks like she enjoys it. Seriously. She doesn't even appear phased, shows no sign of pain or shock. No. What does she do? Well, I'll tell ya', 'cause you'll never fucking guess."

I pause, check myself, make sure my voice stays quiet enough so others in the bar can't hear me. Glancing around, I see none of the few people here appear interested in what this metal chick has to say. But I notice a couple of new arrivals, middle-aged white dudes wearing suits and pointy shoes, have parked their asses on the velvet couch across the room, a couple of dark brews sitting in front of them on the round table. I turn away, take another drink, pull my hood forward a bit more. Good thing I thought to dress down for this meeting.

Chase continues frantically writing in his notepad. Looks as though he's been taking down my every word so far.

I take a deep breath and continue.

"That little hot Goth with the chunk ripped out of her shoulder, she leans in and bites right under the other girl's left tit. The tall one has on a wicked short midriff tank top, and her friend bites such a huge chunk of flesh I can now see part of her ribs. No fucking exaggeration. I know Evan saw it too. So did Jerry. Even Javier behind the kit saw that shit go down. It was kinda hard to miss, right up front like that.

"Why those blind fuckers running the festival didn't shut the shit down sooner…I don't know…It just pisses me right the fuck off. Oh, yeah, security came and hauled those bloody, flesh-eating Goth chicks right outta there, but, ya know, '*The show must go on.*' And it sure as shit did, only for the insanity to get worse.

"Yeah, we halted the music when we saw that shit go down. Javier stopped drumming immediately, yelling at the crowd to get a grip…be kind or we'll end our set. Then off on the side of the stage, I see one of the concert organizers doing a hand-roll gesture, telling us to keep playing. Can't remember the dude's name. I suck at names. But I never forget a face. And he's flanked by two of those UFC-sized men in black, assault rifles and all, and that guy in a white fucking lab coat again. And I'm thinkin', *Man, this is no, like, mad scientist costume or some shit. It's a metal fest, not a cosplay convention. Who the hell is that guy?* I tell the audience we'll give 'em another chance, play another song, but if anyone else goes off the rails, we cut it.

"So, we go right into…"

Seriously? His hand's in the air *again*? Man, this guy's getting on my every last nerve. I just want to get this meeting the fuck over with and get back home.

"Chase, this isn't a college class, and I am *not* one of your hipster wanna-be-trendy buddies who's gonna laugh with you about this over microbrews at some posh local brewery that charges ten bucks for a fucking beer. If you raise your hand one more time…What? *What* is it?"

Chase leans forward, sets his notepad on the table. "What does Epheasos bottled water have to do with those Goth chicks' behavior?"

"Oh, shit. Yeah, I forgot to mention…They both had a couple bottles in their hands when our set started. Before they went all trippin' balls crazy, they chugged 'em and tossed the empties up onto the stage. So, yeah, they drank the Kool-Aid. This isn't random shit I'm trying to force to fit my narrative. None of this is 'coincidental' or 'meaningless correlations.' I've already heard all the naysayers bullshit accusations. Are you suggesting you don't believe it was the water? Do I need to get up and walk…?"

"Just playing devil's advocate," he says with his surrender hands held up, pen laced between his long, skinny, smooth-skinned fingers. "Just part of my job, which also brings me to my next question. With songs like 'Take a Bite,' 'Cadaver Caravan,' and 'Flay the Flesh,' can't you understand why the public vehemently rejects the Epheasos water theory and why they keep screaming, '*Metal music corrupts*'?"

I let his words fully sink in, all the way down to the pit of my sickened stomach, and down the last of my bullshit-eraser.

As I wipe my lips, careful not to smudge my black lipstick, I set my empty glass down gently on the table. I clear my throat. Take a long, deep breath.

"Well, there, *Mr. Chase Levitt*, you told me you're a metal fan. You told me you're a Fleshpeel fan. But I smell your lies. If you knew *anything* about my band, our songs, *anything at all*, you'd know my lyrics are fiction. The inspiration for everything I write comes from horror literature. Yes, *literature*. You may see a fucked-up metal chick sitting in front of you, but I actually fucking read. Not only that, *Chase*, but if you knew *anything* about me, about my band, you'd know I also write horror books. My band helps promote my writing with our music and vice versa. Yeah, *Mr. Judge-The-Book-By-Its-Cover*—clearer than a picture, I *write* more than a measly thousand words."

I reach over and snatch his notepad out from under his resting hand.

"What the…" Chase starts to object as he sits up, rigid.

"I didn't see you writing any of that down. Why aren't you writing it all down? Are you only writing what you *want* to hear, what 'the people' want to hear? What the fuck kind of article is this supposed to be anyway? Are you working for *Them*? Or do you work for the unheard, the underrepresented, the looked down upon, the silenced? Tell me, *Chase*, who the fuck do you *really* work for?"

He starts fidgeting with his glasses, straightening his vest, his bow tie, his messy-trendy hair. Then, he hesitantly reaches his hand across the table, wanting the notebook back.

I grasp his forearm with my free hand, squeeze. "I'm still waiting." Cocking my head to the side, I pin him with my blackhole eyes, stare him down, making sure he holds eye contact.

He remains silent.

Squeezing his arm tighter, I pull, forcing him closer to the table, closer to me. Uncomfortably closer.

"Did you hear me, Chase, or did I fucking stutter? Who the hell do you work for?"

When he finally answers me, his eyes never glance away. I don't even think he blinks once when he says, "*Midcoast Media* and *The Atlantic*. I'm a freelancer, but they buy most of my non-music related articles. But this I'm sending to *Decibel* and *Loud Wire* and *Revolver Magazine*, maybe more. You know, hit where I know your crowd will back you."

Pushing his arm away, I scoff. "'*My crowd*'? Really? No. My crowd's much bigger, much broader than the metal music scene. And this story needs to go big, bigger than metal magazines. No one believes the metal crowd. We're the minority here, Chase. We're the silenced. The lesser than. Don't you get that?"

His demeanor visibly shifts, softens. He nods.

After I release his arm, he pulls the notebook down onto his lap, pen at the ready. "Yes. Yes, I do. And I'm sorry if I offended you in any way. Please, go on. I'll take down your every word and get this story to the biggest media sources I can." He looks me straight in the eye, no blinking, no glancing away. "Maya, I promise you, your story will be heard far and wide."

I nod. "That's more like it. Thank you. Now, where was I?" I really want another drink, but that can wait until I'm back home. That thought makes me remember a key point I need to make.

"I forgot to mention—unlike popular beliefs about metalheads and rock stars in general, my band never plays under the influence of alcohol or drugs. So no one can blame chemical-distortion for my memories from the festival. Clearheaded all the fucking way, man." I glance at my empty glass. "Well, tonight, you know, tension's a bit high. I needed to keep my nerve, make sure nothing but the blatant facts come out uninhibited.

"Now, the festival…Where did I leave off? Oh yeah, the hand-roll gesture. We go right into the next song on the set list, and the next one too. Unaware of any weird shit—weirder than normal—going on around us. Just focusing on the music, focusing on giving the best performance we can. We pound out *almost* the rest of the set without any psycho incidents happening in our crowd. But then we go into the final song. Not until what happens next do I realize what's really going on with this water and all the freakish behaviors that erupted all over the festival.

"We play 'Flay the Flesh,' our biggest hit from the new album. Are you familiar with the lyrics of that song?"

Chase shakes his head. "Sorry, but I haven't had a chance to download the new album yet. Are the lyrics important to your story?"

"Download? Have you forgotten you can actually buy the hardcopy album right at your local music store, hold it right in your hot little hands while also supporting indie music stores?" I shake off my irritation, realizing it's just prolonging this meeting to a dangerous amount of time. "Never mind. Yes, the lyrics are very important, Chase. At least if you want to understand my theory about the water. And please, write this all down. Don't leave anything out. If anything gets left out, my story sounds just as batshit as the carnage that took place.

"So, things seem fine at first. But then the chorus kicks in.

"Flay the Flesh
Remove their masks, reveal the truth
Flay the Flesh
No need to ask, they're covered in lies
Flay the Flesh

Their evil hides, demons disguised
Flay the Flesh
Flay the Flesh
Flay the Flesh
Don't you cower in fear.

"The mosh pit activity goes berserk. Nothing new, except it grows to epic proportions, like no pit I've ever seen before, filling the entire front half of the crowd. Their energy feeds ours. It feels fucking amazing! But then, something wet and sticky hits my bare left shoulder. Upon impact, I'm singing, can't look away from the mic until…Just as I go into the solo and look at the neck of my PRS, I'm able to see what's still sticking to my shoulder." I pause, trying to erase the visual from my mind. Unsuccessful, I just blurt it out. "It was someone's fucking face."

His hand freezes upon his notepad. He rolls his eyes up, looking at me over the top of his glasses.

"Yes, you heard correctly. Someone in the audience took my lyrics literally, flayed someone's flesh, and threw their skin on stage. Needless to say, I freaked the fuck out. Javier noticed what happened right away and immediately stopped drumming. After using the neck of my guitar to fling the skin off from me, I scream into the microphone, 'What the fuck is going on out there?'

"In the center of the pit, amidst a littering of Epheasos water bottles, I notice three bodies lying on the ground. Three people who didn't just get knocked down. No. Those metalheads, I knew in that moment, were never getting up again. And how did I know that, Chase?"

He doesn't attempt to answer. Just glances up at me, shrugs, shakes his head.

"*Because they had no faces*. Nothing but blood." I close my eyes, take a deep breath before continuing. "My heart drops. I don't know what the fuck to do. I glance around, looking for security but see no one. I scream into the mic, 'Show's over! We need a medic in the pit right now! Someone help!'"

I pause. Wipe my brow. I need to end this. Get out of here. Right fucking now. I feel too exposed.

"I repeated the emergency request a couple more times, then I took my guitar and hightailed it off the stage along with the rest of the guys in the band. Jerry told our roadies to pack it up ASAP.

"We didn't hang around to find out what happened next. That's where I must confess—none of us stopped to help anyone. Screams erupted in various spots around our crowd as we weaved our way toward the parking lot. As much as we wanted to hang with some of the other bands, check out more of their sets, we wanted to protect ourselves more. The roadies cleared the stage, and we all got the fuck out of Psychoville before the festival went up in flames. Part of me feels regret for not stopping to help others, but in the battle of fight-or-flight…Well…if I chose fight, there's a good chance I'd be ashes right now. And ashes can't speak."

Knee bouncing like Javier's behind his kit, I wait for Chase to finish writing. When his pen finally stops, he glances up over the rim of his glasses, waiting for more. By this time, I'm already on my feet.

"That's it. Enough said."

I take a chance, step over beside him, turning my back to the rest of the bar. I glance over at the busybodies on the couch, make sure they're busy looking elsewhere. Then I reach into my satchel, lean down toward Chase.

"Hide it," I whisper. "Don't let anyone see you with it. *No one.*" I hand him an empty Epheasos water bottle. "I snatched it from the stage. One from those Goth chicks." I pause. "It's the only one I managed to snatch," I lie. "Use it to prove my theory. I'm done. Hands washed." I straighten up, strategically adjust my hood. "Thanks for listening. Your cell will be with the doorman. I'm out."

As quick and inconspicuous as when I arrived, I get the fuck out of there and never look back. But first, on my way out, I hand Pasquale Chase's cell and whisper, "Do me a favor. Give this back to that guy after I'm gone. If anyone tries leaving here soon after me, don't let 'em." I nod toward the suits on the couch, as well as Chase, still hesitant to trust him. "Then text me."

He nods. "Done deal."

*

Three weeks later and I still haven't seen or heard of Chase Levitt's article about my experience at Dethfest through any music media outlets, not even his usual places that publish his work. I've called him numerous times, sure to block my number. No answer. I refuse to text him. Leave no trail.

Wanting to get in touch with him to find out what the hell the deal is, I manage to contact an administrative assistant at *The Atlantic*.

"Sorry, we don't know anything about that article. Mr. Levitt hasn't sent us anything in over a month," she tells me.

Revolver Magazine, *Loud Wire*, and *Decibel* also haven't heard anything about Chase's interview with me. They don't even know who Chase Levitt is.

Unable to sleep and about ready to climb the fucking walls of my home studio, I call Jerry.

"Nope. Still haven't heard a thing," he tells me. Then he keeps insisting I try calling Chase again.

"All right already! But, man, I have a *really* bad feeling."

We hang up.

Pacing the studio and clenching my cell so tightly it feels like I might crack it in half, I dial Chase's number one more time. Like Jerry said, "You never know. Maybe he'll finally answer."

His phone rings into my ear, and I step over to the tall window overlooking my long driveway. Always worried someone's listening, watching, I pull the curtain aside and peek out.

"Motherfucker!"

My phone hits the hardwood floor with a crack and a clatter. I stand frozen, unable to look away.

Someone's outside my window, hanging by a noose from my roof, swaying like a pendulum in the moonlight.

Tick-Tock, Tick-Tock...

They're wearing a paisley print vest, a bow tie, and...

I can't breathe.

...a pair of black, thick-framed glasses perched on their skinless face. Blood, muscles, and sinew fill my vision.

Chase Leavitt. Faceless.

"What the fuck!"

I drop the curtain, jump back. With my heart revved so high it sounds like a blast beat pounding against my skull, I crouch for my phone. When I pick it up, I see the cracked screen.

Damn thing better still work.

I dial 911. It rings once.

My phone dies.

Dammit! What the fuck do I do now?

Just as I reach out to set my phone down next to the mixing console, it rings in my hand. *How the hell?*

I turn it over, check the caller ID.

Slashed through by broken glass, an *Unknown Caller* message stares back at me.

Renee S. DeCamillis

A Note from the Author

When Mark invited me to join the *Dethfest Confessions* team and write a story for the anthology, my metal horns immediately raised high and I yelled, "Hell yeah!" After immersing myself in the *Dethfest* world and all that took place at the festival in the first book, I immediately joined Team Kyle and knew the road my story would traverse. Since metal is to mainstream music what horror is to mainstream literature, my mind went down Conspiracy Street. Crushing the stereotypes of metal music and rock stars in general, my story, "Faceless," examines the lengths people will go to make that which they don't understand look like the real evil in the world. The overarching theme: trust no one, especially the ones running the show. Of course, I also pulled a lot of inspiration from performing in many different bands over the years, including my current band, Scars Aligned. Thank you to everyone who gives my story a read!

Renee S. DeCamillis

It Stared Back (Extreme Warning)

by

Thomas K.S. Wake

The whiskey bottle smashed against the backstage room mirror, shattering both it and the looking glass.

"Motherfuckers!" Spittle sprayed from Lord Tenebratis's lips as he seethed.

The door to the backstage opened, and the guitar player, Sanquinox, walked in with drummer Mallum Infantum, bass player Perkele right behind him.

"Dude! What the fuck was that?" Perkele asked.

Gilbert looked at himself in the broken mirror, his face fragmented in the spidery web of cracked glass. What stared back was not Lord Tenebratis—the one who spit on God's face—but Gilbert Johnson, age fourteen, overweight and awkward.

Mallum, who usually stayed out of the arguments, joined the conversation. "We need to get back out there."

"The fuck we do. Did you hear those sheep chanting?"

The outrage in his bandmates subsided a bit. Sanquinox laid his hand on Gilbert's shoulder.

"They are just American teens being American teens."

Gilbert slapped the hand away.

"Necrotitties? Necro-fucking-titties!"

Perkele's mouth twitched, fighting off a smile.

"It is not funny!" Gilbert shouted. "Dethfest is our chance to get back into the game, and those goddamned fucking clueless morons are making fun of us *during our soundcheck.*"

Sanquinox closed the door.

"Exactly. This is our chance at a comeback. Our ONLY chance. And whose fault is that?"

"Don't," Gilbert warned his friend, his face tightening in rising anger.

"No! It was you who were drunk off your ass at God Doesn't Live Here. It was you who forgot the lyrics, slurred through the songs, and shat yourself on stage." Sanquinox walked up to the vocalist and stuck his finger in his chest. "It was *you* who started chucking that said shit at the audience, like the fucking ape you are. So get your head out of your ass and get ready to get on stage in a few hours."

Gilbert balled his fists.

"That was seven years ago. Seven years that I have been sober."

"Precisely, and I commend you on that. Now use some of that resilience you had to get off the bottle and get your shit together. Let's do this and become the black metal legends we were destined to be!"

*

The air in the forest surrounding the festival was stifling. The merciless sun saturated the shadows between the trees with an almost tangible heat.

Gilbert stormed through the forest, further away from his band and the rude, gathering fans. The rivulets of sweat made his corpse paint run, and he looked like a black and white character melting. He didn't care.

Gilbert fingered the plastic bag in his pocket—Bag of Contemplating. He had stormed backstage and out of the festival area, but not before buying a bag of shrooms from a girl wearing a Carach Angren T-shirt. Gilbert thought those guys were posers, but he had enjoyed looking at the massive boobs making the trio printed on the shirt bulge.

Seven years. Seven *long* years without a single drink. Not a sip. He hadn't smoked as much as a cigarette since getting out of the police station after the shit-flinging incident.

Something was different this morning. The mockery cut deeper than it should have. For years, Gilbert hadn't given a shit what other people thought. But today, there had been an echo mixed in with the chant of the teens. An echo he hadn't heard in almost twenty-eight years. The malignant whisper inside his head had stopped the night of the fire…

"Fuck it." Gilbert opened the bag. The dried mushroom cracked under his teeth. He took a deep breath and waited, leaning against a tree and listening to the muffled sounds of the festival about to start somewhere in the distance.

Then it came—the rush of psilocybin through his veins.

He took a wobbling step as the forest spun and became a verdant canopy of swooshing shapes. The trees around him bent like rubber and reached with their branches. But they weren't branches; they were slender arms of women. Fingers beckoned him to come closer. And he did.

The tree trunk split open, and a lithe woman with radiant red hair stepped out. Her round breasts were firm and inviting. She licked her lips and sighed. The entire forest sighed with her, and Gilbert got hard.

The woman's red hair flowed down her shoulders and covered her breasts. She winked and sat down, leaning on her elbows and spreading her legs, pubes the color of the morning sun.

"Do you want me?" she whispered.

Gilbert nodded and fell to his knees. He kissed her ankles and made his way up to her pubic mound.

"Uh-uh," the redhead said playfully, pushing Gilbert on his back. Like a snake, she slid her body down so her face stopped at his crotch, just a breath away from his bulge.

"Can I, please?" she asked, looking Gilbert in the eyes.

He could do nothing but nod. The woman purred and caressed Gilbert's crotch. An electric shiver shot from his testicles up to his stomach, the pre-cum wetting his underwear.

The woman unzipped Gilbert's pants slowly. His less-than-impressive manhood jumped out of its confinement and almost touched the woman's lips. Gilbert felt like he was already cumming.

"Fuck me, that feels good." Gilbert moaned as his penis disappeared into the warm, wet mouth of the forest nymph.

Gilbert closed his eyes and bent backward in ecstasy, the woman working his shaft. He felt a slight rasping against his stomach and inner thighs every time the nymph moved her head past them. Gilbert was about to look down, when her tongue wrapped around his cock and found the crevice between the tip and foreskin.

The vocalist came harder than he ever had.

"Jesus Christ, that felt good."

"I am happy you liked it, my son," Jesus said, rising in the air while wiping Gilbert's cum off his beard.

The Lord and Saviour hovered ten feet above the ground, then exploded into a bright burst of light, leaving behind a cloud of tiny unicorns being propelled by the rainbow mist shooting from their uni-holes.

Gilbert chuckled.

The unicorns zigzagged and disappeared into the forest.

He looked around. It had gotten dark. How long had he been out?

Gilbert got up on his elbows and winced. Something was rubbing against his inner thighs and balls.

What had appeared to be Jesus's beard was, in fact, a clump of moss, twigs, and leaves wrapped around his cock. The vegetation gleamed with his semen.

"Not again." He sighed and cleared his crotch of the makeshift wank sock.

"I have to say, that was glorious," came a voice breaking the silence.

Gilbert jumped and turned around, locating a figure concealed in shadows, sitting on a tree stump. He regained his composure and buckled his belt. "Who the fuck are you?"

The figure, draped in a tattered monk cloak, moved, and the movement sent chills running up Gilbert's spine. It was not so much that the figure walked, but *slid* across the forest toward him.

"Oh, I go by many names. Belial, Behemoth, Belzebub, Asmodeus, Satanas, Steve, Lucifer, Mephistopheles. Take your pick."

Gilbert scoffed. Some lunatic from the festival.

"But you might remember me as…"

The figure's voice deepened and gained a malignant echo. An echo Gilbert remembered from his childhood. An echo he had heard underneath the audience's chants.

"No…," Gilbert said.

"…The Dark."

Gilbert's knees buckled. This wasn't happening. He was still high from the shrooms. Gilbert tried to collect himself.

"And yes, it is. I have been waiting. Watching. Listening. All these years, I've heard every dark prayer and blasphemous thought you've uttered. It has been delicious."

The forest spun, but this time differently than before. The trees melted into black spirals, like oily taffy.

"You are a hallucination."

The Dark chuckled.

"I assure you I am not."

"You are. I took a hit for the first time in years. You are in my brain. Not here."

"Oh, but I am." The Dark slid closer, like a maleficent dervish. "And I am not alone."

The Dark's cloak bulged and quivered. The hem lifted, and a small, naked boy crawled out. The boy stood up. Gilbert did not recognize him, but he seemed to be around seven or eight.

Gilbert backed away from the two figures. "Stay the fuck back!" He turned to leave. "I am going to get the police!"

"Gilbert," the naked boy said.

Gilbert froze. He had never heard his little brother speak but somehow knew it was him. He had been only eight months old when the fire took him.

"Sampo?"

The little boy took a step toward Gilbert, but The Dark stopped him by placing a hand on his thin shoulder.

"Yes," The Dark gloated. "He has been with me all these years. Waiting. Growing. Suffering. Your gift to me."

Gilbert ran his fingers through his hair, trying to process the madness.

"Wait." Gilbert grasped the sliver of sanity rearing in his mind, frantic to keep itself intact. "If that is Sampo, he would be, like, twenty-five."

The Dark's laughter boomed and rattled the blackness swirling around them. The forest was now completely gone, replaced by depressing darkness.

"Time works differently where I am from."

"And where is that exactly?" Gilbert said with newfound defiance in his voice. "And please, don't say Hell."

"Okay, I won't." The Dark pulled Sampo closer and leaned in.

"Gilbert?" The boy's voice was frail, scared.

Gilbert didn't believe the boy was his dead little brother, but he was not going to leave him alone with a freak in a cloak. He liked many dark things and even believed in some, but pedos weren't one of the things he accepted.

"I can show you instead." The Dark took a deep breath and smelled the little boy.

Gilbert shuddered, first in disgust and then in horror. The skin on the boy's cheeks evaporated like mist and drifted inside the figure's hood. Underneath was a rugged surface of cindering flesh. Gilbert smelled gasoline, and the scent awoke a memory.

The boy whimpered. "Gil…"

"Oh, yes." The Dark purred and inhaled again, sucking in more of the evaporating skin.

"It really hurts." The boy raised his arm, a plea for help. The skin on the forearm bubbled and popped. Black smoke and pieces of flesh burst out. The boy screamed, but it was not a scream of a seven-year-old.

It was the scream of a baby.

And Gilbert recognized it.

"Sampo. How is this possible?"

But the boy didn't answer. He kept on screaming—the same scream Gilbert had heard that night when he doused the upper hallway of their home with gasoline.

Their mother had been asleep. Gilbert had gone into his little brother's room. Sampo's steady infant breath moved his chest up and down.

The gasoline had sloshed when Gilbert raised the canister above the crib.

Sampo had stirred, his hand searching for the little stuffed bunny he always slept with. The seeking hand found the animal and pulled it closer. The stirring stopped.

Gilbert had heard the slow laughter of the thing he had beckoned to come forth using a ritual found in an old book—a birthday gift from a friend. He didn't take the ritual seriously, but whatever had been on the other side of the abyss did.

And that same thing had been in their home. In the utter darkness caused by a power outage. Gilbert hadn't wanted to do it, but it compelled him. He was afraid, and the only thing that could keep the thing, The Dark, away was light.

Gilbert tilted the canister, and his little brother gasped and screamed as the acrid fluid invaded his nasal cavities and eyes. The baby squirmed, and the scream reached a frantic peak when Gilbert dropped the lit Zippo into his brother's crib. The fire had consumed everything.

He never remembered how he got out of the house. By some miracle, the fire was deemed an accident, and instead of juvie, they sent Gilbert to foster care.

"I feel it every day now, Gil," Sampo said, whiffs of smoke puffing from his black mouth. "The fire might have driven The Dark away from you, but it pulled it to me."

Gilbert felt nauseous. All the years he had devoted to the dark arts, to mocking those who believed, to rebelling against the system, not for once had he thought there was anything beyond the physical world he could see and touch. He had forgotten his run-in with the thing in front of him, the entity inhaling his brother.

Gilbert's stomach churned.

"What do you want from me?" he asked, clutching his abdomen.

The Dark consumed the rest of Sampo and savoured the sensation. It let out a satisfied groan.

"I want to help you, Gilbert."

"Help me?"

"More specifically, I want to help Sampo. See, it was not his fault that you immolated him in his crib. But regardless, he is paying the price. And I want to change that."

Gilbert hissed between his teeth. Something that felt like a ball of glass shards turned inside his stomach.

"I can make the pain go away—Sampo's…and yours."

Gilbert tried to speak, but only drool came out of his mouth. The pain inside was excruciating.

"I am a fair being. Just agree to help me, and Sampo is free."

The ball of shards expanded, and Gilbert was sure he would pass out from the agony.

"What do you say?" The Dark asked.

Gilbert nodded. He didn't care, just wanted the pain to stop, wanted Sampo's torment to stop. In fact, he wanted the entire world to stop.

The Dark let out a howl of victory.

Gilbert's stomach churned, and whatever was inside him started making its way up his esophagus. He was gagging. The drool changed colour to crimson, and something elastic and pulsating was coming out. Gilbert's eyes turned in his head as he struggled to breathe.

The tissue of his throat ruptured when the thing finally came out. It splattered on the forest floor, and the first thought that came to Gilbert was he had vomited out a placenta.

A sinuous cord still snaked from the dark red mass and coiled inside his stomach. He tried to bite it off, but it was too strong. Gilbert retched again, and the cord bulged and shook.

The placenta expanded, and its blotched cellular surface erupted, spewing out tendrils of black and red. They hit the ground and the trees, overtaking whatever surface they came into contact with.

Gilbert grabbed the cord with both hands and tried to pull it out of him, but to no avail. He heaved again, and the process repeated. The placenta thing grew, and more tendrils spooled out of it.

The entire forest was changing into a landscape of red, glistening, putrid flesh.

"Don't fight it, Gilbert. There is an entire world inside of you, waiting to get out. This will take a while."

The Dark turned as Gilbert's innards pushed out more of the hellish flesh.

"Oh, one more thing." The Dark pivoted to face Gilbert. "One of the names I am also known as is 'Prince of Lies'." The Dark smiled, and a small naked Sampo emerged from under the cloak.

Gilbert tried to protest, but another convulsion choked the words in his throat. The cord swelled, and the expanding placenta spewed more tendrils, consuming more of the forest around them.

Gilbert fought to take a breath but could only huff through his nose. He grabbed the slippery cord snaking from his mouth and tried to pull it out. This only caused him more pain. The roots of the cord were lodged somewhere deep inside him. It was spreading, like the living flesh overtaking the forest, now a black membrane with diseased red tendrils criss-crossing on its surface. And like the thing coming out of Gilbert's mouth, it, too, was growing.

Rancid bile burst from his nostrils, clogging the sinuses and taking away the last medium of air. A deeper darkness overtook Gilbert, and he welcomed it. Unwittingly, he had unleashed Hell, and he wasn't man enough to live and see through the consequences. He just wanted this to end.

Right when his lungs were about to cease functioning, a bright, shimmering light pierced through the membrane and lit the darkened forest. The red tendrils squealed and thrashed when the light touched them.

Gilbert fell to his side as a group of soldiers rushed in from the hole the flare had torn.

The soldiers fired multiple additional flares, and the illumination scorched the infection Gilbert was vomiting out. The stench of cindering, rotted flesh filled the air.

One of the soldiers rushed toward Gilbert, unsheathing a combat knife. With one clear strike, he severed the suffocating cord, which shriveled into nothing in a blink of an eye.

Air rushed into the lungs deprived of it, and Gilbert gasped and jerked up. He was about to say his thanks but was interrupted with a strike of a rifle butt into his face.

*

The steady rattle of wheels on tile woke him. Gilbert opened his eyes to a white sterile ceiling rolling past overhead. He was being hauled somewhere on a gurney.

"Where…?" He tried to get up but was held down by tight straps around his wrists, neck, thighs, and ankles.

The gurney was surrounded by six men in hazmat suits.

"He is awake, sir," said someone with a thick Russian accent.

The gurney stopped.

One of the men turned to look at Gilbert.

"Good morning, Mr. Johnson," he said with perfect English.

"Where am I?" Gilbert asked, panic setting in.

"Do not worry about that. You are safe here."

"Safe from what?"

The man said something unintelligible, and the other man on Gilbert's left nodded, typing on the tablet he was holding. He read the text popping on the screen, then gave a reply, also in Russian, that sounded like a confirmation.

"Good news, Mr. Johnson," said the man who had spoken first. "They are ready for you."

"Who is! Where am I? And what the fuck is going on?"

"You'll soon see."

All the rest of Gilbert's questions, shouts, and profanities were ignored. His captors silently moved him to his destination.

It was a large operating theatre. Bright spotlights were aimed at the centre, where Gilbert's gurney was placed. Along the wall stood barrels marked with a single word: "EPHEASOS." Twenty feet above him, the walls were glass. Behind the glass stood a dozen men looking down on him. Some of them wore Russian military uniforms, some American, and others Gilbert didn't recognize.

"Hey, hey! Wait!" Gilbert pleaded, but he was silenced by a scalpel appearing in his field of vision.

"Gentlemen," said the surgeon holding the tool, "we are ready to begin."

"Begin what?" Gilbert asked. "Untie these fucking straps!"

The corners of the surgeon's eyes wrinkled when he smiled under his mask.

"Begin making history, of course, Mr. Johnson. You have something unique inside of you, and we intend to take full advantage of this opportunity."

"Opportunity to do what?"

"To bring Hell to those who oppose us, of course. Dethfest is the perfect opportunity. And if we begin now, it will be ready just in time. Some would choose a more *pharmaceutical* approach, but we prefer a more *natural* method."

The surgeon brought the scalpel to Gilbert's stomach.

"Unfortunately for you, there will be no anaesthetic. The connection works best under extreme pain."

Gilbert screamed.

"Hush now, Mr. Johnson." The surgeon pulled the blade across the skin, opening a pathway of tissue, fat, and blood. "And please, try not to die."

Jon Cohn

Fighting Fire With Fire

by
Jon Cohn

All right, Doctor. The first thing you need to know about my involvement in Dethfest is, *none* of my equipment misfired—I want to make that absolutely clear. There were no mistakes. At least not in the way you would probably think, considering how bad the fires got.

Let me start from the beginning…

The first moment I felt something off about the festival was early that morning, when I stepped onto the stage, licked my finger, and held it up to the air. It's a trick my grandfather used to do all the time, which took me decades to truly embrace.

You gotta understand, I live at the intersection of science and art, and I take my craft extremely seriously.

The morning winds whipped south, toward where hundreds, maybe thousands of metalheads would be gathered in just a few hours. The skies were blue and crisp, but I could feel an energy in the air—something I usually attribute to the calm before the storm. This time, there was something else to it as well, an unexplainable feeling sending a chill through me, even in my black fireproof costume.

I still don't know exactly what that feeling was—a gut reaction? Some sort of portent of the shitstorm to come? I don't know.

Even though the weather conditions seemed perfect, I went back and re-checked all my pyrotechnic rigging for the show. The propane tanks and remote firing mechanisms were all primed and ready. The firework displays had been measured and packed properly, then meticulously angled for maximum effect…and minimal danger.

I double-checked the backpack flamethrowers our backup performers, Heidi and Kirsten, would be using, making sure the pump pressure was set to four out of a possible ten. In a large arena show, we might crank the flamethrowers all the way to eight, to really give the folks in the nosebleed section something to see. But this was Dethfest—a three-stage outdoor festival. The space wasn't huge, and no matter what, safety at shows has always been my top priority.

I feel like, before I get any further into this, you need to understand that fire *is* chaos.

It consumes everything in its path while fighting like hell to search for a way to spread. It hunts for fuel. Errant sparks dance around the always unpredictable breeze for a curtain, piece of clothing, patch of hair, or even a piece of paper. Once it finds something to consume, it can move faster than a lion on a pack of gazelles.

People see it on the news, when forest fires seem to jump over five-lane freeways. One simple ember is all it takes to hop throughout a crowd or a building, and suddenly, instead of one little flame, you've got ten. Five seconds later, you have fifteen.

And they aren't little fires anymore.

They're growing, literally feeding on the screams of the victims, crawling in and devouring homes from the inside out. It blows along all the wiring in the walls, hunts through cabinets to find a bottle of accelerant hidden away. It burns, feasting on the very air we breathe, until there is nothing but ash in its wake.

All of this happens in just a couple of seconds if you don't do everything in your power to understand and control all the variables in the situation. Wind can change direction at any moment, which often makes outdoor festivals hardest to coordinate. But there's also humidity, barometric pressure, cloud cover, fluctuating temperatures, and about a hundred other factors to figure out before you go off, playing with man's earliest and deadliest invention.

If it sounds like I'm talking about fire as if it were alive, it's because sometimes, I feel like it is. Fire demands respect, Doctor.

In the twenty years since I formed the band, I've seen fire behave in ways defying all my understanding of science—which, to be frank, is a fair amount. Back before I was Morton Grimes, lead singer of Flamethrower, I was Morton Allscythe, a graduate student in organic chemistry, working toward my PhD. I don't know how much you dealt with this in med school, but in the science community, there's a bit of a stigma around chemistry students. As much as I hate to admit it, it's true for a fair portion of us: we play with fire, we cook up our own pharmaceutical drugs for recreational use, and a weirdly disproportionate amount of us love metal music.

I fell mostly into the former category, at least in the beginning. In my spare time during my PhD program, I was building my first flamethrower—a little contraption with hidden compartments that, when switched, injected different powders to make the fire change colors. With just a few simple clicks, I could mix in potassium chloride to turn the flame purple, then rotate over to copper chloride to turn it blue or copper sulfate to make it green. It was the project that attracted the attention of Anne Paulson, my fellow chemist and soon-to-be lead guitarist.

You probably knew her as Crystal Paulson, for reasons about to become obvious. While I was off playing with color-changing fire, Anne had taken to cooking speed and quickly became a supplier to any and all chemistry students who wanted a little something to help them stay up a night…or three. I wish I could say it took more than a simple offer to turn me from a pretty straight-edge lab geek to an addict, but us chemists know better than anyone that sometimes, the conditions for a specific reaction are just right. We were young, stressed beyond belief from school. On top of that, I was going through a rough personal time, and Anne had this magnetic quality about her, making it impossible for me to say no. It also didn't hurt that she was far and away the most beautiful woman in the entire program.

Over countless long nights at the lab, we got high and blasted metal while working on our graduate projects. We did eventually hook up a few times—I won't lie—though it was nothing serious. There was an understanding, at least from my end, that we had some sort of an unspoken connection. At first, I thought it was simple attraction, but I quickly learned it was a force beyond romance. It was darker and soon started to feel as important as, if not more than, my studies.

Anne and I frequently went to metal shows, where I learned that despite the outfits, wild hair, moshes, and occasional fist fights, most metalheads were just like us. Over-educated, under-paid, and mad as hell at…*something.*

The rate at which I got hooked on Anne's speed was alarming, to say the least, but it felt like it was a long time coming. Much like the little flamethrower I kept in my desk, it was something with the power to thrill but also the constant threat to destroy. Honestly, I don't know which aspect I found myself more drawn toward.

And before you go asking about my past…I'm not going to sit here and blame all my problems on my childhood. I'll just say it was a shit time that didn't do me any favors, aside from forcing me to work like hell to get out of there as soon as I turned eighteen. Let's just leave it at that, okay?

So, one night, while especially revved up and all alone in the lab, I spent hours staring at my little kaleidoscope flamethrower, watching it change from red to green, to pink, bringing it closer and closer to me, wondering at what point it would singe off my eyebrows, fry my nose hairs, or light my head on fire.

Obviously, much of that night was a blur. The one thing I clearly remember was Anne catching me holding my hand over the flame, blisters beginning to form on my fingers. That was the night we decided we needed an outlet for all our regrets and frustrations.

We agreed we never felt more alive, freer, than when we were at shows. I proposed a hypothesis—we could amplify that feeling even more if we were the ones giving the performances. With our combination of passion, drugs, and the scientific know-how to put on a literally explosive performance, we were ready to go. It also helped Anne absolutely shredded on guitar, and my singing voice wasn't too bad either.

The idea of a band had been born.

We created our stage names—Morton Grimes and Crystal Paulson—grabbed a couple of other metalhead musicians we knew within the graduate program, and formed *Flamethrower*, with me as lead singer and initially as lead writer.

Our first album was full of songs about personal angst. I sang about my addiction to speed—the self-destructive obsession gnawing in the back of my head. The flamethrower gimmick was an analogy describing my compulsion to self-sabotage and the near-constant tickle in the back of my head telling me nothing I did was any good. That I should set my whole life ablaze.

We put on shows in ratty clubs with no safety codes, where I would cook up more and more elaborate pyrotechnic displays, a flourish to my metaphors for self-immolation. Crystal, as it turned out, had just as much anger inside of her, though when she wrote, her lyrics were directed outward rather than expressing the feelings of self-loathing I tried to convey. Like a lot of music in our genre, her lyrics were aggressively progressive, a feeling I shared, for the most part. However, her songs served more as a call to action. She wanted to raise awareness of government and police corruption, inequality, racism, sexism, and she wanted to inspire people to get up and do something about it.

"What's the point of having a platform if you're not going to use it?" she always used to say. "People are actually listening to us. Why not give them something to think about?"

Despite some of her more caustic lyrics, the fans had spoken, and by the time our third album came out, we had dropped out of school, and Crystal had moved up to lead writer. Her songs consistently got crowds riled up and clamoring for more, and the merch booths always sold out of shirts boasting her lyrics. The fire gods had spoken, and Crystal was the one to lead our band to stardom.

I thought the fire motif would burn out after a couple of years and then we'd go back and finish our PhDs, but gimmick bands these days are the most popular they've ever been, with groups like Ice Nine Kills, Ghost, and SeXXX ruling the scene. Combined with our inspiring anti-fascist lyrics, Flamethrower became unstoppable.

We're now twenty years in, and I'm writing maybe one song per album. The rest are all Crystal calling on people to rise and burn down our government, to take the recent rise in domestic terrorism head-on, with ultra-aggressive songs like "Annihilate with Hate." I'm sure you've probably heard our song about a certain demagogue reality-star-turned-politician called "You're Pyred."

For Dethfest, Crystal came up with this idea to really step up our performance by adding some new props. She had me build guitars shaped like AR-15s, which, when a button on the neck was pressed, would let out a *brrrrrap* of faux gunfire from the nozzle, using a pneumatic piston and homemade mini-flame cartridge. I didn't love the idea of insinuating the non-violent sect of our population should arm themselves with the very weapons they were rallying to ban, but Crystal felt it delivered a poignant message to our new setlist, particularly our big single, "Fighting Fire With Fire."

As I was checking the gun guitars, one of Dethfest's coordinators came and called the band together for a check-in. You know, scheduling stuff, re-hashing the rules of the show—all that jazz. But this is when things started to get weird.

These shows are always sponsored by all sorts of companies. It's nothing new to have them handing out the next energy drink—or whatever—for us to consume on stage, for us to awkwardly plug some skating shoe company at a random point in between songs about us waging war against late-stage capitalism. And most of the time, especially at shows like this, it's a simple "yeah sure" kind of thing, and then you go back to doing whatever the hell you want.

But the guy from this Epheasos Water Company was weird. He was in a full suit and tie, head inflated like he had come straight from some corpo headquarters, with this smirk on his face, demanding we drink nothing but this water. He even had an armed guard, a dude with a *real* AR-15, drag in a chest full of the water bottles for us.

Now, I don't need to remind you, I've been touring for two decades. I've never seen security like this before. Of course, with what we know about the tainted water, it makes sense why they would try to scare us into using their product, but in the moment, most of the band grabbed a bottle just to get them out of our faces. Even Crystal, who I was sure would throw it back at them, glugged down half a bottle in one swig. The day was already threatening to be hot as hell, and we hadn't even started jumping around and blasting fire.

They didn't bother forcing me to drink like everyone else. I was elbow-deep in lighter fluid, fixing up the rapid-fire mechanism on a gun guitar. It was one of those seemingly insignificant moments that, looking back on it, I'm pretty sure saved my life.

I don't drink water at shows. With all the pyrotechnics we have and the thick, fireproof black suits, it gets to be well over a hundred degrees on stage, even before you factor in the sun from a festival. Instead, I have a concoction I brew up for maximum hydration, something similar to liquid IV but without all the sugar. By the time I'd gotten the gun guitar working again, I poured out a bottle of Epheasos water and refilled it with my own drink.

With our props check out of the way and sound checks having been finished the night before, we retreated to our air-conditioned tour van to wait for our set. Through windows and on monitors, we watched thousands of metalheads packing themselves shoulder-to-shoulder to watch us, Bone Rivet, Dethros, and almost a dozen of our peers.

I think after enough years of this, you start to get a sixth sense for crowds and the energy they're going to bring to a show. I don't know if this goes back to the weird feeling I'd gotten that morning, but everyone in our bus agreed that the day felt like things were going to get wild. Guests poured through the gates, and even from our windows, we saw pockets of non-ticketed fans climbing through gaps in the venue's back fence. We weren't slated to perform until about halfway through the event, so we got to watch as the day proved to be every bit as strange as we felt, and then some.

Outside the bus, PAs, EMTs, concert security, and those armed guards scrambled all over the place. We heard word of people biting each other, even a bear attack. I could already feel myself sweating in my thick costume. Things seemed to be going wrong on every stage, and none of them had actual explosions and flamethrowers incorporated into their setlists like we did…

By the time we were called to the stage, I was almost shaking with an energy I kept telling myself wasn't fear. After checking in with Crystal, the band, and our flamethrower girls to gauge their feelings, it seemed I was the only one walking into the performance with any sort of trepidation. In fact, everyone else seemed like caged animals just waiting to be let out. Again, now with the clarity of hindsight, I also realize I was the only one who wasn't actively tripping on weaponized water.

We stepped out onto the stage, and at first, I felt my anxieties disappear. The crowd went wild when Crystal dove into the opening riff of "Annihilate with Hate," and nothing but pure energy poured into me as I screamed the lyrics into the microphone. In the audience, fists were pumping and people jumping, shouting all the words along with me.

As the song neared its ending, I braced for the first of several dozen technical cues and breathed a sigh of relief when the mortars attached to our drummer's base let out simultaneous blasts of heat on both sides of me. The audience erupted into cheers, and I rehydrated using my special drink hidden inside the Epheasos bottle.

On either side of the stage, Heidi and Kirsten emerged in their flame-print bikinis, holding their flamethrowers connected to almost comically-oversized backpacks. We kicked off our next song, "The Flame of Freedom." Streaming jets of fire flew over the heads of the audience from the girls working their machines. They'd been with us for two tours and over fifty shows by that point, so I focused on putting everything I had into my performance, and they worked their mesmerizing magic on the audience.

"Do you need a minute?" Dr. Tahir asks.

My breath catches in my throat, and I fight back a shuddering wave of emotion.

I let out a sigh and try to wipe my forehead, but the metal cuffs pinning my hands to the table stop me from bringing my orange jumpsuit's sleeve up to my face. Instead, I lean down to wick the sweat and soak up the tears forming in my eyes.

"I can keep going. It's just…Everything from here on out is hard enough to think about, never mind having to say it out loud."

The doctor's dark manicured eyebrows soften, and she nods sympathetically. "Whenever you're ready, Morton."

I force out a breath of air, then prepare to tell the rest of the story.

The thing is, I didn't even notice when everyone started screaming. When you're up there on stage, everything in the crowd just sounds like noise. I'm trying to concentrate on my performance, I'm keeping track of positioning so I don't get burned on any pyrotechnic cues, the whole band has earbuds to communicate with each other during the show, and I'm listening to make sure the band's actually playing their instruments right. It's a lot to keep track of at once, and somehow, I didn't realize what was going on…until the smell hit me.

It was pungent, acrid, and made my stomach do a backflip before I could even register what it was. I looked stage right, and that's when I saw it. Heidi had dipped her flamethrower into the crowd, spraying them all with diesel burning at fifteen hundred degrees.

The stream shooting from her nozzle was not the ten-foot blast I would have expected from a level four setting on the flamethrower. She was hitting people two-thirds of the way to the back of the pit. That's more power than we would even use at an indoor arena show.

That horrible sickening smell was the burning hair and skin of nearly a hundred people. They shrieked and wailed, shoving against each other, trying to flee, but there was nowhere to go. Any direction they pushed, all they managed to do was spread the fire further in that direction. Like I said earlier, fire *wants* to spread, and the harder the crowd pushed, the more fuel they provided. And it's not like they could stop, drop, and roll either. That would just have been a way to ensure they got stomped to death by the feet of a hundred other panicked people.

I looked backstage for our designated fire marshal and EMT—which is standard for all of our shows—only to find no one there but horrified PAs and sound technicians. On the other side of the stage, Kirsten was fiddling with the knob on her flamethrower, preparing to roast the other half of the audience.

What happened next—I need you to understand, Doctor Tahir—was one of the hardest moments in my life. I had a choice to make. I knew where the emergency extinguishers were. I could have grabbed one and tried to put out the quickly spreading fire on stage right. I could have saved some people.

Instead, I sprinted full bore at Kirsten, tackling her to the ground and smashing my hand against the emergency shutoff pump on her backpack before she had a chance to burn the other half of the crowd. Kirsten stared at me from the ground and pulled the trigger on the flamethrower in an attempt to burn me alive. Her eyes were wide, and I swear I could see flames burning out of control inside of her.

I had no idea what was going on, what had driven these women to suddenly try to kill all our fans. It didn't make sense. It only got more concerning when I tried to get back up and realized the band hadn't stopped playing. If anything, their performance had only ramped up to bring in more emotion…and more rage. Without missing a beat, Crystal had moved in on my microphone stand and taken over as the singer, playing her guitar and screeching out the lyrics to the song she had written about literally burning down America's infrastructure.

By the time I'd climbed back to my feet, several security guards had made it onto the stage. One had slammed Heidi to the ground, smacking her head into the floor. Blood trickled out around her blond hair as her flamethrower slowly petered out.

The other security guard—oh God. Whenever I close my eyes, there's about a hundred fucked-up things that fight their way to the surface. What I saw next I think will haunt me until the day I die.

The guard charged at Crystal, trying to get her to stop playing, but she clocked him first.

Time slowed.

Her eyes sparkled, and a satisfied grin spread across her face. She lifted her guitar gun as if she were aiming at the guard, then pressed the hidden button on the back of the guitar's neck, triggering the nozzle mechanism. A rapid fire burst of flames crackled out of the head of the guitar, right into the guard's face, and I swear, over all the cacophony I could actually hear the pop of his eyeballs exploding from the sudden extreme heat. Red and yellow splattered out of his sockets, running down his face like a pair of raw eggs thrown against a wall. His scream rose above all others, and he stumbled backward, clutching at his face.

I fell back to my knees and retched up my breakfast, while the rest of my band played on, like they were possessed. Once I had the energy to look back up, another wave of terror shuddered through me.

Standing just offstage were three guards—not just standard security, but the kind with assault rifles and bulletproof vests. They were aiming at us. Everything was too loud, and the band was in some sort of a trance. There was no time to warn them, and I didn't think they would listen to me, even if they could hear me over their thrashing metal. I tried to scramble to my feet as they opened fire.

The music cut off abruptly. Bullets ripped through the heads of our drummer and bassist, sending them crumpling, lifeless, to the floor. This seemed to snap our backup guitarist out of whatever spell he was under. Suddenly becoming aware of the horror around him, he tried to flee backstage amidst a hail of bullets. I don't know what happened to him after that.

The only person still standing there, fingers flying across strings, wailing out her manifesto, was Crystal. Whatever we were, whatever she meant to me, I couldn't let her light be extinguished like this.

I had one trick up my sleeve.

Since I was on the ground and actively fighting against the chaos, the mercenary goons didn't seem to notice me. I scrambled toward them as quickly as I could and hugged the edge of the stage so they wouldn't see me from the wings. Before they had a chance to land the final shot against my partner, I stepped around the corner and faced them, with my fist pointed toward their tight group of three.

Our big finale featured another new prop, one I had hatched up while watching *Star Wars* shows on the tour bus. The fire cue was supposed to be the exclamation point to the end of the song,

"You're Pyred," but instead, I dropped my fist down, pointed it straight at the soldiers, and pressed a button hidden in my sleeve.

From a small fuel reserve hidden in the back of my jacket, gasoline poured down a hose running the length of my arm and ignited. It fired from my wrist like I was the goddamn Mandolorian. Their vests might have been bulletproof, but the guards' outfits burst into flames as if they were made for the job.

My victory was short-lived—first on account of me *intentionally* setting other people on fire. I might have spent the last twenty years shouting for people to rise and overthrow, but deep down, I'm just a scientist. I've never even been in a fist fight, and there I was, burning three men, presumably to death.

The other pressing concern was, in their immolated panic, the guards clawed for safety, finding only the long black curtains running up the sides of the stage. The fire did what it did best—it leaped onto the curtains, climbing as fast as it could to the multiple caches of gunpowder, gas tanks, and other pyrotechnics hidden up in the rafters.

I needed to get out of there, *now.*

I dashed to Crystal, keeping my arm raised over my face to prevent a repeat of the eye-melting performance she had just given to her last assailant. A burst of burning-hot bee stings pelted against my fireproof sleeve when she attacked me too. Once the burst of fire was finished, I shoved her hard enough to get her hand away from the firing mechanism, knocking over the microphone stand in the process.

Our eyes locked.

Hers burned with the same intensity as Kirsten's, though as I shook her and screamed her name, it was as if the real Crystal emerged from some hiding place deep inside her skull. She screamed and looked around, realizing what was happening.

It'd been nearly ten years since the both of us decided we needed to get sober. You can't live this lifestyle for this long without figuring out a way to keep your body from falling apart. For a moment, it almost felt like those out-of-control days, when we were revved up to the moon and felt like we were simultaneously being swallowed by a hole in the world, clawing our way to the top so we could fucking rule it.

I told her we needed to go, ASAP. She nodded, and we gunned it backstage, moving away from the impending explosion as quickly as possible. We weaved through a maze of tour vans, piles of load-in boxes, and pure chaos, trying to make it back to our tour bus.

As we sprinted around a corner, we came face to face with another pair of guards, who immediately pointed rifles at our heads. My wrist flame was a one-shot use, and Crystal's guitar hung limply from her shoulder, completely useless against real guns. I squeezed my eyes shut and clutched Crystal's hand, waiting for it all to be over, when a blast nearly knocked me off my feet. The rest of my fireworks must have finally caught fire on the stage, causing them to all go off at once and sounding like a bomb. The guards quickly diverted their attention to the ball of fire rising in the air behind us, and Crystal and I sprinted the rest of the way onto our bus, where I quickly busted it through the back chain fence of the festival and drove away as fast as I could.

I think you know the rest of the story from there. We were pulled over, arrested, processed, and grilled by cops until you showed up. I'll be honest with you, Doctor. I don't know how to describe what happened any better than that. I may be a chemist, but I have no idea what was in that water that could cause people to act that way.

But I do know this. Whoever was responsible for it, I know it was me who attacked those three guards on the side stage, and

I did it without being under the influence of any substances. Whatever happens, I have to take full responsibility for my actions.

I hurt those men. I watched them burn.

All Men Must Die

by
Duncan Ralston

▶

The following documentary footage concerning the tragedy at Dethfest was recovered from the Barstow Film Academy's cloud storage after the incident at Westview Psychiatric Hospital. It has been edited for dramatic purposes.

Fade in on a man in a white hospital gown sitting at an empty table in a plain white room, a door with a wired glass window directly behind him. His hands are cuffed to a restraint ring in the table. Tattoos cover his arms and knuckles, as well as the top of his head, shaved bald, which glistens under the camera and overhead lights. The tops of his ears are slightly pointed. His eyes are beady and so dark they almost appear black. Tabloids have suggested he wears black contact lenses, but he clearly wouldn't be allowed to wear them in a mental hospital.

Off camera, the interviewer—Harry Mendes, deceased—states, "Omnes Morimur, lead singer Harvard Jensen interview. Rolling." After a beat, he begins, "Thank you for taking the time to speak with us, Harvard."

Harvard, matter-of-factly, in his strong Norwegian accent: "I don't get many visitors."

"No, I don't ima—" A whisper behind the camera causes

the interviewer to pause. "Do we need to fix his mic?" Another pause. "Okay, go ahead."

A young woman—identified as the camera operator, Abigail Jean, also deceased—wearing a black beanie and a flak jacket steps into the shot. She fiddles with Harvard's Lav mic on the collar of his gown. The camera picks up muffled sounds as she does.

"Thanks," Harry says as she steps back out of shot. "Let's start at the beginning, shall we?"

"Of course," Harvard says.

"Can you tell us why you're here?"

"In the Westview Psychiatric Hospital or in this rather small visitors' room?"

"Yes. What brought you to the hospital?"

Harvard grins. It may be noted at this time, that like Anthony Hopkins playing Hannibal Lecter, Harvard has yet to blink. "The doctors tell me I'm insane."

"Can you answer using the question, please? It'll be easier for us to edit later."

"Of course. I've been committed to the psychiatric facility at Westview because the powers that be have deemed me to be *non compos mentis*. They say I am a harm to myself and to others."

"And do you believe yourself to be a harm to others?"

Harvard finally blinks. His grin fades. "Yes. They are correct in this belief."

"Hmm." Harry's mic picks up the sound of papers shuffling, indicating he's looking through his notes. "Can you tell us about what happened at Dethfest?"

▶

Footage cuts to a different interviewee in a studio apartment with exposed brick walls, sitting in front of rows of various guitars, from a Kerry King Flying V with the devil horns on its headstock and Slash's Les Paul November Burst, to Eddie Van Halen's Frankenstrat. A title card identifies him as "JACE LEE, LEAD GUITAR/BACKUP VOCALS." He's wearing an Omnes Morimur tank top from their 2006 Metal Mayhem tour, and the light from nearby windows makes the rugged terrain of mostly healed burns all the way up his right arm stand out clearly.

"You know, we all acted like we worship the Elder Gods," he says, looking off as the sound of a siren arises from outside. "Cthulhu, the Great Old Ones, that kind of shit. But it's just a gimmick. Not with Harvard, though. Those rituals we perform at the start of our shows, I'm pretty sure he believes them. And that night, he crossed a line, using a *real* knife to cut me and Leesa. I think he *meant* to draw blood."

▶

A title card says "METAL MAYHEM, 2006" over assemble-edited live footage of the show. Harvard—in the full black druid getup they all used to wear before some critic wisecracked they looked like Spinal Tap during the "Stonehenge" performance—draws a fake blade across the palm of their new female drummer, Leesa Christensen, drawing blood. (Fans may note they wore these same costumes at Dethfest for the first time in a decade.) He crosses the stage and does the same to a younger version of Jace, then to their rhythm guitarist, Jackson Emmerson, and bassist Shawnie Landers (both deceased). Then Harvard cuts himself. He tastes the (fake) blood, letting it drip down his tongue.

As the band begins pounding out the diminished arpeggio

intro to their biggest North American hit, "The End," Harvard raises his arms heroically. Footage cuts to the crowd going absolutely mental.

"We are Omnes Morimur," Harvard growls over the mayhem, "*and all men must die!*"

▶

Cut to Leesa Christensen, drums, nearly two decades older. Her long jet-black hair is tied up, and she's wearing a white dress shirt with a nametag. Her facial piercings have been removed. She sits at the head of a table in the conference room of the Sheer Plaza Hotel, where she works as a night manager.

"It was *supposed* to be a fake knife and fake blood," Leesa says, looking at the fading scar across her palm. "We do the sacrifice bit and jump into 'The End,' like the crowd expects us to. This time, Harvard says he's making a sacrifice to the 'great winged one,' like usual. You know how he says it, just like that— wing-*ed*—with that accent of his, but like he's quoting Shakespeare or some shit. Then he slashes my fucking hand. Like *really* slashed it. I figured he was just high or something, back on smack, got the props mixed up—"

"Hasn't Harvard been sober since 2010?"

Leesa's dark eyes turn to look at Harry, just slightly to the left of the camera, staring with a penetrating gaze. "Have any of you seen the video?"

"I have," Harry replies.

"Me too," says Abi.

"And do you honestly think someone who's *fucking sober* would do what the hell he did?"

▶

Harry Mendes speaks in voiceover as a series of still shots from the Dethfest music festival crossfade into each other. Tons of metal fans rocking out, making devil horns, cheering each other, laughing, playing air guitar, headbanging, having a great time. Bands thrashing. Singers and musicians drenched in sweat, shredding, beating drums, screaming into mics. Pyrotechnics blasting.

"Unfortunately," Harry says, "our footage from that day was seized by people claiming to be 'with the government.' We can't show you what our cameras picked up from the show, though if you've seen the news coverage of the event or the handful of live reels and TikToks that weren't pulled down before they spread all over the net, you already know what happened. Dancers from the band Flamethrower turned literal flame-throwing guitars onto the crowd, killing dozens of attendees, maiming more. The trained bear from the group Klaaz escaped and mauled a bunch of people. Security turned their weapons on the crowd."

Crossfade to ambulances and police cars lined up outside the festival gates, men and women in various states of injury—though mainly burned—on gurneys, reaching out to friends, shouting and crying in agony. Body bags lined up on the grass. Attendees in handcuffs, led away by police. A young woman stares hauntingly out of the back of a police car.

"We were there to make a film about the Dethfest concert," Harry continues, "but we ended up documenting a literal festival of death."

▶

In a slightly shaky handheld shot, Abi Jean, the camera operator, sits on a bench in the back of a van. She appears uncomfortable being on camera herself, regarding the heap of gear in black bags at her feet.

"It was horrible," she says, shaking her head. "I've seen a lot of awful stuff. My older brother used to show me those…'Member internet shock sites? Bestgore, Rotten.com, and all that? Yeah. When I was, like, five, he'd show me that stuff. Freaked the shit outta me. But nothing can prepare you for actually *seeing* something like that. You know, *in person*." She takes off her beanie and runs a hand over her shaved head, exhaling sharply. "The *smell*, you know? It's not just the screams, but that *smell*. I don't think I'll ever be able to *un*-smell it." Finally, she looks directly at the camera. "You know what I mean, Harry?"

"Don't address me, Abs. Act like I'm not here."

She half shrugs. "Hare, c'mon. I don't wanna do this."

"We don't have any footage from the show. You were *there*. You *saw* what happened. The more interviews we can get—"

"*You* were there too, Harry. *I'm* supposed to be the one behind the camera, not you."

"Fine. You wanna do this?"

The camera makes abrasive sounds as Harry removes it from his shoulder, turning it to pass it to Abigail. She takes it, points it at him in soft focus. He's at least a decade older than Abi, mostly bald, dressed in khakis and an argyle sweater. He adjusts his round-framed glasses and smiles awkwardly. The camera zooms in on his eyes, then pulls out in a crisply focused medium shot of him standing in front of the Westview Hospital sign.

"Tell us about what *you* saw that day, Harry," Abi says from behind the camera.

"All right. Okay. What I saw that day…" He clears his throat. "It's almost indescribable, the…horror of it all. The chaos. If I had to describe it, though, I'd say it felt like *orchestrated* chaos, at least in the beginning. I mean, we all saw those guys with the rifles and black tactical gear, right? What kind of security is that for a rock concert? The Hells Angels did a better job."

"The biker gang?"

"Yeah. From that Stones concert in the '60s."

"They hired one-percenters for *security*?"

"It's a long story. You can look it up when we're done interviewing Harvard. Anyways, my point is…that didn't look like normal security for a concert. And people were going crazy *long* before the Flamethrower set. I've been to a lot of metal shows in my day, and this was *next level*. Even the pit at Pearl Jam in Denmark, where all those people died, didn't get this nuts, or the wall of death at Hellfest 2014. And security just stood there and let it happen. They were *pushing* people into the pit."

"I saw that too."

"This is gonna sound a little paranoid, but it's almost like the whole show was some massive social experiment. MKUltra or Milgram, but on a grand scale and right out in the open. Like they were shoving it in people's faces how easily they could manipulate us." He frowns and looks off, then looks again at the camera. "Sorry. What was the question again?"

"What did you see that day, Harry?" Abigail asks.

Harry sucks in a deep breath, about to speak.

▶

A woman with cat-eye glasses, dressed in a tweed jacket with her hair pinned up, sits behind an oak desk in front of a bookcase. A title says "PROF. ADRIENNE NOWAK, MHIST., GLADDEN UNIVERSITY." She has a large tome spread out in front of her, opened to a page, and she points to something written there.

"Here it is," Professor Nowak says. "Winged creatures are common to many mythologies. Mesopotamians called him Pazuzu. Ancient Greeks called it the Phoenix. Christians call him Beelzebub. The Anishinaabe call it the Thunderbird. But a specific reference to the 'Great Winged One' you asked about is here, from a Greco-Roman cult circa 1350 BCE. Within the Pavlopetri Mystery cult, as it's known to scholars of the era, so-called 'wandering initiates' performed several unique rituals to summon and *subsume* deities. In other words, to become their *living personifications* on Earth through a process called 'immanence.' Several of these mystery cults performed 'holocaust sacrifices,' in which live animals and even fellow initiates were burned upon an altar. This specific cult was centered within a small island city off the coast of Laconia called Pavlopetri. It's known as the oldest submerged city in the world."

As the professor continues, we see a map of Ancient Greece, which zooms in on the water between Peloponnesus and Crete. The map crossfades to several modern photos of submerged stone foundations and stairways, followed by examples of excavated pottery.

"It's speculated that in addition to several of the common gods, they worshipped the immortal Phoenix, which they were said to refer to as the 'Great Winged One.' Allegedly, they believed, like the Phoenix, sacrifices who were 'wholeburned' would return to life, though not as themselves. Instead, they would exist for a short period of time as living manifestations of the deities they worshipped."

Back with Adrienne in her office. "Now, since this is a 'mystery cult,' there is very little data from believers themselves. All of this knowledge comes to us secondhand, from outsiders.

It's possible that the entirety of our knowledge of the Pavlopetri Mystery cult is fabricated. What *is* known is that the island itself lay on fault lines and likely dropped below sea level during a particular severe earthquake, swiftly killing each and every one of its inhabitants."

▶

Cut back to Harvard Jensen in the hospital visitor room. He's picking at something on the chains holding him to the table.

"What did you see that day?" Harry asks.

"I understand you were there yourself. What did *you* see?"

"This isn't my interview."

A smile creeps onto Harvard's face. His chains rattle as he points with both forefingers, his hands clasped to form a gun. "Hiding behind the camera. I see you, Mr. Mendes. I *see* you."

Harry mutters something unintelligible.

"Very well," Harvard continues. "What I saw was humanity stripped to its basest instincts. The purest expression of our base selves is anarchy. Chaos. We are a plague upon this earth, Mr. Mendes. We're lice clinging desperately to a corpse, unwilling to believe our home may no longer be meant for us."

"Are you talking about climate change?"

Harvard sputters, turning away in disgust.

"Who is the world meant for, then, Harvard?"

"You know the answer to that."

"What? This Great Wing-ed One?"

Harvard smirks. "Among others."

Harry lets the moment hang before asking his next question. "The ritual you did that day, Leesa thinks you accidentally used the wrong prop. She thought you'd relapsed. But you didn't have any drugs in your system when the police took you in."

"No."

"So, what was it? Was it an accident?"

"Did it look like an accident?"

"It looked exactly like it always did. Only Leesa reacted like she'd really been cut, and you moved on to Jace, who couldn't even start playing because you cut him so bad. Jackson and Shawnie took off, or you would've cut them next, right? Then you cut yourself and let the blood drip on your tongue. But you didn't open the show with your trademark line, did you? Because over on the other stage, Flamethrower started burning people alive."

Harvard bangs his fists against the table, rattling his chains. "*Flamethrower*! Please. We are not concerned with tearing down human power structures or saving the world like those *pathetic* charlatans. The world is not worth saving! We wanted to burn it *all* down. And we *would* have, if those *freaks* hadn't gone berserk!"

"'We'? Your bandmates seem to think your occult worship is all fun and games."

"For them, perhaps."

"But you said 'we.'"

Harvard gives Harry a dark smile.

"Right. Your, uh…your tourmates, the Great Wing-ed One and Friends," Harry says sarcastically. "So what was the purpose of your ritual, Harvard? Why did you cut Leesa and Jace—"

"You will soon discover why. He is patient. He *waits*."

"Who waits?"

Harvard's smile widens. "My tourmate, as you call him."

▶

Cut back to Harry outside the hospital before the final interview.

He's almost frantic, obviously in the middle of a tirade.

"I mean, you *saw* it, right? How is something like that even *possible*? He's not even *injured*. Not a single burn on his body. But Jace has burns all the way up his arm from trying to—"

"It doesn't make sense," Abi agrees from behind the camera.

"I mean…maybe it was the druid cloak. Maybe it was fire retardant—"

"Don't use the R-slur."

"What? That's not—It means *inflammable*, Abs. It's not a slur."

"I just don't like that word, okay?"

"Okay, fine. We'll cut it out in post."

"*Thank* you. Anyway, he wasn't wearing the cloak when he came out again, was he?"

Harry frowns and glances over his shoulder at the hospital sign. "No. No, he wasn't."

"So, we'll just ask him. Maybe, like you said, it was some kind of fire suppressant. Maybe he covered himself in that goop they use to set stunt performers on fire. We're *film people*, Harry. We should *think* like film people. We're not watching a train on a screen, thinking it's gonna run us over. We know all the tricks, right? So, what was the trick? How did he walk right into that crowd of burning people and walk right out again like nothing happened?"

Harry considers it a moment. "What's the trick?" he repeats with a decisive nod.

▶

A YouTube video plays, vertical with black bars above and below. The title says "OMNES MORIMUR SINGER SURVIVES FIRE, LEAKED FOOTAGE GRAPHIC, NSFW."

It's a chaotic, shaky shot from a cell phone camera of the blaze, dozens of people screaming, running away, *melting*, their clothes charred or burned off. The camera zooms in and settles on a man in a black cloak approaching the worst of it. His face isn't visible because of the angle, but even with the footage zoomed in and slightly pixelated, we can see it's the same kind of cloak Omnes wears in their opening number, and he raises his hands just like Harvard does before he shouts, "*All men must die!*"

Harvard strides toward the writhing mass of burning people. The person holding the phone struggles to keep it focused on him while people bump into them, screaming, terrified, some literally on fire.

Within the cacophony of chaos, Jace shouts, "*Harvard!*"

Then Harvard is swallowed up by the blaze.

"Did you see that?" the woman behind the phone cries. "*Did you (beep) see that?*"

The crowd surges toward the camera, running at a sudden breakneck pace away from the fire. Bodies slam into the woman, battering her from all sides. As she's shoved back and forth, the phone itself hurtles into the sea of people, landing face up. Shoes and boots trample it, and the woman cries for help.

▶

An exterior shot of the F/X Studios warehouse. Inside, it's filled with all kinds of props and power tools and massive shelves containing body parts of creatures and robots and human lifecasts. A man in his early fifties, beefy with a crew cut and safety glasses, talks to Harry, who's standing nearby. The title says "LEW STANLEY, PYROTECHNICIAN, F/X STUDIOS."

"You asked if it's possible to do what we saw in those videos with special effects. The answer is…maybe. If we had a cloak made out of flash cotton—that's nitrocellulose, which burns away very fast with a lot of heat, same thing the flash paper magicians use is made out of—I could show you exactly what *coulda* been done."

He raises a butane torch in his left hand, turning it on with his right. The camera shot pulls back, revealing a man in a dark jumpsuit, his clothes, face, and hair dripping with clear, thick fire-retardant gel, like he was involved in an explosion at a lube factory.

"If he wore a cloak made from flash cotton and underneath that he'd covered himself from head to toe in burn gel, he coulda walked into those flames and right back out like he did, feeling a little hot."

Lew raises the torch until the blue flame touches the stuntman. Fire licks up the gel as the pyrotechnician touches it elsewhere on the stuntman's body. Suddenly, the man's entirely engulfed. He lurches forward, raising his arms like Frankenstein, flaming gel dripping from his clothing. Harry reacts in awe, blinking and adjusting his glasses.

Lew grabs a fire extinguisher and puts the stuntman out. He sets the extinguisher down and says, "You put on a layer of burn gel and it'll protect you from fire, but eventually, burning real hot like that, it's gonna start to hurt. It'll give you second-degree burns right through the gel. Especially wearing something like flash cotton on top. So, it's *possible* he coulda done it that way, but unless he's done a lot of practice, it's not likely. Not only that, in the video, you can see the guy's not dripping gel like Carl here was. It'd be unlikely he could survive something like that *without* burn gel, and to my knowledge, there's no such thing as a *dry* burn protection."

"So," Harry says, "you're saying it's not possible."

Lew chortles. "Well, I mean we all *saw* it. It's obviously

possible. I just can't explain or replicate it with the tools I know of."

▶

"What's the trick?" Harry asks Harvard from behind the camera.

Harvard cocks his head. "Trick?"

"You walked into the fire and walked out without a scratch."

Harvard leans back, relaxing. "Ah."

"So, what's the trick?"

"There is no trick."

Harry waits a moment before asking the next question. "Considering the riot on stage during Systemic Collapse, Klaaz's pet bear rampaging through the crowd, and those people crushed in the Dethros pit, there was probably a lot of stuff going on in your mind before the show. Is that what caused the mix-up with the prop knives?"

"There was no mistake."

"So you meant to cut your bandmates' hands. Jace, Leesa. That was intentional."

"Very much so."

"But you weren't able to cut Axyl and Steen. They ran off stage before you could. They were, how did Leesa put it? 'Paranoid and high as shit'?"

"It would seem so, yes."

"Was that necessary for your ritual? To cut all four of them?"

Harvard smirks. "'The blood of three will set me free.'"

"I'm sorry, what was that?"

"It's a lyric," Abs says from the other side of the camera. "From 'Rain of Terror,' off their debut album."

Harvard smiles in her direction. "A fan, are you?"

"My mom is. I'm not really into metal."

Harvard's smile becomes a sneer of distaste.

"So you only needed the three of you," Harry says. "Jace and Leesa both confirmed you tasted the blood, just like you usually do. Only this time, it was *real* blood, not fake."

Harvard's dark eyes widen in reverie as he leans forward. "It was *sublime*."

▶

In another cell phone video from a different angle, we hear the same voice shout after Harvard when he enters the churning mass of burning people. It looks like something out of Dante's *Inferno*, blackened bodies like matchstick heads writhing within the flames. Three cloaked figures chase after Harvard, one after another. The first two howl in agony as the fire consumes them. The third reaches into the blaze but pulls back, the arm of his cloak catching fire. He staggers out with a wild scream, patting the arm frantically before dropping to the ground and rolling in the dirt.

A moment later, a man calmly strides from the midst of the chaotic conflagration. He's naked from his bald head to his feet, a pixelated blur over his groin. It's clear from the tattoos this is Harvard Jensen. He spreads his arms wide as if in welcome, like the figure in the cloak did when he stepped into the fire and how Harvard always did during their opener.

Harvard walks straight to his bandmate on the ground and offers him a hand. Jace pushes himself up on his uninjured elbow, breathing heavily, not accepting the assistance. His other arm is ruined, glistening black and red raw, the entire arm of his cloak burned off. Behind Jace, Leesa has taken off her hood and stares at Harvard in disbelief.

▶

In the hotel conference room, Leesa looks at her hands folded on the table. "I don't know how he did it. It's fucking impossible. But you saw it. You were there."

"We didn't get it on camera, but yeah," Harry says. "And the YouTube videos after, we downloaded them before they got scrubbed."

She looks at Harry, to the side of the camera. "Then explain it to me."

"I can't."

Leesa nods definitively. "Neither can I. But we all saw it. And *he's* the one in the insane asylum."

▶

Jace sighs. He's absently tuning an electric guitar in his lap, the Boneshredder Stratocaster he used during Dethfest, shiny black with a glow-in-the-dark skull on the headstock, vertebra on the neck, and ribcage on the body.

"As soon as I saw where Harvard was headed, I chased after him. Sure, he's unstable and nihilistic, and he cut me and Leesa pretty bad, but we spent the past twenty years in that band. We formed it together. Ups and downs. Rehab, breaking up, reforming. I didn't wanna see him get roasted like a campfire marshmallow." He looks up apologetically. "Sorry, that was in bad taste. And that's not a pun, so don't cancel me. I didn't wanna see him die. That's all I'm saying. So yeah, I chased after him. I thought Jacks and Shawnie were too, but I guess they were high on whatever made all those people go crazy, and they just…never came out of the fire. And I got way closer to the fire than I wanted to, I'll say that much."

He raises his burned arm and regards the raised scars, wriggling his fingers. "At least I can still shred," he says and plays a lick from the first "Death by Devastation" solo.

▶

Outside the Magic Castle in Los Angeles, Harry shows a man in a black fedora and a slim black suit a video on his cell phone. The man watches with interest, the screams just barely audible, then he nods as if he understands what's happened. A title identifies him as "JACOB STEEN, ILLUSIONIST."

"I've seen this before."

"And?" Harry asks.

"You've seen the movie *The Prestige*? Hugh Jackman and Christian Bale?""

"The Nolan movie? No, I haven't seen that one."

"Fucking awesome flick," Abi says.

"Well, okay. They explain how an illusion works. First, you show the audience something ordinary." Steen puts a cigarette in his mouth and lights it with a Zippo. "Then you do something extraordinary, like make it vanish." With the smoke held between his lips, he flips the cigarette into his mouth and closes it. "But that's not the part that amazes people," he says, with no trace of the cigarette. "Anyone with a couple of bucks can get a trick at a magic shop to make something disappear or catch fire, or whatever. The trick is making it *reappear*." He reaches behind Harry's ear, producing the lit smoke, and puffs on it a couple of times. "And that's the basic structure for pretty much every magic trick."

Harry applauds.

"So, you've got your ordinary," Steen says. "This guy up

there on the stage, doing the same phony ritual thing he does every time he's up there. It's flashy, but it's a gimmick. It's misdirection. Then you have him walk off stage. That's something different, something the audience isn't expecting. Then he does something extraordinary. He walks right into the fire. Now people are paying attention. They're following him with their cameras. Then he does the trick. He steps out of the fire, no cloak, completely unharmed."

"So how does he do it?"

"Well, in *The Prestige,* he uses doubles for his illusion. I mean, that's only one part of the big twist, but it's really pretty clever. Everything you need to know for that big reveal is carefully placed within the story. You're *expecting* magic, but it's really something else. And that's the trick. That's what makes it work."

"So you're saying he used a stunt double? That's him coming out of the fire but not going into it?"

"That's how *I* would do it, but it's uncontrolled. I wouldn't walk into a burning building if I didn't set fire to it myself and have a plan of escape. I'm just saying, with the angles of the cameras, he *could've* done it that way."

▶

Leesa shakes her head. "That was Harvard on stage. He cut my hand, not some stunt double. I toured with him for fifteen years. You think I wouldn't be able to tell?"

▶

"A stunt double?" Jace says, looking skeptical. "It was Harvard, or I wouldn't have chased after him. What the fuck. I'm on meds, sure, but d'you actually think I'm *that* crazy?"

▶

Harvard sits smugly in his chair at the table. He blurs, and the camera zooms in and focuses on his black eyes before pulling out again to a medium closeup.

"So…how did you do it, Harvard?" Harry asks.

"Do what?"

"How did you survive the fire? You said it wasn't a trick. We talked to a pyrotechnician. He demonstrated how they do fire stunts in the movies, but he couldn't pinpoint how you were able to do what you did in those videos. We talked to an illusionist who said you used a double, but both Jace and Leesa confirmed it was you on stage."

Harvard chuckles bitterly, leaning forward over his chains.

"So how did you walk into that fire and walk out again? Like nothing happened?"

Harvard looks up, his head tilted forward with a slight smirk, like Anthony Perkins at the end of *Psycho*. "The Great Winged One is *immortal*."

He stands abruptly, raising his arms as far as the chains allow.

"We are Omnes Morimur," he bellows, "*and all men must die!*"

Fire dances in his black eyes moments before Harvard bursts into flames. The image flashes white, the camera struggling to deal with the sudden change of light as he's engulfed. Shouts of terror rise over the crackling blaze. Abi and Harry race to the door, pounding on it, screaming for help. The rumble of fire thumps like the opening double-kick drumbeat of "The End."

"The handle's too hot!" Abi says desperately.

"Open the door!" Harry shouts to the guard on the other side.

The camera falls sideways with a loud clatter, leaving only their legs visible. They continue to beat on the door, out of step with the rhythm of the pyre.

Screeeeeeee!

A horrendous avian screech joins the steady beat of the fire, like the shriek of violins. Abi and Harry turn abruptly when the massive shadow of this sudden interloper falls over them.

"*No—*" Harry says.

"*What the fuck?*" Abi cries. "*What the fuck?*"

The heavy flap of wings accompanies the fiery percussion, and a huge taloned foot slams down in front of the camera, entirely ablaze, shaking the floor. In the next moment, what looks like a giant wing, feathers aflame, swoops into view. The filmmakers scream in terror as it swings in an arc toward them. Their screams rise in a crescendo of agony, their bodies entirely devoured by the inferno.

Wholeburning.

Then the footage cuts to black.

Silent.

Memento Mori

by

John Palisano

Backstage can get tedious, especially after months on the road, so these rig checks are always a treat. *Ace Guitar Magazine's* been doing them for ages now. They send two people to a show—one talks, one shoots—to go over a musician's rig. In my case, they want to know all the details about my guitars, my pedalboard, my amps…and anything else.

Yeah, we play live.

Always have. Always will.

No backing tracks with us, so the gear we use to deliver the goods is vital.

We're in Louisville tonight for another big bill. Forge Fest, like blacksmiths forging metal. Pretty cool and is respectful of the art and craft it takes these bands to deliver the goods. The air is humid, with that earthiness specific to this part of the country, somewhere between the Midwest and the South. The people are cool here. I always feel taken care of without it ever coming off as phony.

"Yo," Terry hollers over at me. "*Ace Guitar's* here."

I look up from my iced tea and give a nod to the two youngins by his side. The girl's got long hair and wears her intensity on her sleeve. The fellow next to her wears his hair long too, tied in a ponytail. He carries a small camera on a monopod with a mic on top.

"This is Dolly and Jim." Terry's usual raspy voice is in a rare happy tone. He likes these rig checks too. A nice break from the routine.

I put out my free hand. "Pleasure to meet you, and thanks for coming out."

Dolly grips my hand stronger than I expect. "Back atcha, Archie. This is my colleague, Jimmy." She nods at him. "Go on. Shake his hand."

He does. His grip is light. So light, in fact, I think he must have been a fighter in another life.

"Pleasure, sir."

"Don't 'sir' me," I say. "It's just Ace. No one calls me Archie."

"Like Sting," Jimmy replies. "I get it."

I'm taken aback for a moment. "Yeah. Something like that. I mean, we both dig jazz, so…"

Dolly almost stands in front of him. Pretty sure she must be a Leo. "Anyway, can we see where we're shooting?"

"Sure. Follow me."

"Everything smells like Nag Champa." Dolly's pretty on the ball.

"Yeah. Cleanses the bad juju out."

"Huh. Was not expecting that, considering your lyrics and image."

We make it past the rear of the PA column's back stack and to my corner of the backstage area. "Here we are. The crew affectionately calls this 'Ace's Space.'"

Dolly looks around at the neck-high Anvil cases, open to reveal their contents. "This looks like an apartment on a spaceship."

"Sure does. And it's all on wheels so it can come and go in a flash. Pretty wild." I point to one case with drawers. "That one has my clothes and personal items. I dress the same on and off stage, which makes things easier."

Then I point out the next case, also lined with drawers.

"Here's all my extra guitar stuff: picks, cables, pedals, straps. All the little things." I open the pick drawer, where there are three bags stuffed with hundreds of diamond-shaped plectrums. Reaching into the open one, I grab a bunch and hand them to Dolly. "Any interest in these? They're pretty cool. Just ignore my signature stamped on them."

She receives them like she's taking Holy Communion, palms out, eyes wide.

"These are gorgeous." Dolly picks one up and shows it to Jim. "They're little purple diamond things." She spins it. "And it has the Dethros logo on one side. How rad? These will definitely be popular at the office."

Jimmy's eyes are wider than hers. She slips one into his front pocket before he has a chance to react. Her hand lingers inside for a moment, and she grins almost as wide as Steven Tyler.

"Don't say I never did anything for you." Dolly leans in close to his face for a moment, then pulls back. She is a terrible flirt. Knows what she's doing to the poor schmuck.

A bead of sweat rolls down from his forehead. Poor bastard. He can't even manage to say anything back, he's so rattled.

"Anyway," I say. "What about the amp heads and such?"

"Fuck yeah. I'm totally into how much power *you're* packing."

Dolly's hilarious. The double-entendre is not lost on me. No wonder they're getting tons of hits on these little videos. Not too many people give a crap about the details of some middle-aged metal guitarist's road gear. Add in a charismatic, funny host and folks will tune in, especially if she's pushing the line a little. Brilliant.

The third case glows with power switches and lights. "I'm a Boogie guy, so I've got three classic Dual Rectifier hundred-watt beasts. Believe it or not, I just use one at a time. They're all pretty much identical and there for redundancy. A, B, and C."

"Look like you've got a Kemper going too," Dolly says. "Surprised to see that from a tube snob."

I laugh. "I'm a total cork sniffer when it comes to tone. It's our sound. The Kemper is there as a safety. My tech profiled my Boogie and my pedals. If the other stuff goes down, she can switch to the Kemper line, and the show can go on without a hitch. Even if we lose the backline, we have a direct line out to the house PA. We've only had to use it once."

"Sounds like a good story."

"We were in the UK, and some radical group snuck backstage and started pulling plugs, trying to kill our show. They unplugged some of my cabinets and some of the bass cabinets, but if you watch the video, there's not even a second lost. Amazing."

"What happened to the perps? They get sent to hell?" Her laugh sounds way more evil than I expect.

"I just remember seeing McGovern, our security head, dragging someone wearing all white by his hair through the mud. His nose looked like it exploded from the inside out."

"Shit. Don't mess with Dethros."

"I'm in the band, and I wouldn't." I shake my head. "Let's check out the axes."

"Oh, yeah." Dolly turns to Jimmy, that same shit-eating grin. "Make sure you're ready for the money shot."

"I'm ready." He's got the camera up, and he's looking through the viewfinder as he follows her.

I lead them around the back of the Anvils, where there's a workbench and guitar cases. "We've got a custom flight case for the three ESPs. They travel upright, and it's even climate-controlled so they don't overheat." I look around. "Not sure where my tech is. Probably getting lunch." I reach in and grab one by the neck, taking it out. "Here it is. The ESP Ace of Deth."

"Holy Grail moment," Dolly says. "It's actually a very dark purple with subtle dark specs in the finish. And the whole thing has that same color."

I flip it around. "Yeah. It's supposed to be like the coals in hell. The back of the neck matches. The headstock too. The hardware is all blackout style. Everything."

"The coals of hell," Dolly says, "burning your flesh. Unreal. What about the pickups?"

"Classic EMG 81s. Volume only, just like Eddie Van Halen."

"Sick." Dolly points to the other guitars in the case. "What about those?"

"They're all identical. Just backups."

"Wait? So, you only travel with three guitars?"

"I probably only need two. Three feels a little luxurious."

"We interviewed Joe Bonamassa last week. He travels with more guitars than most mom-and-pop stores even stock. You're completely on the other end of the spectrum."

"First of all, I freakin' love Joe. I listen to his stuff all the time. And I have tons of very different guitars at home, believe me. Y'all will have to come over for that. Show another side of Ace."

Dolly turns to the lens. "Did you hear that? We have it on video. Ace is inviting us to his house for another shoot." She looks back at me. "Holding you to that, Ace, hate to tell you."

"I wouldn't have said it if I didn't mean it. It'll be fun. I'll order us some good Mexican. It'll be a blast. Contact me when the tour's over."

"Damn right I will."

"So, yeah. When I'm touring, I like to keep it simple. It's very spiritual for me. I don't want to be worried and just want to be able to tune into that Dethros channel and groove, you know?"

"I bet."

I strap on the ESP. "All right, let's head to the front of the stage and let this baby fly." As I do, I look right at Jimmy. "You play, right?"

"Yeah," he says, sheepishly.

"Cool." I look at Dolly. "You know how to use that camera?"

"A little," she replies. "But wait, Ace. We have very strict orders from our boss never to touch any of the gear. It's forbidden."

I shrug. "My house, my rules. You've got it on tape. And I need help checking the front-of-house line, and my tech is off hiding somewhere." I point at Jimmy. "Get ready."

He looks like he's going to pass out.

"Okay." His voice is barely audible.

I get it. Lots of musicians I know aren't exactly type As. In fact, most are pretty reserved. I was too when I was Jimmy's age, before Dethros hit the big time.

At the front of the stage, we stop.

"Holy crap. Your mic stand looks like something Giger would have designed. It's even more intricate up close." Dolly doesn't miss any details.

"My brother, Mitchell, designed all the mic stands and a lot of the stage props we use. Giger was a huge influence on him…and us. Check out my pedalboard." I point down.

"That does not look like the normal tray of pedals," she says. "It looks like an alien egg or something."

I shake my head. "Close. It's the cocoon of a giant moth." I tap the side with my foot, and it lights up an eerie orange. "The buttons are built-in to look like the dark spots. I hate the bucket switches most pedals use. Way too small for onstage. Even the wah is built-in and is made to look like an organic part of the cocoon." I gesture to Dolly. "Can you take over the camera for a few minutes? I need to show you something while Jimmy plays."

"Are you sure about this?"

"I am. I need to hear the front-of-house system and make sure my guitar is going through all the monitors before the show."

"Okay," she says to Jimmy. "You heard the man." Dolly gestures for the camera, and he hands it over.

"All right." He wipes his hands on his pants, his eyes bugging out.

I hand Jimmy the ESP. "Here you go. I'll walk you through this."

Jimmy's got the ESP over his shoulder and strung perfectly, like he's done so a million times. I reach into my pocket and hand him a pick.

"Nah," he says. "I already got one."

I laugh. "Of course, you do." I knew he was a closeted player. Guitarists always carry their own picks. Just in case. "Ready?"

Jimmy nods.

"Okay. Roll up the volume. Press the top-left black spot on the cocoon. That's Mute and Unmute."

He does. There's no sound, though. He looks around, nervous.

"Go ahead. Play something."

Jimmy strums an E, and the system roars. Even I'm a little surprised at the sound level.

To his credit, Jimmy goes right into riffing. His picking hand is fast and tight, his fretting hand fluid and confident.

He looks at me for a moment, and I nod, making a rolling keep-going gesture with my arms.

I motion for Dolly to follow me, and we walk stage right to check out the monitor wedges. No doubt they're working. It's loud as hell. We go center stage. Stage left. Up on the drum riser to check the speakers. All are kicking.

Jimmy's playing some impressive classical-tinged lead work. Dude obviously has spent some time deciphering Yngwie.

I'm grinning ear to ear because of the look on Dolly's face. I try to holler over the PA, "Did you know he could play like this?"

She leans out from behind the camera, her face shocked, and shakes her head.

"Crazy."

We saunter back to Jimmy, who is in bliss and doesn't notice us. He's killing it. Dolly's filming him, and I just cross my arms, loving every second.

Jimmy gets to a natural conclusion, sees us, rolls down the volume, and looks back up at me. "Holy shitballs."

"Damn right, brother," I say. "And you, m'man, can shred. That was impressive. You in a band?"

He shakes his head. "Wow. Well, thanks. And no band at the moment."

"When this video comes out, I'm sure you'll have your pick."

Jimmy reaches for the strap on his shoulder.

"Keep that on a bit longer," I tell him. "Dolly? We need to turn off the camera for this, okay?"

"Sure," she agrees. "Sick of holding that damn thing anyway." She presses a button and puts it on the stage.

"Grazie. Appreciate the understanding. I need to show you all something interesting inside the cocoon now." Bending down,

I reach for the back and unlatch a small hidden door. From there, I slide out an oversized green and yellow pedal with a yellow sun wearing sunglasses. "This is something special. I asked Analog Man Mike Piera to build it for me. But no one outside of my circle knows about it."

"What's the big deal?" Dolly asks.

"It's a looper pedal called the Memento," I say. "But it's not digital. I don't like the artifacts and clinical sound of the digital ones. I wanted the weird, subtle wobble from something like an old-fashioned tape delay. So, Mike figured out how to do something similar but using cassettes. So, it's warm and a little unpredictable. And I can even run it backward and slow the speed if I want to, all with three buttons."

I press one of the top buttons, and Jimmy's performance plays back, filling the arena. He looks around, dumbfounded, and mouths "wow" to Dolly. She nods and mouths it back.

Clicking another button, the recording slows. A third button plays it backward.

"That is sick," Dolly says. "Love it."

Letting it play for a few more moments, I watch their faces. Also? Where the hell is the crew?

I click it off. "It's so quiet now. No buzzing." Dolly looks around. "That's wild."

"Some very advanced noise suppressors are happening. But it's weird to not even hear any voices or people mucking about." It gives me an idea. "I bet they broke for lunch. Perfect timing, speaking of the looper pedal." My blood feels cold. Why am I bringing this up? "I'm sure you both know about the incident at Dethfest a few years back?"

"Yeah, man," Jimmy says. "My cousin was there, believe it or not."

"Is he okay?"

Jimmy points to his head. "He has mental scars, but that's the extent of it."

"Ever wonder why there wasn't much in the way of footage of what went down?"

"Now that I think of it, none really comes to mind." Dolly's put her hands in her pockets. She's eyeing the camera, probably bummed she's missing a scoop.

"Everyone has camera phones. And we recorded all our shows, but something happened when we went to play back the files. It was just a series of pulsing sounds."

"So, the rumors *were* true. They were using electromagnetic pulses that day to kill all the electronics," Jimmy says. "Crazy they had that military-grade tech."

I shake my head. "I don't know about the conspiracy stuff, although some of the arguments are really compelling. Something was strange that day. One of our engineers thought it could also have been a sync pulse from the lighting controllers that was put on the wrong frequency."

"But what about everyone's phones?" Jimmy asks. "My cousin said everyone he was with had to get new phones. They were all fried somehow."

"I don't know about that. Who knows? Maybe we were all drawing too much current? The crazy thing, though, is, lucky or unlucky, it only affected digital devices."

Dolly pointed at the cocoon pedalboard. "I think I know where you're going with this."

"Yup. That's right. My looper pedal was not affected," I tell them, "and somehow—because of seeing kids being pulled up and over the dividers, some obviously blacked out—threw me off my game. I didn't stop the loop from recording."

"But it was recording your guitar," Jimmy said.

"Yeah, but pickups are just specialized microphones. So, we *did* get something."

What am I doing? Am I crazy? I should shut up. But I can't help myself. There's something about these two that makes me feel like they'd be a good conduit.

"Is it still in your pedal?" Jimmy asks.

"Hell, no. We pulled that tape. Transferred it to digital right away. Backed it up. Hid the original in a vault. The detectives investigating the case asked for the original copy once we alerted them." I shrug. "We gave them a dupe."

"Never heard this," Dolly says.

"Because nothing ever came out publicly. And those kids that died never got any kind of justice. You know how it is. Metal gets no respect. It's still a genre that's seen as junk and filled with trash people, according to lots of authorities. Who cares if some metalheads died at a Dethros show, right?"

Dolly shakes her head. "Evil."

"Yup."

"And the pedal is the memento? Pretty close to Memento Mori. Remember Death. Disturbing and ironic."

"Yup. And that's why we held off further development."

"Smart idea. Can we hear the recording?"

"I was about to ask. But you have to be ready for it. This is not an easy listen," I warn.

Dolly pipes right up. "I can handle it."

"Me too," Jimmy agrees.

We go around to my backstage area. I open the flight case containing my laptop and slide it out on its shelf. Fire it up. "You'll see why I didn't want to play this over the PA." I point at them. "Keep this to yourselves. Promise?"

"I can't write about this?" Dolly asks.

"Absolutely not," I say, knowing she'll still probably leak it. "If people find out, that could open up some seriously dark consequences for each of us."

If it's leaked with no obvious or easy traces back to me or us, we'd have some protection against retaliation. But I don't want them to know my plan. They'll really try and cover their asses if they think they don't have my permission. Then maybe someone learning about this will be able to do something…give those kids' families some justice.

"Understood," Dolly says, Jimmy echoing her.

"'Kay." I find the audio file and press play. The small speakers next to the laptop turn on.

This is what we hear.

After a moment of me making some weird pick-slide sounds, I stop…

My guts go tight. I should not be doing this. I hate hearing the recording.

The tape warbles, probably a spot where one of the EMPs hits. The crowd chatters, and there are crying noises. Security shouting, *"Got her. Get her over the barricade."*

I'm brought back to that moment, can see the young woman's blue and black hair and dark lipstick. She looked like a rag doll being passed over the barricade and received by stage security. They had trouble holding her because she was so floppy, so one slung her over his shoulder.

Later, I learned she didn't make it. Probably dead before they even got to her.

There are more crying, pained sounds. The crowd had surged forward, and many were getting crushed.

"Oh my God."

Dolly's voice isn't loud now. Jimmy's got a hand over his mouth.

"It gets worse." I hate saying so.

There are indecipherable shouts and screams. This is not an audience cheering for a triumphant band; these are the cries of the anguished.

Images play back in my head—so many kids being pulled over the barricades. Some bloody. Several were already pale, their lives drained. I looked out at the mass. People swayed and pushed and shoved, but they were all packed together so close.

Pat. Pap. Pap.

Gunfire.

Unmistakable. Close to fireworks, everyone knows, but the timbre is just a little different.

Screams. Terrified people. Just sitting ducks. Nowhere to go or hide. I remember seeing kids falling near the back. Saw men dressed in black carrying semi-automatics, firing at will, their muzzles glowing white every millisecond, rounds exploding.

Each one could take a life or, at the least, ruin it. For what?

Every five seconds, the sound distorts for a moment—the pulse of the EMPs. An eerie counterpoint to the chilling moans and screams for help.

"Let's go. Get out of here."

The voice on the recording is McGovern, our security head, ushering me off the stage. It keeps going, but I stop it a moment later.

"There's another forty-five minutes of it," I tell Dolly and Jimmy. "But you get the idea."

Dolly shakes her head. "It's like listening to hell. People were being murdered."

"Cripes," Jimmy says. "That's one of the scariest things I've ever heard. You can picture people just getting mowed down, like they're nothing."

"It's inhumane." I shut the laptop lid. "And I've beaten myself up over it so many times."

"There was nothing you could've done." McGovern's deep voice shakes me out of my skin. He's snuck up behind me. "Nothing any of us could have done, more than we did."

When I spin around, he lifts his chin. His gray eyes search me for some meaning. I can imagine he's wondering why I've just spilled the story to two kids who look barely out of college. Makes me feel like a little boy with his hands in the cookie jar.

I shake my head. "We weren't recording this part," I say, sounding guilty. "I was just telling them—"

McGovern puts up a hand. "You owe me nothing, Ace. It's your story to tell. I've always said that." He looks at Dolly and Jimmy and nods.

"This has turned into a confessional," I admit.

Without missing a beat, Dolly says, "Well, drop and give me fifty Hail Marys, and we'll call it even." She smiles and winks at me.

"Sure. But after the show, okay?" I try to laugh, but nothing comes out. "If I have enough energy." I sigh. "Speaking of the show, are we about to open the doors?"

"That's what I was coming to tell you. T-minus fifteen and counting," McGovern says.

"Got it." I look at Jimmy and Dolly. "Of course, you're both welcome to hang backstage and check out the show. I just ask you to give me an honest review after, okay?"

"Absolutely," Dolly says. "Thank you, Ace."

Jimmy puts out his hand. "Thank you, Ace. You're the best."

I shake his hand. "Don't forget your camera. I don't want it getting stomped on."

"Oh, yeah." He bends down, nervous, picks it up, and heads off, McGovern ushering them into the artists' area behind the stages.

Following them, I duck into my trailer, ready to recharge a bit. Can't stop thinking about the cries and screams recorded on the Memento Mori. All those kids lost…Why the hell are we still doing this? Why am I?

I grab a cold espresso from the fridge, sit back on the couch, and look out the window. So many people milling about. Lots of smiles.

Metal is a community that brings people such joy, even and especially during the darkest moments. Music gives people a great outlet to express those emotions. Every time we play, countless people get to exorcize that shit, myself included.

We thought about quitting after the event. One of the other bands had even attacked the audience with flamethrowers. Those kids came for that release and ended up wounded, scarred, and dead. In the end? We decided we'd keep going, to show the fans we were still there for them. We weren't going to let that horrible event define us. We'd make our own future and show them a way out.

That's when I get an idea and send off an email to Analog Man with an idea for the Memento Mori.

He writes back almost immediately. He's down. Loves the idea.

*

After the opening bands play, I meet my tech. She's already cleaning the strings and neck of the ESP, getting it ready for showtime.

"Hey, Ace. How'd it go?"

"Amazing. Love those interviews. Way more illuminating than normal."

"Great. Glad to hear it."

"How was lunch?"

"You mean, Zakk Wylde's birthday? Well, you were missed," Sophie says. "He was asking where you were."

"Now I know where everybody went while I was being interviewed about my gear."

Sophie hands me the ESP. "Speaking of your gear, ready to go, Ace."

I go into autopilot. The intro music from the cult movie *Darksound* plays, the same as it has since our first gigs. We go through the first couple of songs, and it's like I'm not even playing. One of those nights where it feels like something is playing through me. Pure magic.

When it's time for my solo spot, I look over to Dolly and Jimmy. They've been standing side-stage, rocking out the whole time. I step up to my mic.

"All right, you crazy motherfuckers."

The audience roars.

"You havin' a good time with Dethros tonight?"

Another roar.

"I bet."

Can't help but laugh.

"You know, we've been through some serious shit the last couple of years, and we're all just damn lucky to be here with you all, I swear."

They keep hollering, so I make it quick.

"I was thinking about how all of this is all because of you, and I'm thinking about the next wave of heavy metal coming up. Some amazing bands. This afternoon, I met a killer guitar player. You've got to listen to this shit."

I tap the black spot on the cocoon pedalboard to play the last recording. Then the spotlight pans over to Jimmy. He looks terrified.

"That's Jimmy San Quinto. This motherfucker can shred."

His playing fills the arena. I call him out to stand next to me. He does, and I put my arm around him.

"Look at their faces," I say. "Get used to it."

"I can't believe it. Unreal."

"It's all about passing it on, brother."

"I didn't know you were heavy metal's answer to Dave Grohl," Dolly says, slipping an arm around my other side.

Am I surprised she didn't hesitate to get in the spotlight too? Nope.

Hearing the playback at full concert volume, I'm relieved it's as good as I initially thought.

The faces in the crowd look familiar and, at the same time, brand new. They're all here because of us. Same as they were that day at Dethfest. My stomach tightens up. What if it were to happen again? What if there was a stampede or a stage rush? More kids could…

No.

Stop it.

There have been safeguards put into place. And soon, thanks to the two kids on either side of me, the truth is going to leak out. Sure hope whoever was behind the shootings doesn't come for me. If so? At least I had a good run.

The recording stops. I go back up to the mic. "You like that shit?"

They go nuts.

"I'll bet. And guess what? Jimmy's going to do that again for you tomorrow. Live. Ain't that right, buddy?"

He's a deer in headlights, but he nods, then yells, "Fuck yeah, I am, Ace!"

I'm cracking up. "Fuck yeah, man. Love it. And one more thing? You're probably wondering why I didn't just have Jimmy shred tonight. I wanted you to hear this new pedal Analog Man is going to be putting out. It's called the Regenerato. Rebirth. Because who doesn't want to come crawling back from the dead and give some revenge to those who sent us to hell?"

At that, everyone goes apeshit.

The cymbals crash four times.

I turn the volume up on the ESP and play the opening riff from "Gravecrawler," our new track.

Yeah. They know this one, all right.

Off we go.

The crowd hops up and down to the groove. Tens of thousands of souls, all in sync, the energy unstoppable.

There is no place I'd rather be.

Long live heavy fuckin' metal!
— Archie 'Ace' Atkins

Grind Finale

by
Joe X Young

It had been eight months since Kenneth O'Brian discovered a wall is never *just* a wall.

Kenneth sat in the doctor's office, his eyes looking anywhere to avoid positing his own future, however long that might have been. He knew he was obviously fucked; he just didn't know if the reaper was going in dry.

The office walls showed attempts at personality. The expensively framed certificates from heavyweight official bodies were intended to put the patient at ease by providing masterpieces of penmanship on high quality vellum, proof the specialist was, at the very least, qualified to do her job. Every so often, he would catch a glimpse of other pictures, those seemingly created by one or more of the children in the sparse family photographs at various stages of their development, pictures deemed unworthy of beautiful frames. Kenneth knew the score; he had a lifelong habit of putting work before family.

"Mr. O'Brian?"

"Sorry, it's just…"

The doctor had been totally proficient, cold in her delivery of the news.

The Day of Dethfest
6:04 a.m.

Beyond the cordoned-off area outside the compound, what was once an ocean of leather and spiky studs had given way to looser night apparel and clothing more befitting of a Burning Man festival.

Kenneth showed his pass to a slab of beef masquerading as a security guard, who grunted something barely intelligible and allowed Kenneth into the enormous backstage area of marquees comprising the Stage One green rooms of the three-staged festival grounds. Golf carts had been lined against the inside wall. Kenneth took one and drove it to where the bands were going to hang out between sets. He worked fast, checking that each of his misting machines was still connected to every unit's air-conditioning. The weather report had stated the day could exceed a hundred degrees Fahrenheit, the kind of heat guaranteeing folks would be cranking up their AC units.

Satisfied it was all in order, he went on to Stage One, the entire platform decorated in swathes of acid-green cloth. Black light strips had been positioned to illuminate blue plastic barrels. Pumps and tubes leading out of them would spray a fine fluorescent mist of a popular soft drink into the air, which, being backlit, would look like toxic waste. The huge video wall at the rear of the stage that would show the Bare Knuckle Bastards logo in between songs, the live feed of them playing during their set, and crowd close-ups all checked out as working fine. Kenneth's heart banged hard and steady in anticipation of what he had told the band would be his masterpiece.

He drove his golf cart alongside the nine-foot wall of hay bales separating Stage One's field from Stage Two's, making his way through the woodland border, past another wall of bales, and over to Stage Three, where the first act was going to be Red Jolly Roger at noon. Kenneth set about attaching a chemical spray unit to one of the wind machines positioned to make the stage curtains billow like sails on Vykyng's set. Now it would blow out more than just air. By the time Gothika took to the stage at 1:45 p.m., everyone would be having the time of their lives, and the mist blower would have been pointed at the bands to help keep them cool during their performances and push Kenneth's mist out over the crowd.

He headed back to Stage One and was still there at 8:30 a.m., when his men in black arrived. They parked their Humvees around the event arena and exited, looking like the multiple versions of Agent Smith in *The Matrix*.

Humourless. Dangerous.

Kenneth smirked.

Outside the arena, the sounds of early revelry escalated. More people were arriving, and those who had camped out overnight to get pole position in the queues were indulging in a plethora of pre-show activities—not all of them legal or moral— as booze, drugs, and even lovers got passed around.

12:00 p.m.

The Bare Knuckle Bastards ascended the stage. Hedgehog was first, and the crowd went wild. He walked over to his drum kit, took two pool cues from a stand, and twirled the cues like they were nunchucks before slamming each one in turn across a guard rail, splitting them in half. He carried the two remaining pieces back to his drum kit, sat his huge frame down, and used the pieces of pool cue as his drumsticks to deliver a riff Dave Lombardo would have been proud of.

Some of the crowd cheered in appreciation, and Hedgehog finished his check by smashing into a cymbal on the Hi-Hat, which was Biffer's cue. He plugged in his Rickenbacker 4004LK, pulling a few meaty chords for good measure.

Next up the steps was Bluey, with Kenneth right behind him. Bluey ran across a third of the stage, dropped to his knees with his axe raised above his head, and slid almost the entire remaining distance to thunderous applause.

Kenneth grabbed his microphone.

"Can you hear me at the back…? Are you motherfuckers ready to get K.O.'d?"

Kenneth looked out across the thousands of attendees in front of Stage One. From the audio perspective, everything was good to go, even if the crowd was not so enthusiastic.

"*Not* good enough. I said *are any of you motherfuckers ready to get K.O.'d*!"

This time, the answer was deafening, with most of it being affirmative, interspersed with shouts of "Fuck you" and "Fuck off, Grandad."

"Oh, well, in that case…*Fuck you too*! We'll come back when you fuckers learn some manners!" Kenneth led the band back down the steps, like he'd done a thousand times before. They went backstage and put on the hazmat suits they'd transported to the wings. Each band member turned on their air purifier, and Kenneth checked that his inbuilt microphone was synched to the stage mic.

At the back of the stage, the huge screen burst into a video display of street fighting. A lot of the assembled audience stopped to watch the brutal takedowns and punches knocking teeth out of the pugilists involved. The scene changed, and animated green goo dripped across the footage. Radiation symbols flashed, and a siren went off. A murmuring travelled across the audience, who tried to figure out what was going on.

Kenneth stepped back onstage to his now-redundant mic stand. The rest of the band took their positions, instruments at the ready.

"I…am…*K…O…Pugnus*…and we…are…*Bare…Knuckle…Bastaaaards*…"

Behind him, the screen stopped flashing the warning and now displayed a mutant monster fist with three knuckles facing forward, as if to punch through the screen. Across the knuckles was tattooed "BKB."

Hedgehog battered the drums with his pool cue drumsticks, tapping out the intro, and the image of the knuckles behind them started bleeding cartoonish green slime. K.O. Pugnus took a step forward and slammed his foot down on a large button, initiating the effects he had rigged up. Black lights illuminated particles of a fine green mist, which had begun to emanate from spray nozzles situated around the front of the stage, and the backdrop image turned into a scorched earth scenario.

He started singing "Deadworld."

"In a world polluted, darkness looms,
toxic waste, deadly monsoons.
Venomous rivers, a sickly flow,
as into this poisoned world we go.

"Radiation's embrace, the deadliest kiss,
a wasteland of danger, a vile abyss.
Permeating toxins, a noxious brew,
in this Deadworld, we soldier through.

"Toxic waste, a vile disgrace,
in our death-metal fury, we'll find our place.
Screams of mutation wail from the beguiled,
A maelstrom of poison, this earth defiled."

Out among the audience, fans' faces turned skyward, and the green mist descended, temporarily providing a cooling break in the ninety-plus-degree heat. Kenneth saw girls loosening their shirts and people sticking their tongues out to catch the moisture, perhaps in the hope it was alcohol. Some looked disappointed when the particles hit their tongues.

Kenneth sang on…

"Flesh and bone start to decay.
In the murderous onslaught, we fade away.
A cancerous blight, a planet's plea,
in this wretched wasteland, we're no longer free.

"Barrels of horror, toxic streams,
an apocalypse nightmare of deadly extremes.
A torrent of sickness in a world decayed,
a toxic nightmare, mankind betrayed.

"Toxic waste, a vile disgrace,
in this death-metal fury, we'll find our place.
Screams of mutation wail from the beguiled,
A maelstrom of poison, our earth defiled."

"Screams of anguish, a venomous cry,
as we face the horrors from which we'll die.
Heartbeats of doom, thundering dark,
as on our deadly journey we embark.

"From this earth's ashes, no phoenix will rise,
in this poisoned wasteland where everything dies.
We show our resilience in the face of despair,
but in the end, there's nothing there.

"The earth's lament, a mournful dirge.
From this ravaged landscape, we'll not emerge.

No chance of survival, a pointless fight,
it's our end of days and our last goodnight.

"Toxic waste, a vile disgrace,
in this death-metal fury, we'll find our place.
Screams of mutation wail from the beguiled,
A maelstrom of poison, the earth defiled."

Kenneth's voice dropped deeper, and he growled out the final verse of the song:

"As the world's last cries fade out to nought,
we cannot think of the fight unfought,
of the lives unlived and the words unsaid,
in this death-metal anthem, *everyone's dead*."

The screen changed. It showed a live feed of the crowd. But with the A.I. Filters, they were now corpses in various stages of decay, some zombified, others with parchment skins stretched taut and splitting. Some people's faces were fleshless, their skulls laughing and chattering. They pointed cell phones at the screen, only to find none of their phones would record. The event managers had deployed signal jammers to prevent piracy.

The emptied-out mist machines clicked off, and the stage lights dimmed. The awning cast a shadow across the screen, making the faces in the crowd easier to see, which resulted in cheers of delight. The backing music slowed to a fade, and all that could be heard was Hedgehog's thrumming beat.

On the screen, the word "Bare" was overlaid, giant across the crowd's dead faces. It flashed red and turned into the word "Knuckle" in a warm amber glow, becoming the word "Bastards" in the same toxic green colour as the cartoon slime had been. It remained on screen longer than the previous words, as it was customary for their fans to yell, "Bastards," whenever the word came on screen.

They didn't disappoint.

After a brief pause, the word "Bastards" changed into the red, white, and blue of the Union Flag of the United Kingdom, draped across the knuckles of the BKB Monster Fist.

Bluey launched into a guitar solo. Kenneth looked out over the crowd, trying to judge the mood but finding it pointless. Most of the audience were scrutinizing their cell phones, trying to figure out what was preventing them from recording.

Hardly the response Kenneth had hoped for.

A fight broke out in the crowd. It looked to Kenneth as if some guy had bitten a girl's nose off, while several people were pulling at him, trying to stop him from continuing his attack. Genuine security guards had already spotted them and were forcing their way through the revellers, but some of the guards detoured toward a circle of spectators who were watching a naked threesome fucking.

Kenneth smiled. His formula had taken effect. Far more people started making out in public than usual. While the mood in the crowd seemed to consist mainly of anxiety regarding the lack of cell phone capability, the Bare Knuckle Bastards launched into their next song, and their next. The crowd grew more unstable, and it became difficult to discern the larger group: those fucking, those fighting, or those trying to escape the escalating mayhem.

The Bare Knuckle Bastards ended their set with their most recent hit, "BKB: Undefeated," which once got rousing cheers but hardly seemed to register with these otherwise occupied metalheads.

Hedgehog conducted a comic rimshot, dropped his pool cues, rose to his feet, and separated the Hi-Hat. He grabbed one of the cymbals off the stand and flung it out like a Frisbee above the crowd, sending it veering to the right, where it scalped a guy.

Kenneth turned. Hedgehog had removed his protective hood.

"Get Hedgehog the fuck out of here!" Kenneth yelled to Biffer, who slung his Rickenbacker around his shoulder.

Biffer and Bluey ran to the gigantic drummer, who was destroying his drum kit until he saw his bandmates.

"Oh, hi, guys! Is it time to fuck off? I think it's time to fuck off…Good gig, though!"

He calmly turned toward the steps and left the stage, followed by Biffer and Bluey, both of whom were relieved they didn't have to physically handle Hedgehog.

Kenneth took one last look over the crowd as a final farewell before heading for the steps, dodging the roadies who were taking away BKB gear and prepping the stage.

No more Bare Knuckle Bastards on tour. The rest of the band had returned to their green room and were getting stoned to come down from the adrenaline rush of the gig. Kenneth had other plans. He had to disconnect the blue barrels, clear the aerator pipes, and destroy any evidence linking him to the activity at Dethfest.

*

The news reports that followed were sketchy. *Something* had gone seriously wrong at Dethfest. A fire, possibly caused by the band called Flamethrower, had ignited bales of hay separating the stage areas and had turned the arena into a giant oven, which claimed an estimated tens of thousands of lives. There was speculation of sabotage with a chemical accelerant, as fire marshals had previously given Flamethrower the all-clear.

Eye-witness testimonies from the survivors proved unreliable. They reported seeing monsters, murders, and cannibalism before the inferno, which were immediately ascribed to bad drug trips.

The government promised a full investigation. From the bedroom of his mansion Kenneth knew it would become unnecessary.

"Do I get a countdown?"

"I can count you in whenever you're ready."

"I tell you what, Chrissy, I thought that influencing shit was just kids playing dress-up; I didn't know you were a fucking tech genius."

"Most of us can do this nowadays. We'll begin as soon as you are ready."

"I'm ready now."

"In which case…Five…Four…" She raised her fingers, counting off the remaining *three, two, one*, and pointed at him.

He cleared his throat.

"Grphh. Right. Welcome to the K. O. Pugnus show. As you can see, the reports of my death are a load of bullshit, but you might see me kick the bucket on this livestream…" He paused, looking beyond the camera to Chrissy, straining through milky eyes to see whatever emotions she might be showing. "I've had the best doctors—and all of them agree I am fucked. So I've accepted that, and I want all of you to know that I love every motherfucking one of you for every single record you bought, every album, every CD, the downloads…all of it. You've all given me so much, but now it's time for me to give something to you."

He reached to the bedside table, grabbed a white enamelled metal mug with a straw in it, and sipped something so unpleasant, he grimaced as he swallowed.

"Now I'm going to tell you the truth about Dethfest. And yeah, I am only saying this because I'm on my fucking deathbed. The music company assholes can come at me when I'm pushing up daisies in my new pine overcoat.

"Anyway, you've heard all that crap about cover-ups, but nobody knows the truth, except me. So I'm about to drop the fucking motherlode on you, exactly as it happened."

He winced as he drank more, spat phlegm into a cardboard dish, and continued.

"I'm not saying my life was all bad. I did a roaring trade at gigs with my homebrew 'Class-A Pharmaceuticals.' I made so much money I decided that starting a metal band was the right choice. At least from the 'supplier' perspective. That's the real story of how Bare Knuckle Bastards got started. Good times."

The old man sipped some more of his drink, the straw making a noise when he had drained the metal mug. He stopped sucking and offered the mug to Chrissy, who took it from him.

"Be an angel and fill this up for me from that jug over there. I'm getting dry with all this talking, and I need my spit…Right, Dethfest…I've always been angry about how the music industry screws everyone over. And yeah, I know we've had plenty of hits and made millions, but that's not been down to the record labels. We couldn't get signed; we didn't even get a sniff from the indie labels until we'd already sold over a million records.

"Our shit was banging. Even the early stuff was raw and powerful. We stayed loyal to that. We had dreams and needs like everyone else, but one of my dreams was not to be a sell-out to corporate greed.

"They hated that. BKB struggled to get gigs. The events managers and record companies want the whole nine yards for events, y'know—all of the pyrotechnics, flames belching out of the guitars, giant frigging' robots yomping across the stage. Fuck that bullshit! They sure as fuck punished BKB for not doing it, though.

"Dethfest…Just look at that. I mean, what was the fucking deal with the billing? It was fucking daytime, man. Back in the day, I'd be getting wasted and waking up at four in the afternoon with a couple of groupies playing with my junk. Twelve fucking thirty! Before fucking Vykyng, man. Don't get me wrong, they're good. But if we were going to be on the breakfast shift, at least we could have been put on Stage Two, right before Flamethrower. I mean, yeah, those babes with the bikinis…Something to look at instead of the audience, who are just killing time until their favourite bands get on stage. For fuck's sake, we're the Bare Knuckle Bastards. We were headliners before half of those wankers were born!

"I've been disillusioned for decades, but being an opening act was the last fucking straw. I decided to do something really fucking metal. A final 'fuck you' to the whole capitalist road train. I'll give them a Dethfest to remember, go out on a high, and not a natural one either.

"You know all of that bullshit with the Big Pharma and government cover-up? That was all on me, and yeah, I know there's been a shitload of people saying that already. But I'm going to show you the fucking receipts…"

He turned toward Chrissy, who sat at a table, preparing a video file for the broadcast.

"Movie time?"

Chrissy nodded.

"Then Roll VT!"

She started the video footage of K.O.

Pugnus in overalls and a leather apron. Behind him stood several blue barrels, a banner displaying "EPHEASOS," and a rack on which hung five hazmat suits. Pugnus tapped the microphone pinned to his collar, and spoke.

"Welcome to the Final Testament of Kenneth O'Brian, better known as K.O. Pugnus of Bare Knuckle Bastards, and this is part of my 'confession.' My apologies for the Super 8mm footage, but I'll explain more in the livestream that my granddaughter, Christina, and I will do after Dethfest. For now, I need you to know that I am making this video for the benefit of the legal system, as I want it understood that Chrissy has no idea what I am really doing. She believes I am going to be broadcasting a 'farewell to fans' and nothing more. Therefore, I take full responsibility for everything that is going to happen at Dethfest.

"What a lot of you don't know is that while Queen's Brian May was getting his degree in astrophysics, I was getting PhDs in chemistry, molecular biology, and neuroscience. The banner behind me is for a company I created called EPHEASOS, a fact that can be derived from the name. I'll not bore you with the chemistry stuff, but what I have in the barrels behind me is EPH, or Ethylphenidate. It's a psychostimulant. The 'EAS' is for 'electrophilic aromatic substitution,' for modifying the compound so it can cross the blood-brain barrier. And the 'OS' stands for 'oxidative stress,' the use of free radicals in breaking down the body's natural defences so the EPH can do the business. Got it? Good!

"Most of you don't need to know that shit anyway. I'm just explaining how the whole EPHEASOS Water Company came about for 'The Man,' as it'll end any speculation. Also, yes, I am dying of the effects of chemical poisoning, but not from experimenting with EPH. And I know the band's wardrobe has always been more in line with Black Flag than these hazmat suits we will wear at Dethfest, but the protective gear is functional so BKB are not going to be affected by the EPH I am going to spray into the crowd. They're expecting me to spray a 'Toxic Waste' mist over the crowd in protest of how toxic the music companies are, but instead of a watered-down fluorescent green soda, it'll be EPH and food colouring.

"The EPH is designed to give everyone the trip of a lifetime. It'll unleash their innermost desires, free the darkness from their souls, and should be pretty fucking spectacular, even if I do say so myself. Once airborne, the mist will carry on the wind, and the whole festival will get a lungful in minutes. Even those who don't drink the bottled water laced with EPH that my stooges will be handing out will still get a low-level dose…Plenty of ways for it to get around the crowd.

"Picture the scene—thousands of metalheads getting wasted, unleashing their real selves, being as one with the music. It's going to make the orgy at Woodstock look tame! The event organizers are going to be using cell phone jammers at Dethfest to prevent people from live streaming the bands, but thanks to my staff and a bunch of 8mm cameras, the whole thing will still be recorded for posterity, and the entire world will see what a real fucking metal concert is supposed to be like.

"So there you have it—my confession. If you remember me for anything at all, remember me for making thousands of people lose their fucking minds, their inhibitions, and having the best time of their lives!"

The video footage ended. Chrissy sat, tears in her eyes, and pushed some keys on the laptop.

"You caused it?"

"I didn't think it would go the way it did."

"But you said it in the footage…About unleashing their inner darkness!"

"I meant letting it go, having fun instead, but hey, I've taken enough drugs to know that not every trip is all sunshine and roses. A few people were bound to have bad trips."

"Bad trips? That wasn't the Summer of Love. They were killing each other, *eating* each other. What the fuck, Grandad!"

"I wanted to show them Bare Knuckle Bastards could get the crowd going, and everyone would know that the good times began when we did our set. We'd have been legends."

"Thousands dead, and you planned the whole thing. Is that legendary enough for you?"

"You don't understand."

"You're damned right I don't. Why all of that crap with EPHEASOS? Why the fake security men with the Humvees?"

"I had to get thousands of gallons of EPH into the event, so I set up a fake water brand, paid people to make it look legit, and got reps to approach the festival organizers with a sponsorship deal the greedy bastards couldn't refuse. The organizers were very happy with the size of the offer, so I had free reign to do whatever I wanted. Some of the security men were actors I had hired for what they thought was a movie. Their guns fired blanks, so I'm not responsible for the actual shootings."

"People died!"

"People have forgotten how to live. They hardly even lift their heads up from their devices anymore. First thing in the morning, they grab their cell phone, go to the shitter, and take it with them as they can't bear not to have it near them…They photograph every fucking meal they have so they can impress other people with their shitty imagined lifestyles and fake bullshit. They needed to see that there's more to life—"

"So you killed thousands of people?"

"They were supposed to get high, that's all. I mean, really fucking high. I didn't think there'd be—"

"Carnage? Mass slaughter? For what?"

"For the kids…For the future of metal…For BKB!"

"Fucking hell, Grandad. I'm sorry, but BKB is a pathetic bunch of has-beens. You've not had a hit in years, and you're never going to return to the glory days."

"How dare you—"

"Oh, I fucking dare, all right. All my life, I've taken your shit about the Bare Knuckle Bastards. Christmases spent wondering where the fuck you were, only to have you turn up on boxing day too stoned to speak…Mom crying in the bathroom as Dad tried to defend you. Even throughout his own illness, he stood up for you and your stupid fucking band, and you couldn't even attend his funeral. Your own son! And I'm not even going to talk about Mom's suicide. I'm surprised it took her as long as it did. If you were my dad, I'd have eaten a suitcase full of your Class-A crap, just to be finally free of you, so show some fucking accountability for once."

"This livestream is all about accountability! I want the world to know that I didn't want to hurt anyone."

"You haven't 'hurt' people; you've killed people, destroyed entire communities. Every one of those kids who didn't return home had families, people who loved them, and this whole deathbed theatre of yours is still all about you, isn't it? It's about your beloved Bare Knuckle Bastards. Those serial fuckwits are hailing you as a fucking hero for making them wear hazmat suits on stage, as it probably saved their lives. And there's you, thriving on the attention after the worst mass poisoning since Jim-fucking-Jones dished out the Kool-Aid. I wish you hadn't worn a hazmat suit. I wish you'd been right there, filling your lungs with the same toxic shit you made everyone else have. But no, you got away with it all, and now you're going to die and leave me with, what? This mansion, the other houses, the cars, millions in art, jewellery, shares, bonds, cash—everything you've signed over to me as your sole heir, it's all going to be taken by the government when the Dethfest Inquest ends. If you think I'll ever have anything resembling a normal life after this, you're a fucking idiot. So, well done, Grandad. Well fucking done."

"I don't want to bow out like this, not fighting with you in front of the world."

"You're not going to die in front of them."

"You don't understand."

"What don't I understand, you murdering fucker?"

Kenneth raised the metal mug. His hands shook as he tried to get purchase on the straw with his lips. He finally caught it between his teeth, and noisily drained the contents of the mug before dropping it beside the bed.

"The juice I've been drinking for the past hour has enough EPH in it to kill a whale."

"Oh, well, bon voyage! Have a nice fucking trip. You couldn't even do your confession sober, could you!"

"This is my swan song, Chrissy. I'm probably going to lose consciousness in the next few minutes, become comatose soon after, and dead before you can get an ambulance out here."

"Oh, you dumb bastard! It's going to look like I've poisoned you for the inheritance!"

"No! You're forgetting the livestream. There are probably millions of people watching us right now. They've heard my confessions. They've just heard me tell you that I'm poisoning myself with a lethal amount of EPH. I'm looking straight into the camera now…

"To all of you watching this, you've heard the truth. My granddaughter, Chrissy…Christina…is not to blame for anything and that I have taken my own life. She had no idea what was in the drink she was giving to me."

He turned away from the camera and focused on her, a pleading look on his face.

"Is that supposed to make me feel better?"

"It's my admission of guilt and a declaration of suicide. No court will convict you with that evidence and millions of witnesses."

"There are no witnesses. We haven't been live streaming, just recording."

"But the V.T.!"

"Cutting and editing, that's all. Did you really think I would allow someone who can't stay sober to embarrass me in front of the entire fucking world?"

"Tell me you're kidding!"

"Fuck no, and it seems like I made the right choice. You're going to just slip away in your sleep. No fuss, no final farewell to your fans…Just a sad old man going off to spend eternity in Hell."

K.O. Pugnus groaned, a spasm arching his back. His heart skipped a couple of beats, his numb left arm gave out from under him, and he flopped against his pillow. His eyes rolled back into his sockets, the whites now more a sickly fluorescent green, which matched the coloured froth slowly emanating from his open mouth.

Christina checked him for signs of life but found none. She transferred Kenneth's Dethfest confession onto an external drive, which she locked in the safe, then moved the camera and laptop out of Kenneth's bedroom and called for an ambulance.

She never showed the footage.

Do You Want to Die at Dethfest?

We hope you enjoyed the stories in this anthology. If you've already tried not to die at Dethfest in the interactive novel, perhaps you've gained a deeper understanding and appreciation of the devastation that occurred. If you haven't read it yet, then it might be time for me to send the Men in Black to have a talk with you. Thank you for reading and supporting indie authors!

Mark Tullius

A Note from the Publisher

This collection of stories nearly didn't happen. Five months ago, right before *Try Not to Die: At Dethfest* was released, my co-author and I considered writing a few stories as told by the bands. These bands were our creation, so it made sense for Glenn and me to explore them. It didn't take us long to realize neither of us was up for the task, but that didn't dampen my desire to know about these bands and what had happened on the day of Dethfest.

Instead of putting out an open call for short stories, I sent out invites to some of my favorite indie authors, people I knew could pull off a great story, several of whom I'd already collaborated with: Duncan Ralston, who came up with the title and subtitle for the anthology; John Palisano and P.W. Feutz, who already have *Try Not to Die* books out; and Caitlin Marceau and Jon Cohn, whose will be here shortly.

Once I had the foundations set, I sent out more invites, relying on recommendations. Some of the authors I'd never read before, but while waiting on their short stories, I picked up several books. The book *Arcranium,* by Dameon Manx and Mark Towse, impressed me so much we're now starting work on *Try Not to Die: Arcranium.* And this will just be one of the many collaborations this anthology has sparked.

While I enjoyed watching the stories develop, I only did a bit of the overseeing, with light edits and suggestions. This was so different from collaborating on a *Try Not to Die,* where we blend styles. I figured the less I interfered, the more you would get to experience that author and their writing style. Plus, I had such an incredible editor in Lyndsey Smith, who worked tirelessly on this, encouraging me whenever I had my doubts. This book would not have happened without her.

I've loved short story collections since I was a kid, never knowing what I would find, but certain I would discover a couple of new authors I'd want to read more of. That's what I'm hoping this anthology does for you and why I included all the bios and links to newsletters, where you can get ahold of free books, stories, and updates of what these writers have coming out next. I hope you discover some favorite new authors and encourage them to keep churning out killer stories.

Mark Tullius

About the Authors
(In Order of Appearance)

Daemon Manx

Daemon Manx is an American horror author and member of the Horror Writers Association (HWA). He has been featured in magazines in both the U.S. and the U.K., is a recipient of a HAG award for his story "The Dead Girl" (2021), and a Splatterpunk award nominee.

Daemon plays both bass and guitar (poorly) and is infamously known for a motor vehicle accident he was responsible for, involving President Ronald Reagan's limousine. In 1999 he was a contestant on the gameshow Wheel of Fortune in which he used a good thirteen of his fifteen minutes of fame.

Daemon has eleven years clean and sober and uses his platform to help others. After struggling with addiction, he served an eight-year prison sentence where he found recovery and learned to write horror.

He is best known for his latest release, *Manx-iety: A collection of Disturbing Stories*, and his debut novelette, *Abigail*. With seven publications and inclusion in numerous anthologies, Daemon considers himself blessed as he prepares for his upcoming four book series, *The Ojanox*, to release next summer. He currently lives with his sister, author Danielle Manx, and their narcoleptic cat, Sydney, where they patiently prepare for the apocalypse. There is a good chance they will run out of coffee far too soon.

Recent Publications

Abigail

Piece by Piece

Drawn & Quartered

Hacked in Two

These Lingering Shadows

Tales from the Monoverse

Arcranium

Manx-iety

The Ojanox Series – Coming Soon!

Try Not to Die: In Arcranium – Coming Soon!

www.daemonmanx.com

www.lastwaltzpublishing.com

Grab Your Copy of Manx-iety

"Manx-iety" a must-read for fans of horror, suspense, and dark fiction. Highly recommended for those who are brave enough to delve into the depths of their fears.

Download a free copy of The Dead Girl by signing up for Daemon's newsletter.

Steve Stred

A two-time Splatterpunk Award nominated author, Steve Stred lives in Edmonton, Alberta, Canada, with his wife and son.

Known for his novels *Mastodon* and *Churn the Soil* and his series, *Father of Lies,* where he joined a cult on the dark web for four years, his work has been described as haunting, bleak, and is frequently set in the woods near where he grew up. He's been fortunate to appear in numerous anthologies with some truly amazing authors.

He is an Active Member of the HWA and can be found at stevestredauthor.ca.

Jay Bower

Jay Bower is a horror author living outside St. Louis, Missouri, in the forest of Southern Illinois. He spends his time reading, writing, and convincing his wife the dark stories he writes do not involve her.

One time punk-rock skateboarder and heavy metal kid of the 80s, Jay approaches his work with the same indie attitude as those early punk bands.

Author Website: https://jaybowerauthor.com/

Violet James McMaster

Violet James McMaster (she/they) is a bookseller, writer, Horror Writers Association member, musician, and voracious reader based out of the rural labyrinths of Pennsylvania. A lifelong lover of the horror genre, Violet is currently working on a book of essays engaging with the intersections of body, cosmic, and folk horror, and the experience of gender dysphoria. You can follow her on Instagram @violetjamesmcmaster, Twitter @vithelibrarian, and Bluesky @violetjmcmaster.bsky.social.

Robert Essig

Robert Essig is the author of twenty books such as *This Damned House*, *Baby Fights*, and *Broth House*. He has published over 100 short stories and edited three small press anthologies, one of which, *Chew on This!,* was nominated for a Splatterpunk Award. Robert lives with his family in East Tennessee.

https://linktr.ee/robertessig

Caitlin Marceau

Caitlin Marceau is a queer author and lecturer based in Montreal. She holds a Bachelor of Arts in Creative Writing, is an Active Member of the Horror Writers Association, and has spoken about genre literature at several Canadian conventions. She spends most of her time writing horror and experimental fiction, but has also been published for poetry as well as creative non-fiction. Her work includes *PALIMPSEST, MAGNUM OPUS, A BLACKNESS ABSOLUTE*, and her debut novella, *THIS IS WHERE WE TALK THINGS OUT*. Her second novella, *I'M HAVING REGRETS*, and her debut novel, *IT WASN'T SUPPOSED TO GO LIKE THIS*, are set for publication soon. For more, visit CaitlinMarceau.ca or find her on social media.

Get the Free Story on Caitlin's Website

Everly and Brooklynn are excited to be starting the next chapter of their lives together. With a baby on the way, they're eager to get settled in their new home where life is perfect. Well, except for the rusted car stuck in their driveway…and the cracks that have started appearing around the house… not to mention the eyes that watch Everly when she's all alone…

Determined to uncover the secrets hiding at *23 McCormick Road*, Everly embarks on an emotional journey that both tests her empathy and teaches her when to hold on—and when to let go.

Simone Trojahn

Horror author Simone Trojahn was born in 1980 and lives with her family in a small town south of Munich. Trojahn wanted to be a writer as a child and sent her books to various publishers. However, she was rejected again and again, often on the grounds that, at her age, she should stick to her own experiences rather than write fictional thrillers. After graduating from high school, Trojahn worked in various social institutions, including a kindergarten classroom and a home for severely disabled adults, but never lost sight of her goal of making a living from writing.

Her debut novel, *Mörderherz,* was published in 2014. Overjoyed to have finally found a small readership, Trojahn then revised and published some early works she had written between the ages of fourteen and twenty-one. Among them are the novels *Sommertränen* and *Das Leben nach dem Sterben*, in which the author shows her 'softer' side.

In late summer 2015, Trojahn's hardcore thriller *Kellerspiele* was released and made it into the Amazon Top 100. Many fans of realistic horror still celebrate this relentless psychological thriller as a masterpiece of the hardcore genre. It was followed by the kidnapping drama *Das Kinderspiel* and the psychological thriller *Blutbrüder* in 2016. Trojahn's fan base in the horror genre grew. In 2017, *Selina's Way* was published, and the eBook cracked the Top 20 of the Amazon bestsellers list.

In the same year, the author shocked her readers with the revenge thriller *Weil ich dich hasse* and the abuse drama *Todsonne* by finally blurring the boundaries between perpetrator and victim beyond recognition. In 2018, Trojahn published her first book with REDRUM BOOKS. *Wutrauschen* describes the dramatic love story of a psychotic couple that—how could it be otherwise?—ends in disaster. In the same year, the hard-hitting apocalyptic thriller *Am Ende der Hoffnung* was released, in which loyal readers could see a reunion with the unlucky hitchhiker Fred Manson from two of the author'' early works—*Tage der Vergeltung* and *Straße der Gerechtigkeit.*

At the beginning of 2019, Trojahn published the horror thriller *Bad Family* with REDRUM BOOKS and once again lived up to the title given to her by a reader—the "uncrowned queen of hardcore noir." This was followed by other thrillers for readers with strong nerves: *Selina's Way 2* (2019), *Schaffenskrise* (2019), *Giftiges Erbe* (2020), *Toter Schmetterling* (2020), *Mutterfleisch* (2020), *Das Tiefste Schwarz* (2021), *Selina's Way 3* (2021), *Hassnacht* (2022), *Blutland* (2022), *Liebe böse Schwester* (2023), and *Das Vermächtnis des Grauens* (2023).

In addition, all of the author's older novels have now been reissued by REDRUM BOOKS. These include the horror thriller *Kaltes Lächeln* and the short story collections *Schicksalshäppchen* and *Dark Menu.* The short story "Hexensaft" was printed in a limited edition comic to spoil regular readers with a very special goodie.

Since 2019, some of her thrillers have been published in the English language.

Furthermore, there will be a movie based on the hardcore thriller *Kellerspiele/Basement Games* in the near future.

For more information, questions, and critique, you can contact the author here:

Facebook – facebook.com/simonetrojahn
Facebook groups – Simone Trojahn Fans
Redrum Books – Nichts für Pussys
Instagram – simone_trojahn_autorin
Email – t.simone80@gmail.com

English books available on amazon: https://t1p.de/0s1fb

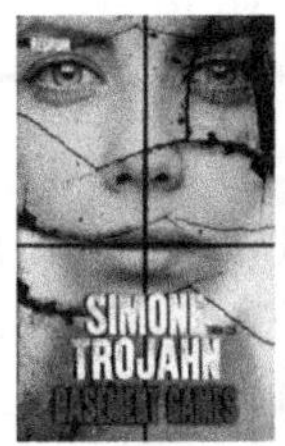   

Zachary Ashford

Zachary Ashford is the Aurealis-nominated author of *When the Cicadas Stop Singing* and a 2023 nominee in the Ditmar Awards Best New Talent category. His debut novel, *Polyphemus*, was released through Darklit Press in November. It's a balls-to-the-wall barrage of heavy metal goodness, and it features a playlist to match. His other books include highway-patrolling serial killers, hordes of rampaging drop bears, post-apocalyptic landscapes rife with lizard people, and tonnes of heart, tonnes of action, and tonnes of monsters. He is an educator, occasional speaker, and cat-lover. In the past, he's been a heavy metal journalist, a radio copywriter, and a teenage headbanger. You can buy his books in the usual places and find him on the modern hellscape we all call social media at www.instagram.com/zac_ashford.

Now...a preview of *Polyphemus*:

Anton momentarily disappeared and the deep bass of a ritual drum began to pound. There was movement outside the circle and then it parted again. Anton, his hood down and his face daubed in smears of blood-red paint, reappeared and stepped forward. On a rope, he led the biggest fucking goat Oaks had ever seen. It must have weighed two-hundred pounds. It was the size of a great Dane; built like a brick shithouse. Screaming and skittish, it jerked at the rope like a dog that wouldn't heel. Its fur was stygian black and its four horns reached out from its head like the star in Baphomet's sigil. The spike of its beard tapered into a terrifying fifth point. As if it were a fly disturbed from feasting on putrescent roadkill, its dilated pupils capered from side to side, but always alighted on that one focal point. For the goat, that point was Oaks. But as much as it jerked its head, trying to escape Anton's hold on the tether, it kept focusing on Oaks. No, not at him. Beyond him. As if there was something huge and predatory there. Oaks tried to catch a glimpse of whatever the goat was seeing, but he couldn't find it. There was only that hungry, horny, desperate shape loitering there like a monkey.

Anton dragged the screaming beast into the circle, and the ritual drum pounded as slowly as a dying man's heartbeat. The hollow booming hung heavily in the air. The lurking shape swelled with each resonant thud. The goat bleated, apoplectic with fear. It reared and kicked its forepaws, but Anton kept pulling it forward, unperturbed. Then, when the next drumbeat struck, the entire black-robed audience chanted in unison. With each successive strike, they chanted again and again. A single ominous 'Om'. The hairs on Oaks's arms and neck stood on end and the shape began to coalesce. Wispy tendrils of black smoke crept in front of his eyes.

Anton gestured for him to stay put and remain calm as he approached with the scrambling, bucking goat. He produced a long and ornate knife from inside his robe and shortened the goat's leash by winding the rope with looping twists of his wrist. The wailing animal was dragged inexorably closer and closer to the blade and there was nothing its braying could do to stop it. A stream of piss sprayed out from beneath its shaggy belly. An acrid stench steamed up from the growing puddle, then its bowels released and the smell grew worse.

Transfixed, Oaks wondered briefly if India's initiation had been anything like this. Was she watching him; a black-robed voyeur of this bizarre and electrifying ceremony? He had goosebumps. He could have sworn the entity that had followed him all night was caressing him. The hair on his neck stood on end and his balls tightened. Anton's knife flashed and arced through the air. The goat gave a pained scream then fell silent. It had shat and pissed everywhere, but that made nowhere near as much mess as the blood spraying arterial geysers of red.

The goat tried to thrash. To escape. Anton was too strong for it. He held it firm, stoic determination on his blood-drenched face. He pushed his hand into the wound and reached down, feeling around for something. When he pulled his hand free, he pulled the beast's heart with it. He threw the sinuous thing to the floor and let the goat fall to its shaking knees. Its hind legs scrambled in the mess. It slipped, collapsing onto its side. Using the heart, Anton painted a bloody pentagram onto the ground around Oaks. When it was complete, he plunged his hands into the mutilated animal. When he withdrew them, his arms were blood-red.

Oaks watched, wide-eyed. Barely able to process what was happening, he stepped forward as Anton reached for him and grabbed his face. As the bald man drew a spiral of blood on his forehead, he felt the shifting shape from his peripherals manifest and become corporeal. Something seized him and as the booming drum and the strange chanting continued, he felt himself pass out of existence.

Read more...

Polyphemus is available now through Darklit Press in print, digital, and audio.

You can get it wherever books are sold, including Amazon, Barnes & Noble, and fantastic independent bookstores like Little Ghost Books and Godless.

P.W. Feutz

P.W. Feutz is an author of horror and supernatural fiction. His first novella, *The Sun Is A Circle Meant For Serving*, came out in 2023. He's also the coauthor of *Try Not To Die: Back At Grandma's House* and the forthcoming *Try Not To Die: At Meadow Spire Mall*. He lives in Michigan with his wife and two rabbits, Sherl and Watson.

An excerpt from *Try Not to Die: Back at Grandma's House*

This should be easy. East or west on the highway, just pick and follow. But I'm sitting here clutching the steering wheel of Grandpa's car, the consequences of everything I've done wrapping their charred, flaky hands around my heart. People are dead because of me.

"David," Sam says from the shadows of the backseat, the whites of her eyes all I can see. "What are you doing? Get us the hell out of here!"

Her needing me makes this so much worse. I'm supposed to protect her, but I don't want to be responsible anymore. Every decision I've made has kept my sister alive, but for how long? I hate choices. You never know if you've picked the right one. No matter what you choose, you can't know how the other turns out. I'll tell myself that the one I picked is right or wrong, but it's all just in my head. I suppose there will be a moment I'll know, the last second before I die. That's the moment I'll be able to say, "You should have picked the other path." That's all any of us get. That's the only clarity we'll have. The rest of our lives are left or right, up or down, east or west; then cross your fingers and fall into the unknown.

"David, I swear to God! Get us out of here!"

It's hard to think, the image of Grandpa's evil creatures about to rip Sam's head off or stab me through the seat with their claws. "East or west?" I ask her. "Which?"

"I don't know, David. You just have to go." Sam's usual anger has drained. I can't tell if it's from exhaustion or she's scared I'm close to snapping and becoming as useless as the "person" taking up the seat beside her. He's definitely not going to help with the decision-making process. Barely breathing, pale, and shaking, he's like a corpse, electrocuted with enough volts to make him appear to be alive. I'm trying to take Grandpa's word that he's our brother and not going to turn back into the monstrosity he was, but until he starts speaking, I won't believe it's Tim. I won't accept that the person we buried in his grave was someone Tim tore apart with his teeth and claws.

Fifteen minutes ago, this *thing* had been tied to a table connected to Sam, tubes in their veins, Grandpa's last-ditch effort to undo what had happened, to turn Tim back into a human being.

"Please pick, David." Her voice isn't more than a whisper.

I hate myself for making this worse on Sam, but my hands are trembling on the wheel. I have this awful, twisted feeling things would be better if we hadn't made it out of the lab alive.

There aren't any cars on the road, but for all we know there's a trail of bloodthirsty Torpions on our tail or waiting around a curve. But it's not just those vile creatures. The fire from the house must be spreading. With my luck, it's gonna ignite this entire mountain, both east and west about to go up in flames.

I can't believe we might burn alive when we could have drowned with our parents. That's the age-old question, right? Burned alive or drowned? Which would you choose?

"David, just go," Sam says, sounding like she's going to cry.

My foot punches the gas. East. The highway is narrow, one lane each direction. Between the huge green formations of earth that rise off to the sides is a drop into nothingness. The small guardrail wouldn't be able to stop us from careening into the foggy abyss.

This road gets smoother, no potholes or cracks to slow us down, but I keep it at 50 mph, just above the speed limit, my fingers practically the same color as the thing next to Sam. Read more...

Renee S. DeCamillis

Renee S. DeCamillis is a horror author and editor and the author of the psychological thriller/supernatural horror novella, *The Bone Cutters*, originally published through Eraserhead Press and set for republication in 2024 through Encyclopocalypse Publications. She is a member of the Horror Writers Association, the New England Horror Writers, and the Horror Writers of Maine. Renee is the singer/songwriter and rhythm guitarist for the punk-metal band Scars Aligned. She's also a tree-hugging hippie with a sharp metal edge.

Her next book, *Chisel the Bone*, will be published in 2024 through Encyclopocalypse Publications. It is the sequel to *The Bone Cutters*.

Renee's short fiction appears in: *Horrors of the Deep: Starling Sea Stories*; *After the Burn*, a post-apocalyptic shared-world anthology; the *Wicked Women* anthology from NEHW Press; *Northern Frights, The Journal of Horror Writers of Maine 2.5— Mud Season 2021, lost*; *Deadman's Tome: The Conspiracy Issue*; *Siren's Call* eZine Issue 37, the 6th Annual Women in Horror Month Edition; and *The Other Stories Podcast*. Her poetry appears in *The Horror Writers Association's HWA Poetry Showcase Volume IV*.

Renee earned her BA in psychology from the University of Southern Maine, earned her MFA in Popular Fiction Writing from the Stonecoast Graduate Program, and attended Berklee College of Music as a music business major with guitar as her principal instrument. Renee is a former model, school rock band teacher, creative writing teacher, private guitar instructor, A&R rep for an indie record label, therapeutic mentor, psychological technician, and preschool teacher. She is also a former gravedigger; she can get rid of a body fast without leaving a trace, and she is not afraid of getting her hands dirty. Renee lives in the woods of southern Maine with her husband, their son, and a house full of ghosts.

Visit her online:
Website: reneesdecamillis.com; Facebook: Renee S. DeCamillis Author; Instagram: @renee_s._decamillis; Twitter: @ReneeDeCamillis; Facebook: @scarsaligned; Instagram: @scarsaligned

Thomas K.S. Wake

Thomas K.S. Wake became enamoured with horror at the tender age of six when he saw *Re-Animator* on VHS, and it led him to a darkly lit path he still happily treads.

Thomas consumed book after book along with an endless stream of movies, and a thought popped into his head. One of being a writer and conjuring something that would intrigue the minds of readers like him.

Living in Finland presented an obstacle, though; there wasn't a horror culture to speak off there. Very few novels and even fewer horror films were made in the Land of Northern Lights. Horror was, and still is, considered less, something not worthy of the creative efforts. This forced Thomas to seek publication abroad, and finally, slowly but steadily, his stories are gaining traction. After almost a year hiatus, he is back at the keyboard, ready to—hopefully—horrify and terrorize readers.

Jon Cohn

Jon Cohn is the author of multiple books, with the latest, *Everything Is Temporary,* now available on Amazon, Kindle Unlimited, and coming soon to Audible! Jon's debut novel, *The Island Mother*, won a big award - Publisher's Weekly's Booklife Prize for Best Indie Horror Novel of 2022.

His novel *Try Not to Die: On Slashtag* will be released February 2024.

Jon is also a professional board game designer based out of San Diego, California.

You can follow him on Instagram and Twitter @joncohnauthor.

An excerpt from *Try Not to Die: On Slashtag*

In the heart of L.A., there's a sort of competition between studios to see who can push billboard sizes to the absolute limit.

The largest you'll find are typically plastered to the backlot walls keeping gawkers from getting into the coveted studios, making sure they tune in on Wednesday nights. Today, I'm not just one of those unwashed masses hoping to make it past that security gate. I *am* the talent.

Well…sort of.

I'm greeted by a thirty-foot mural of reality TV queen Britt Holley, with an even larger KMC Network logo staring down at me, when Chrissy and I pull up to the guard station in her '94 Impala.

The guard leans forward and squints at us, probably not used to seeing such a fine vehicle pass these gates.

"Names and IDs." He checks his clipboard and reaches out his hand expectantly.

"Chrissy Holtz," my driver, and best friend, says, digging through her purse and producing one.

"Jeremy Talbott." I reach across Chrissy to hand him my license.

He studies them for a few seconds, then cross-checks our printed names with a list in his booth.

My pulse pounds. What if there's been a mistake or a miscommunication along the line and our names aren't on the list? There are already several cars behind us—Mercedes and Porsches. How humiliating would it be for us to have to turn around after getting this far?

The guard steps back out and hands Chrissy our licenses. "Welcome to Krentler Media Studios." He uses a highlighter on a paper map, drawing a path for us to park and find their reality TV casting office.

Hollywood, here we are.

"Don't gawk," Chrissy says, exiting the vehicle. "Act like you belong, and you can get anywhere."

She would know. For the last two years at film school, while I've spent almost every waking free hour working on student film sets, Chrissy has been getting non-stop work as an extra on just about every show I can imagine. At this point, I don't even think she remembers her own filmography, and occasionally, I will spot her in the background of some cop drama she has no memory of participating in. Then again, that could also be partially because she's stoned roughly ninety percent of the time.

I follow Chrissy around the labyrinthine studio filled with monolithic and historic yellow buildings, pretending to walk with purpose. She heads straight for the office. We're about to walk in when a building to my right catches my eye.

"Oh my God," I say, completely starstruck.

Jared Collins, the star of the hit series *Unnatural,* walks past me and through a door of a neighboring building.

"Where are you going?" Chrissy asks when I divert from the path and follow the actor.

<u>1A. Explore the studio</u>
<u>1B. Follow Chrissy</u>

This book will be published February 2024

Duncan Ralston

New standalone horror novel PUZZLE HOUSE available now!

Author of the cult smash-hit *Woom* and *Ghostland* and more than fifteen other books that aren't the cult smash-hit *Woom* or *Ghostland*. His debut collection was blurbed positively by the legendary Jack Ketchum. In ten years of publishing, Duncan Ralston hasn't won or been nominated for sh*t outside of screenwriting awards, and is definitely not bitter about it.

For seven FREE dark fiction short stories/novellas including the prequel to *GHOSTLAND*, *The Moving House*, signed copies of *Woom*, bookplates, and merch, please visit www.duncanralston.com.

An excerpt from *Try Not to Die: At Ghostland*

Ghostland, Opening Day

April 20th, 2019

Everyone I know wanted tickets for Ghostland on opening day. "It's like *Jurassic Park* but with ghosts," the ads used to say, before they got sued and had to stop. They claim it's a haunted theme park, only not like something out of *Scooby Doo*. According to the website it's this huge 108-acre park filled with haunted buildings and cursed objects. Who wouldn't want to see actual ghosts in real life? Even *I* thought it sounded awesome, and I'm a huge wuss. So of course, opening day sold out fast.

"Ask Lucky," Gabby said the day the tickets went on sale, three of us sitting in her room. My name is Lucy, but everyone's called me Lucky since forever. My parents and little sister, all the kids at school, my teachers and track coach, even my boyfriend.

Gabby was sitting in Jordan's lap at the computer trying to get tickets that day, and I was sprawled out on her bed texting Eli after football practice. When I switched places with them it went from "*This event is sold out*" to "*Hurry! Only four tickets remaining!*" I bought the last four, which was exactly how many we needed.

Ask Lucky.

I've always had good luck. I don't know what it is about me. Not like, "win the lottery" good luck. Just… things always seem to kind of *work out* for me. It's hard to explain. Take yesterday after school. I was so excited to go on our little road trip weekend to Ghostland that when I saw Eli parked across the road, I ran out in front of a school bus and would've gotten run over if my feet hadn't slipped out from under me. I sat there, staring down at the laces on my shoes, feeling like an idiot for nearly getting myself killed, but even worse for falling like a doofus in front of the whole school and the rest of the track team. As a runner I should have known better than to leave my laces tied loosely, but if they *hadn't* come untied just then I would've been roadkill instead of just painfully embarrassed with two scraped knees.

See? Lucky.

We got to Ghostland just after breakfast and we've been walking around for a bit, but not very long. No ghosts yet, just this hologram of the guy who "invented" the park and some other holograms here in the Visitor Center. It's kind of interesting so far, like a museum of all things supernatural. I like the old photos of ghost hoaxes. There's a feature on this Scottish lady, Helen Duncan, who took photographs of herself with ectoplasm coming out of her nose and mouth. It says they put her in prison for practicing witchcraft in 1944, which seems weird because it's pretty obvious the "ectoplasm" was actually just some kind of fabric. My first reaction is to think that people were way more gullible in those days, but then I remember the internet.

"Hey, Lucky," Eli calls over. "C'mere."

He's standing with Gabby and Jordan in front of a glass case on a stand, the excitement on his face giving him those dimples I fell for in the sixth grade. The three of them are watching this three-foot-tall sailor doll dance like it's doing a TikTok. It stops dancing the second I take off the Augmented Reality glasses they gave us at admission. It's just sitting in its chair, with its weird little sort-of monkey face. They say the ghosts in this place are safely contained by something called a "Recurrence Field," like animals in invisible cages—only they call them "spectral beings" on the foldout park map—forced to repeat the same things on a loop. It all sounds like a load of bullcrap, as my dad likes to say, but when I settle the glasses back down on my nose, the doll's back up on his feet, doing a jig.

So is it real, or is everything we've seen holograms? I can't say for sure. That creep with the thin perv mustache who welcomed us to the park, I'm pretty sure *he* was a hologram. But the rest of them? I don't know. It's almost like being in a real-life video game.

"Yo, check this out," Jordan says, waving us over.

Continue reading…

John Palisano

John Palisano's novels include *Dust of the Dead, Ghost Heart, Nerves*, and *Night of 1,000 Beasts*. His novellas include *Glass House* and *Starlight Drive: Four Halloween Tales*. His first short fiction collection *All that Withers* celebrates over a decade of short story highlights.

He won the Bram Stoker Award© in short fiction for "Happy Joe's Rest Stop" and Colorado's Yog Soggoth award in 2018. More short stories have appeared in anthologies from Weird Tales, Cemetery Dance, PS Publishing, Independent Legions, Space & Time, Dim Shores, DarkFuse, Crystal Lake, Terror Tales, Lovecraft eZine, Horror Library, Bizarro Pulp, Written Backwards, Dark Continents, Big Time Books, McFarland Press, Darkscribe, Dark House, Omnium Gatherum, and more.

Non-fiction pieces have appeared in Blumhouse Online, Fangoria, and Dark Discoveries magazines and he's been quoted in Vanity Fair, The Writer, and the Los Angeles Times.

You can find more at: www.johnpalisano.com

NOVELS

Night of 1,000 Beasts
Dust of the Dead
Coming Soon in a new edition!
Ghost Heart
Nerves

NOVELLAS

Placerita with Lisa Morton

Glass House
The Bipolar Express
in Surreal Worlds

COLLECTIONS
Starlight Drive—Four Tales for Halloween
from Western Legends
All That Withers—Stories
Collected Short Fiction
from Cytraxis Press

An excerpt from *Try Not to Die: In the Wild West*

My back's resting against the west wall of our house, the only
side with shade. It's nearly ten and already hotter than a blister
bug in a pepper patch. These four walls of wood are the only
thing separating me and Pa from all this emptiness. Desert as
far as the eye can see, a flimsy cloud, thin as my bedsheet,
creeping across the brightest blue sky, barely casting a shadow.

Our house outside of Placerita Town might not be much, but
it protects us from the blazing California sun while keeping out
all the critters. Except for these dang red ants. Inside or out,

they're always a problem, chomping on you if they're given half a second. It's my fault for sitting in one place, but I'm saving my strength.

The little guy on my boot is headed for my leg. I flick gently enough to send him to the sand but not enough to teach him a lesson. He's determined and heads back for me. I meet him halfway with the heel of my boot, feeling a little sorry for sending him to his maker.

Bang! Bang! Bang!

It doesn't matter I knew those bangs were coming, I still jumped at the first one. Pa's finishing up in the blacksmith shop, the last piece for the trip.

Bang! Bang! Bang!

The blows are loud, but the echoes die down quickly. I get up, brush off my jeans, slip on my light duster coat, and strap on my canteen. I wait for the next set of bangs to come and go before I open the shop door. My ears are used to the noise, but the smells always hit me hard, the earthiness of hot metal and fire filling the shop.

Pa's inspecting a red-hot stirrup, setting it down on the forge, his massive hand raising the hammer. He slams it down and sparks bloom like a cloud of raining fire. He looks like a god to me—like someone forging the great cities of Ancient Greece or Rome. I can only hope one day he'll come to look at me with some sense of pride.

The first few seconds in the shop are suffocating, the sweat streaming down my face.

Pa takes off his hat and wipes his forehead with the back of his hand, smearing the black smudge. "Nice timing, Rocky," he says, his voice a deep rumble.

I nod but keep my lips shut 'cause Pa's still talking.

"Make sure you carry enough water with you to get to town." He slips his hat back on, puts down the hammer, and raises the pincers. "This load is gonna be a clip heavier than usual, boy."

The leather saddlebag beside the forge is stuffed with horseshoes and stirrups. I nudge it with my foot. "Maybe if we do well, I can put some away toward a four-legger to help out. Tack of the Town has got a couple on the cheap."

"We'll have to see." Pa uses the pincers to lower the stirrup into a cauldron of water. He disappears in the steam for a second and reemerges, his face glistening. "It's been a real light year," he says. "Not that I like the idea of you having to carry so much by hand."

My grunt surprises me when I pick up the bag. I play it off with a laugh. "My back's already mad at me."

Pa puts the stirrup on the drying rack. "Take the wheelbarrow."

"I don't want to risk it getting broken or taken."

"I trust you."

"It ain't me I don't trust," I say. "It's all the people in town. Someone's apt to steal it. Plus, it ain't gonna be no fun pushing it over the hill."

Pa uses the pincers to pick up the last stirrup. "More reason for you to hustle as much of the haul as you can. Less to carry home."

Even though it's never happened, I say, "I aim to carry only coins back."

Pa nods and laughs with approval. "That's the spirit. None of those bank notes." Pa gestures for me to open the left satchel and sets in the stirrup. "They ain't ever no good when we go to cash 'em in."

"Don't have to tell me twice about them notes." I close the clasps on the bag and say, "Biggest scam going."

Pa grins. "Right you are."

The bag's heavy as a hay bale and I have to use both hands to raise it. "Here's to this being empty."

"More important, be smart and be safe."

"Always."

The fresh air cools my sweat and gives me a bit of energy, making me think the bag's not so heavy after all. I set it down and double-check my pockets, comforted by the folding knife and the handful of nuts. More out of superstition than reason, I slide a horseshoe from the bag and stick it in my duster's long pocket. A piece of Pa keeping me safe.

Continue reading…

Joe X. Young

Joe Young is a British expat living in Germany.

His short fiction appears in a wide range of publications alongside such talents as Jack Ketchum, Joe R. Lansdale, Ramsey Campbell, Christina Bergling, Guy N. Smith, Graham Masterton, Mercedes M Yardley, Wrath James White, and Clive Barker.

Joe's non-fiction articles, reviews, and interviews have appeared in various publications, including reviews for the British Fantasy Society and three articles in Angel Leigh McCoy's *Another Dimension Magazine* which won the Serling Award for Best Anthology in 2017.

Joe's work isn't restricted to writing fiction, non-fiction, and reviewing. He has provided illustrations for various works, created book covers and logos, and generally assists the horror writing community with mentoring via his various Facebook groups, such as Get Writing Horror. He is currently curating a horror author resource website but took time out for the *Try Not to Die* project, which he is proud to be a part of.

Mark Tullius and Joe X Young

Download Your Free Copy

Includes the first two chapters and one death scene from each of the first seven books in the *Try Not to Die* series.

VINCERE
PRESS

Published by Vincere Press
65 Pine Ave., Ste 806
Long Beach, CA 90802